The Ugliest Man on the Mountain

Mark Laming

First Published in 2021 by Blossom Spring Publishing
The Ugliest Man on the Mountain © 2021 Mark Laming
ISBN 978-1-8384972-2-4
E: admin@blossomspringpublishing.com
W: www.blossomspringpublishing.com
Published in the United Kingdom. All rights reserved under International
Copyright Law. Contents and/or cover may not be reproduced in whole or in part without the express written consent of the publisher.
This is a work of fiction. Names, characters, places and incidents are either products of the author's imagination or are used fictitiously. Any resemblance to actual events or locales or persons, living or dead, save those clearly in the public domain, is purely coincidental.

Life is like a rainbow which, in difficult times,
we only see as black and white.
Keep searching for the colours.

Chapter 1

In downtown Harrow, grey clouds were building into monstrous charcoal hills, threatening a horrendous downpour. The mid-morning traffic was stationary along the tree-lined street as the roadworks continued for a second week. The three-way lights took forever to change and, when they did, a maximum of three cars managed to move forward before the next change. Adding to the chaos, a bin lorry was struggling to reach residents' houses. Operatives, wearing high visibility orange coats and trousers, momentarily leant against garden walls as they checked their mobile phones.

With a frisson of excitement, Amber walked up the street carrying her two supermarket *bags for life* and entered a block of flats. On the way up to level two in the lift, she momentarily questioned if she should have walked up the short flight of stairs. The lady doctor had told her to look after her health and slim down but she had ignored the advice.

Gazing into the mirrored wall, her eyes drifted to the large stomach that was straining against the fabric of her pale blue jeans. At fourteen stone, and with more pounds piling on at a weekly rate, she had been warned that her health was at risk. Even after the scare earlier in the year that resulted in a visit to casualty, her thoughts were anywhere but on keeping healthy. She shrugged her shoulders and, on reaching the flat in question, concentrated on the job ahead; drilling out those door locks was always tricky. Keeping down the noise with the towel over the drill was the difficult part. There was no sign of security alarms on the outside of the building or any cameras. Hopefully, the occupants would have left for work by now but she would still be cautious. She yanked up the grey hoodie over her curly black hair and round, dark skinned face.

Amber pulled on grey gloves and within fifteen seconds the lock had been penetrated. She wiped up the dust with a damp cloth and slipped quietly into Flat 7, pulling the door shut behind her. Similar to previous times, the necessity to use the bathroom was becoming an issue. Even with the knowledge that she was alone in the apartment, she still closed and locked the door. Her face hardened as panic set in noticing the two remaining pieces of toilet paper that looked ready to fall off the cardboard holder. Somewhere, the person living here would have a spare roll and she quickly located it in the cupboard under the sink. After using the facilities, she wanted to leave everything in order but had the toilet seat been up or down? Men usually left it up, didn't they? At home she was untidy but, in someone else's home, it was a different matter. Straightening the hand towel, she observed a razor and expensive aftershave.

There were no clues to a female residing in the flat. Leaving the room, she switched off the light. The gentle hum of the fan was to go on for the entirety of her visit.

There was the smell of toast that made her feel hungry and she pictured a rushed breakfast as the man left for work. Inside the kitchen everything was in its place and that was when she saw her first item. The large screen iPad was dropped into her bag along with the charger. The thrill of being in control was once again pleasing her.

Dispelling any feelings of guilt, she spied the pastel-painted rooms with expensive furniture and comfortable carpets. She wondered how clean her trainers were and slipped them off. This was a luxurious flat with no expense spared for the better things in life. Was he a doctor or a banker? What puzzled her was why she was taking so much interest in the victim. Normally her rule was not to speculate, simply remove saleable items and swiftly exit.

A picture on the lounge wall certainly prompted a second glance and would be recorded in her photographic memory. The crudely painted unicorn galloping in the air over a backdrop of the River Thames fascinated her. Cars on the bridges were replaced by sheep and hideous coloured cow faces that grinned. A forest of skyscrapers that adorned the London skyline were painted in purple. This was an artwork that Amber knew she would never forget. She hated it and wondered if it was an original work or simply a print.

She glanced at the enormous seventy-five-inch Samsung TV with a games box tucked neatly below on the glass stand. It was a reminder of her own home and the joy of being able to stream movies and box sets. She enjoyed the cushioning sensation of her feet on his blue, deep-pile carpet and moved backwards and forwards as the sensation of warmth crept through to her toes. In contrast to her large, stained carpet back home, his floor covering was of high quality and perfectly hoovered.

She allowed her mind to wonder about the man and if he had a girlfriend, or whether he could be gay? For one brief moment, she felt sorry for him coming home to discover the break-in.

Moving gingerly from room to room and weighing up further items to remove, it was only when she caught sight of her reflection in his bedroom mirror that she felt like her image had been lasered onto the glass as well as her conscience. Staring at her skin and wet hair, that hadn't escaped the fury of the downpour, she wished she'd worn a coat. Aware of the dampness that had crept through her shirt and jeans, she longed to get home to a warm bath. She was now panicking and checked her watch again for the fourth time. Six minutes – soon time to go. With the adrenalin pumping like a steam engine struggling to move its heavy load, an inner voice in her head kept repeating the word: *Thief*.

For a brief moment she was saddened. Once again, she was breaking the law and someone's heart. The excitement of pulling off another burglary was short-lived as the fear of being discovered set in. She was visibly shaking and momentarily touched her chest in an effort to control the manic breathing – she would have to leave shortly. Scanning a shelf in the bedroom, a phone charger came into view and she was convinced it would work with her own mobile, so added it to the haul. She spied a paperback book on his bedside table and frowned. A little voice inside said, *this guy isn't much of a reader, is he?* Her preferred choice of book fell into the category of biography and factual. Amber's inner alarm then warned her that she should leave immediately.

On the dining table his passport was visible and she wondered if he was about to go on holiday as she resisted the temptation to take a peep at his photo. A mixture of thoughts bubbled away in her mind as she imagined herself accompanying him to some far-off place and falling in love. Her reveries were disturbed by the ping sound of his iPad in her bag as an e-mail was delivered into the inbox. In a desperate effort to turn off the device, she yanked it out and came close to dropping it.

She turned her attention to a drawer in the bedside cabinet and sucked in breath as she saw an envelope containing money. Grasping the bundle of notes, she quickly estimated there must have been over two hundred pounds there for the taking. Her mind was already processing how this windfall was going to be used. In a rush to leave, she stopped in her tracks. There really wasn't time, but she needed the bathroom again.

***

Amber McCarthy was a strange and troubled person but also kind hearted, who looked out for others. It was hard to comprehend her always being there for people whilst inflicting so much grief by carrying out these burglaries.

She was so laid back she couldn't even be bothered to sign her name with a capital letter. Always taking the easy route, her toxic combination of laziness and devil-may-care attitude did little to enrich her life. In complete conflict to her outlandish behaviour, there were times when she appeared to be making an effort but she soon slipped back to her old ways. It was as if she had pressed the self-destruct button a number of times yet she kept returning to ensure it was still activated. Deep down in the corners of her mind, Amber longed for a peaceful life, but why did everything always have to come at such a price?

Her idea of relaxation lay in streaming films on her sixty-five-inch TV with the sound system set to booming. Curled up on the sofa and wrapped in a grubby, popcorn-coloured duvet, forking oven-ready meals and downing Malbec wine was how she spent most of her evenings.

Sunday mornings were reserved for tidying up and fell short of the deep clean that was long overdue. Rank smelling plates, coated in leftover food from days gone by, littered the crowded worktops of the unhygienic kitchen. Her cursory hoovering sessions with the ten-year-old Dyson failed to remove dust from the flattened carpets. Ignoring the red warning light for the dust container, the effectiveness of the appliance was limited. Amber's bedroom looked more like a storeroom with plastic storage boxes crammed full of clothes. Tired woodchip paper on the walls and yellowing white paint afforded little comfort. A washy grey cobweb, with a trapped decomposing fly hung from the ceiling waiting for the hungry spider to return. Ignoring the chaos and filthy state of the apartment came easy to this woman.

A solitary pillar-box red bra hung at an angle from a broken wardrobe door handle and discarded clothes lay on the floor. The unmade double bed was pulled away from the damp-smelling wall with black patches. Contacting a builder to rectify the problem was low on Amber's priority list.

Boyfriends came and went and the latest, a man older than her thirty years with buckled teeth and a mouth full of crowns, was about to receive his marching orders. Her not so regular texts had become acrimonious as love was replaced with bitterness. Relinquishing her hold, she told the man from Wembley that he was not for her.

By day Amber worked for an insurance company. Her desk was the untidiest in the office and she was always getting told off but she was good at her job. She had a high IQ and a thirst for soaking up information. Despite her idiosyncratic behaviour, she was popular with her colleagues and always had a good word for everyone. In essence, she was an intelligent woman who held down a responsible job.

Not so long ago, she had helped one of her office colleagues through a financial crisis by offering practical advice. Miriam Foster, a divorcee, was struggling to settle her monthly bills and clearly needed a hand. The middle-aged woman who had always left the banking and household payments to her wayward husband, brought in a cupcake to give to Amber.

'You shouldn't have worried, it was nothing. I was just trying to help.'

Miriam gazed around the mostly empty office and then up to the battery clock that was running five minutes fast. 'I wanted to thank you before everyone gets in. I've taken on board everything you said about budgeting and

I'm beginning to get on top of things.' She withdrew from her handbag an envelope and held it out at armslength.

'What's that?'

'Sixty-six pounds, the money you lent me to pay the electric.'

Amber observed the shaking hand and the gold band on her ring finger. 'Put that away, won't you? Someone once helped me when I was having a rough time and I wanted to be there for you. End of matter, do you understand?'

It was at this point that many of the office staff streamed into the room and Miriam lowered her voice. 'I'm just so grateful. You are so kind. Thank you from the bottom of my heart. I still think you should have let me pay you back though but I can't imagine you ever taking anything from anyone.'

Amber tried to smile but the irony in what this woman had said cut deeply. A voice in her head kept repeating: *If only she knew the truth.*

Chapter 2

Kane Boulter was celebrating the sale of his business with his girlfriend, Carol, in a small Italian restaurant off St Martin's Lane, close to Trafalgar Square. It was midweek and his favourite table in the window had been taken, but nothing was going to spoil the excitement as plans for the future were discussed.

At forty-five years old, he had done well for himself. His career with a large successful travel company at their head office in Greenford High Street had paid off. As co-owner he was in for a big windfall as one of their competitors had made an offer they couldn't refuse. For the period of three months, he was to manage the business to ensure a satisfactory handover. He also owned the leases on two flats in Middlesex and the rents were affording him a great lifestyle. Life was panning out just fine. His restored silver Porsche with a 3.0 L engine never failed to attract the attention of his neighbours as he roared away from the garage.

Kane's plan was to purchase a holiday home close to the village of Frigiliana in Andalucía. Not too far from Malaga, the hillside location held happy memories of holidays with his ex-wife. There was no sadness in returning as the couple had parted on good terms.

Seated in the quaint restaurant with backdrops of Venice and the prow of a gondola that served as a bar, the ambience and incredible food made this a popular place to dine. The owner, Giuseppe, spoke perfect English with no trace of an Italian accent.

Kane was a regular customer to the bistro named Florence. On this occasion, the owner insisted Kane and his partner stepped into his kitchen. The scene that greeted them was organised chaos with two chefs anxiously moving around the cramped space. They looked up briefly before returning to their work. The heat was intense and, despite the cold weather, the back door was swinging in the breeze and revealed wheelie bins in the yard. Bubbling saucepans with Italian sauces were being stirred by a young woman with purple hair and tattoos on her arms and neck. What had once served as a white apron was now stained with a thousand traces of food in varying shades of red and brown. The distinct and appetising smell of oregano and basil wafted through the air and prompted the couple to comment on the mouth-watering cuisine being prepared. The proud owner pointed to an enormous cooker with eight burners that had recently been installed and joked that chef Ramsay would die for one like this.

Back at their table, Giuseppe placed their drinks on the colourful tablecloth and said too loudly for Kane's liking, 'Is this your new lady friend? You need to make the introductions.' He tapped Kane on the hand and added, 'I liked your previous lady, Kirsty. Are you not friends, any longer?'

Kane fidgeted with the cuffs of his immaculate, white, office shirt and nodded as he nervously checked that the diners on the next table were not listening. He grasped his glass and proceeded to prod a finger around the ice cubes and lemon slice.

Giuseppe adjusted his tortoiseshell glasses and with a stern face asked, matter-of-factly, 'Still only drinking the tonic water?'

Through clenched teeth Kane replied, 'I'm sure I don't know what you are talking about.'

When they were finally left alone, Carol whispered, 'Now, big boy, who's Kirsty?'

She often called him by this name, despite the fact that he was in his mid-forties. He was slim and six feet in height – it was her idea of a bit of fun. She was shorter and carried extra weight. Kane preferred his women on the large size and enjoyed nestling up after a hard day's work.

Kane's voice was quiet and reflective. 'Oh, just someone I knew and had dinner here with. I'm sure I mentioned her.'

'No, I think I would have remembered.'

When their olives and bread arrived, Kane momentarily held his girlfriend's hand and gazed into her brown eyes. He was suddenly aware of other diners who were smiling. Their talk switched to the mundane matters of work and how Carol longed to leave her profession as a nurse. Working for the NHS, her dreams had diminished with the long hours and uncertainty on funding for patient care.

Kane, the sophisticated man who looked smart in his pin-striped suit, ran an imaginary comb through his hair with his hand; his attention to detail was completed with a straightening of the red tie. He checked his mobile and apologised saying an important e-mail was expected.

Carol threw him a stern look. 'Didn't we agree that during our leisure time, we let go? I don't want you getting stressed over the sale of your business.'

Pocketing the phone, he conceded and turned his attention to the excitable chatter of three young girls on the next table discussing boyfriends. He was suddenly aware of a hand on his shoulder and turned to face Carol. Her pensive face worried him.

'What's up?'

She whispered, 'You know you said you would stay over tonight at my place, well I just remembered my flatmate has started to decorate her room and is sleeping on my floor to avoid the smell of the paint. Yucky yellow the colour of sick! Just our luck – you won't be able to come.'

Kane inwardly groaned. He was looking forward to making love to Carol and had been thinking about her on his way up on the train to London. Picturing her slowly undress, he longed to satisfy her. As a young woman she had needs and her staying power always excited him. Feeling disappointed he glanced down to his laptop case at the side of the table that held a present for Carol – sexy underclothes that he longed to see her wear and remove. This woman knew how to make him feel good with her sensuous kisses and furious lovemaking. He wondered if they should change their plans and go back to his place but immediately dismissed the idea.

Replacing his disappointment with a cheeky smile he offered, 'Then it has to be tomorrow at my flat.'

His hand disappeared under the thick, white, starched tablecloth and onto Carol's knee. He felt her leg stiffen as the caress made her jump. She pushed him away and her flushed face left him in no doubt that her feelings of desire were riding high.

'Don't do that!' With raised eyes to the ceiling, she quickly added in a low voice, 'Sorry about tonight.'

Kane played with the edge of the table and grinned.

Carol turned her attention to the owner who was bringing their first course. In unison they both smiled at the sight of their food.

Giuseppe worked his magic with his diners. 'I was hoping you would come this week for some of my pasta.' He carefully lowered two steaming bowls of minestrone before swivelling around to snatch a bowl of parmesan cheese from the adjacent table failing to apologise to the diners.

Spooning tiny amounts of the cheese onto the soup he ignored Kane's request for more and turned to Carol and said, 'Signorina, I thinka you looka mora beautiful every time youa come here.'

Kane broke into loud laughter before remarking that the accent was getting worse. He quickly added, 'This is Carol's first visit here, so how can her looks be getting better?'

Giuseppe nodded his head in Kane's direction and switched the subject to Italy. 'I've never even taken a holiday there but would like to see Rome sometime. You probably eat more of the food than I do – I can't stand pasta.'

Grasping his girlfriend's hand Kane said, 'Now I have heard everything – an Italian who hates pasta.'

Expanding on his life story, Giuseppe ran a hand through his thatch of greying hair and sighed. His birthplace was Brixton and his roots were firmly in the UK. In essence he was a Londoner who loved the city with all his heart. He embraced all things British and his parents' previous homeland inspired little or no interest whatsoever. The decision to run an Italian restaurant was purely for business reasons. London was a haven for lovers of Mediterranean food.

After their meal, Kane and Carol walked down the Strand and battled with the excitable theatregoers making their way to tube stations and home. Their topic of conversation was about her spending the following night with him and the meal he planned to cook.

Just before they said goodbye, Kane pulled out the small silver carrier bag from his case and handed it to her. He recalled his embarrassment on visiting the lingerie store in Harrow High Street and the queue of shoppers standing behind him. Passing over the skimpy knickers to the cashier was embarrassing. He caught the expression on the young girl's face as she held up the expensive and flimsy garment to scan the barcode. There was no rush to put him out of his misery as she slowly folded the purchase and placed them in the bag. The girl's mouth twitched as she muttered the cursory farewell, 'Have a good day.' Kane felt the sweat soaking the back of his white office shirt and hurried out of the store.

***

Kane cautiously pushed open his front door with the drilled-out lock and his voice rose to hellishly loud as he swore a number of times. Some low-life had invaded his space. In a stern voice he shouted through the aperture of his broken door into the pitch-dark interior of the hallway in an attempt to frighten off any would-be burglar but, of course, the offender had long since fled. With all the lights switched on he was relieved to discover there was no mess, everything was as tidy and orderly as he had left it before setting off for work.

Moving swiftly from room to room, it was obvious which of his possessions had been lifted. He made his way to the bathroom and his eyes strayed to the toilet seat that was in the upward position – he always shut the lid. And the toilet roll had been replaced. Remembering that he had intended to do this when he got home, his body shook with fear. The thought of someone in his home really unsettled him.

When his nerves calmed enough to call his girlfriend, Kane swiped the screen of his mobile. It felt like a long wait, but was probably only seconds, before Carol picked up.

'Hi Kane, you got back in good time.'

'Yeah, only I can't tell you the shock I had when I got back.'

'God, what's wrong, are you okay?'

'I'm fine, just really upset – I've been burgled. They took my new iPad and other things.'

'Oh, no, how awful.'

'Yep, and you know that money I raised for the charity – it's all gone. If only I'd banked it. The thief who did this is going to get his comeuppance.'

Casting his mind back to the fund raising, the generosity of his immediate neighbours and work colleagues, he was saddened. He acknowledged the thief wouldn't have known what the money was intended for but it still grated on his nerves. He vowed to raise more funds that would require him to go out on the London streets with his collection tin.

Turning away from his phone he glanced in the direction of the bathroom. 'He even used the wretched toilet and left the seat up!'

'How did they get in?'

Kane laboured his words. 'Drilled the door lock. The odd thing was they made no mess and cleared up the dust and put it in the bin – that's odd behaviour, don't you think?'

'Yeah, really scary. Burglars don't do things like that, especially using the loo.'

'It freaked me out when I spotted the thief had even put a new toilet roll on the holder.'

'Considerate and tidy thief this one. Have you contacted the police?'

'No, I rang you first. Anyway, the police don't come out for this sort of thing anymore. I can't stand the thought of someone going through all my personal things, let alone using the bathroom. What really hurts is the feeling of intrusion. No mess, no drawers upturned or anything like that, it's really eerie. He must have watched me leave for work.'

'Do you want me to come over?'

'No, I'm okay. I have to go as I need to call out a locksmith and report the break in, not that they will come out, but the insurance guys will need an incident number.'

***

After an unsettled night Kane rose early and searched through the rooms thoroughly to ascertain the extent of the missing items that included an iPad and all the money. He estimated the loss was close on eleven hundred pounds. What grieved him most was losing the charity donation that he had personally raised over the last three months. The funds were destined for a hospice. It irked him imagining someone wasting it on booze or drugs. Firing up his office laptop, the computer that had escaped the robbery, the task of completing the online insurance claim form commenced. He kept repeating to himself there would be no forgiveness for the person who had served up so much misery.

***

Over the next few weeks, the process of getting on with life took over with a new lock fitted to the front door and camera surveillance linked to his iPhone. A state-of-the-art burglar alarm with a sophisticated intruder camera system added to the security. Apartment 7 now looked and felt, to all intents and purposes, like Fort Knox. The heart of the property had been ripped out. Even with all the security measures in place, Kane decided a move was in order. Shortly, he would put the property up for sale.

For the first time since purchasing his flat, he attended the residents' committee meeting that highlighted a run of burglaries in the neighbouring area. Kane speculated on the intruder being the same guy who had forced his way into his home. He was convinced it was a young man, probably a druggie financing his next fix.

As was Kane's way, after an annoying or sad event, he would dust himself off and start over again – the stolen items could be replaced. The pilfered charity money he would personally finance, only this time it would be a larger sum.

Positive thoughts streamed through his head at the prospect of taking Carol to Spain on a short break. They would stay in a small hotel a few miles inland from the coastal town of Nerja. He was convinced he was going to find the perfect holiday home amongst the narrow, cobbled streets with whitewashed houses and colourful pots of brilliant red geraniums. Researching estate agents in the area, there was one particular property that was of interest to Kane. It was literally perched on a mountain with spectacular views and within walking distance of the picturesque village of Frigiliana.

As the weeks flew by, the revelation of Carol's infidelity brought the relationship to a thundering halt. In truth they were polar opposites with the main attraction hinging on the physical side. Most of their dates ended with a quick tumble in bed and her smoking one of her disgusting vapes.

Like so many times before, Kane promised himself that the next woman he took up with had to be on his wavelength and not just another bedfellow. He turned his attention to the imminent sale of his travel business that would eventually result in him living abroad in Spain. He dreamed of a new home that overlooked the beautiful Andalusian countryside with hills that rolled gently upwards to his favourite village.

Chapter 3

Six miles east of Harrow, Amber was arguing with a man in the carpark behind the Devonshire Arms pub. The money on offer for the iPad she'd recently stolen was disappointingly low. The dealer in the black hoodie, a man in his thirties, claimed he would have trouble moving it on.

Amber became incensed and snatched back the relatively new appliance shouting, 'Look, Andy, or whatever you call yourself, don't mess with me. This gear is worth more than forty pounds.'

'Keep your voice down, darling.'

'Don't be so condescending and let's agree a fair price for both of us.'

The man with the expressionless face, raised both hands in the air and shook his head. 'I move things on quickly and let things go for a few pounds.'

'I know all that but you know it's worth a lot of money and I risked getting caught,' said Amber who was now concentrating on the wad of notes that he was waving in front of her eyes.

'Just take the money young lady, you know you want it. Or just swap the iPad for some of my sweeties, or perhaps you'd like something with more of a kick.'

'I don't do drugs and that's us done.'

As she marched away from the dealer, she knew that he would get the last word 'Pleasure doing business with you.'

Amber felt sick and vowed never to meet up with the menacing man again. Luckily there had never been any exchange of contact numbers as it was far too dangerous. This was the first time they had met and it was on the recommendation of a third party. Some recommendation.

Whilst Amber got her kicks from stealing and making

money, there was always the risk of being caught. Up until now she had been lucky and avoided prosecution. Deep down she knew the path she was treading was like a clock spring running out of power – her time was almost up. Her mind sped back to her last burglary. Robbing the immaculate property that belonged to that man must have been really upsetting for him. Why was this theft different to the others she had carried out? There weren't many clues as to who the victim really was but, for the first time, her head was telling her that she had done a terrible thing.

Chapter 4

The young woman in the Spanish evening class had everyone's attention as she moved her large dictionary and text book around the cramped workspace she shared with two other people. She was the untidiest of all the students with her bag on the table, notebooks and a half-eaten apple that was turning brown. A crumpled piece of kitchen roll kept falling onto the floor and, out of breath, she leant down to retrieve it with a loud sigh.

Glancing at the clock on the wall that had stopped, she checked her watch. She scanned the tired décor taking in the chipped, white gloss of the skirting board and dated furniture. It was a depressing classroom.

Amber had never been to Spain and had no plans to visit, so why was she learning Spanish? Purely and simply, she needed a challenge and adding a new language to the two she already spoke appealed to her. She disliked the teacher and if it hadn't been for a certain person who attended, then she may well have called a halt to the class. Kane was the man who kept smiling at her and had secretly passed a note with an invitation to join him for a coffee.

Outside in the corridor there was much chatter as people made their way to the various classes in the community centre that included a writer's group, dance and art sessions. The clunking sound of a drinks machine dispensing beverages seemed to go on forever.

This was Amber's second term studying conversational Spanish and the general consensus was she was an intelligent individual who was keen to do her homework and read out aloud. It was just her messy desk and appalling dress sense that made her stand out from the others. Today, she was wearing a light blue jumper with food stains to the front. The size eighteen denim skirt fell short of hiding her large stomach.

Seated at the top table, the teacher, a Spanish lady from Madrid, in her late forties, was firm but fair with her students. With an overwhelming desire to offer the best language course, she encouraged Amber to contribute to the lesson. 'Thank you for telling us about your fascinating account of your holiday in Barcelona. I have to say you are a fast learner picking up the language. *Muy bien*!'

Amber smiled and in an upbeat voice replied, 'Thanks. I've never actually been to Spain but, with a little help from the internet, I used my imagination.'

The tutor muttered, 'Oh, I see.' She switched from English to her usual frantic delivery of Spanish words that were difficult to comprehend.

Amber was aware that everyone was staring at her. She wondered if their interest was in the amount of clutter in front of her, rather than their teacher's remarks on her flair for learning.

Her attention moved to the good-looking man in his smart, grey suit. Kane was smiling at her again. He had engaging eyes that locked onto hers and made her back tingle with excitement. She wondered if he was married or, at the very best, unattached. She questioned why he would be interested in a woman like her.

Her mind cast back to the previous week's class and the journey home on the bus. Seated in the rear of the vehicle she observed her reflection in the window with a thousand fingerprints and disliked what she saw. With her furrowed brow and large cheeks, surely Kane would struggle to spot any beauty in her. Carrying the extra weight and unflattering clothes that could have come from a charity shop, she was hardly a looker. In contrast, the man she couldn't stop thinking about was slim and attractive and spoke with a distinguished voice.

Her reveries were interrupted as a lady in the classroom raised her screechy South London voice. 'Has anyone got a spare pen – mine has stopped working?'

Amber yanked her coat off the back off the chair and retrieved a silver pen, which she triumphantly held in the air. 'Yep, I have one here.'

To her delight Kane stood up and crossed over to her. She felt a shiver of pleasure as his hand momentarily touched hers. His skin was so warm and there was no sign of a ring on his finger. Aware of the expensive cologne that wafted into her face, she thought he smelt incredible. He accepted the pen from Amber's outstretched hand and turned to pass it to the lady on the far table.

As she watched him return to his seat, there was no connection in her memory of the terrible deed that she had inflicted on him not so many months ago. She told herself that this man could be the one for her and, if given the chance, may bring lasting happiness.

The tutor quickly returned her pupils back to their studies. 'Let's have one conversation at a time please.' She tapped the lid of the laptop with her hand and addressed an elderly man who always had a permanent grin on his face. 'Now Stephen, using as many adjectives as possible, please tell us your thoughts on your perfect Spanish holiday.'

At the end of the session, Amber stuffed her belongings into the supermarket *bag for life*, the very same one she used to carry tools to illegally enter properties. She hastily turned to face Kane who was now by her side.

She hung onto his every word. 'I enjoyed hearing your homework, Amber. I can't believe you have never been there as you described it with such clarity allowing me to taste the chorizo in the meal. Your description of the restaurant in that square with the paella cooking in an enormous pan fired with chopped wooden pallets was so real. I felt like I was sitting there waiting for my meal. I'm impressed.'

Amber's heart was pounding as her reply tumbled out. 'Thanks. How about you, have you been there?'

'Me, oh yes, I have recently bought a villa and will soon live between here and Spain.'

Acknowledging that he was wealthy, Amber asked, 'Does it have a pool?'

'Yes, it's enormous, far too big for me. I adore the idea of living in a true Spanish community. It's important to mix with the locals and converse to the best of your ability.' He paused for a moment. 'My knowledge of the language is nowhere near as good as yours – how long have you been learning Spanish?'

'Oh, not that long, I tend to pick up things quickly. I suppose you could say that I have a photographic memory.'

She chanced what she said next. 'And is there a Mrs Kane you share your holiday home with?'

Kane laughed. 'You are not backwards in coming forward, are you? No, it's just me. I used to be married but we won't go into that.'

'Sorry, I touched a nerve there.'

He waved a dismissive hand in the air. 'Not at all. Tell me, where do you live?'

'In North Harrow, not the posh area where the school is.'

'That's close to where I live. I only moved in last week. We are practically neighbours.'

Standing so close to him she could almost feel his breath. She observed his thin face and kissable lips. He was the best-looking man in the class and the youngest.

Before the coffee break, she had sketched her new friend on the inside cover of her notebook. She wished it was a photo taken on her smart phone to view whenever she thought of him.

As everyone trooped out of the classroom, she watched the tutor packing up her things and wished she would hurry up. She observed Kane pulling on his coat and felt embarrassed with her own shabby appearance. In an attempt to look thinner, she pulled in her stomach and ran a hand through the unwashed curly hair. She should have showered this morning but had chosen to stay in bed longer. It brought home how lazy and disorganised she was. Something clicked inside her, a wish to be a better person and definitely someone who looked more attractive. This man could have his pick of any woman yet, while there was no magic to be seen in her, oddly he was showing interest.

In walked the annoying caretaker, a stocky man in his sixties with broken capillary veins on his nose and a permanent frown. He addressed Kane with his usual sarcastic tone. 'And now the yoga lot need all these tables shifting into place, you'll have to get a move on.'

Kane ignored the irritating man. His attention was reserved for Amber. 'You did get my note to join me for a coffee at Costa's, didn't you? I'll understand if you are busy.' He quickly added, 'I'll throw in a muffin if you say yes.'

A kinder voice than usual whispered in Amber's head: *Just say yes, definitely yes.*

Kane offered to carry her bag but she declined his kind offer. How could she possibly let him carry the one that she used for burglaries? Once again, her inner conscience had something to say – *Smarten yourself up by all means girl for your fancy man, but don't get any ideas about giving up on your little earner – you are so crooked you can hardly lie straight in bed at night.*

***

Sipping scorching hot lattes in giant-sized cardboard cups, Amber listened as Kane briefly related his life story. In essence, apart from his divorce, there appeared to have been no great catastrophes along the way. The well-to-do London accent, privileged childhood and private education obviously led to fast-tracking his career. At this point she had no inkling of his profession or the fact that early retirement had already commenced.

She cast her mind back to the previous week when she had spotted him in the car park climbing into an expensive sports car; she had hung back from waiting at the bus stop until he drove off.

Today, she felt so relaxed being with him and leant forward to say, 'Do you have any children?'

Kane laughed. 'You are not shy with your questions, are you? First, did I have a wife and now sprogs? There were difficulties in that department so no kids I'm afraid.'

'I'm sorry, that was rude of me asking that.'

Kane shrugged his shoulders and said, 'Just one of those things. And what about you, is there anyone special in your life?'

She screwed up her eyes. 'I've had my moments.' She patted her stomach and muttered, 'Not much chance with the way I look. I am trying to lose a few pounds. It's early days.'

Kane smiled reassuringly. 'Well, I think you look great.' He then glanced at his watch and frowned. 'I really must fly now as I have a meeting. I've really enjoyed being with you. Would you like to meet up this Friday night for a drink?'

'Definitely – let's swap mobile numbers.'

***

Gazing through the window of the wine bar in Harrow High Street, Amber caught sight of Kane sitting at a table close to the bar area. She had wished away the last three days for her date to come around and here was the wonderfully handsome man raising her heartbeat to frantic. Dressed in a long, red dress that showed off her ample figure, the adrenalin was pumping around her veins like race horses nearing the finishing line. Pushing open the door she took the few steps to reach him and was thrilled to be greeted with a hug. In an excitable voice she muttered a squeaky hello and felt embarrassed.

Kane eyes momentarily strayed to her dress. 'You look great.' He gestured for her to sit and handed over the drinks card. 'My friends recommend the Pilot's Green Gin; you may like to try one.'

Still grasping her handbag, Amber joked that they had both arrived early. Kane glanced at his watch and laughed. 'Twenty minutes to be precise.'

A young man with a toothy grin and a long white apron brought over a small tray of fancy crisps and nuts. He appeared to be in a hurry and glanced over to the bar where a young girl, a customer, was sitting with her friends. Turning his attention back to them, he took their order for a gin and a Coco Cola for Kane.

'Did you have a good day at the office, Amber?'

Amber's fingers worked on the edge of the uncomfortable wicker chair. 'No, not really. My boss called me into his office and I was worried as the company let two people go last week and I knew something was up.'

'Oh, I am sorry to hear that. I had to trim my staff down in the past and it's never easy especially…'

With a smile forming Amber interrupted, 'My boss

said he regretted having to tell me that head office had asked him to speak to me. I was in a terrible state expecting the worst. Then he playfully punched me on the arm and revealed I was to get a pay rise. My work on revamping the way they handle the budget hadn't gone unnoticed.'

'That's great getting extra money but what a jerk risking upsetting an employee like that. Not something I would do. I always valued my staff and it goes without saying that we treat them with respect.'

'Perhaps I should work for you then.'

Kane pushed his glasses up onto his hair and smiled. 'I think you would be too much of a distraction – I wouldn't be able to take my eyes off you.' He then promptly added, 'Sorry, that must have sounded ever so rude.'

With a smile lighting up her face, Amber blushed and said, 'That's the best compliment I have had in a long time, don't stop there.'

They were interrupted by a waitress, barely twenty years of age, who was dressed in a white apron that was marginally longer than her short, black skirt. She placed their drinks on the table and, holding the silver tray against her body, she turned her attention to a girl close by who was shouting out her request for another drink.

Kane raised his glass to Amber and said, 'I often end up here on a Friday night and it's great being here with you.'

A bolt of electricity shot through Amber's veins as the feeling of excitement bubbled away in her head. Only in her wildest thoughts had she allowed herself to imagine him paying her so much attention.

The wine bar became busy, predominately office staff with an agenda to let off steam after a busy week. The noise was increasing and any chance of having a conversation was restricted by having to shout. Unable to make out what Amber was saying, Kane misunderstood her, believing she had said she had been married.

Leaning over close to Kane's ear, in a voice that was sore from shouting, she said, 'Me, me married? I think not. Who would want me?'

Focusing on his amazingly good looks, Amber looked deep into the blue eyes and down to his lips. He was indeed a handsome man with expensive clothes, someone she was proud to be seen with. She had to stop staring and launched into enquiring about his parents and family.

'My father died a while ago and was only in his sixties.'

Amber put a hand to her lips. 'Oh, that's terrible, no age at all.'

'It was heart-breaking losing him but I still have Mum. I see her every few weeks when I go up to Luton.'

'Any brothers or sisters?'

Kane looked thoughtful and traced a finger around the rim of his glass. 'Just one brother and we have our ups and downs. It's complicated. How about your family, are there any black sheep I should know about?'

'My parents died in a car crash when I was a teenager. Childhood memories are something I don't want to talk about.'

Kane told her that he was sorry. The conversation switched to the Spanish classes. There was much laughter as he recalled an incident when a new student sat through the opening minutes as their tutor wrote on the whiteboard the dates for the next term. The bald-headed man in a poor-fitting suit was clearly embarrassed and explained he was in the wrong room.

The fun stopped as Kane checked his mobile and frowned at the many unread messages. The phone was pocketed in his coat and the sleeve of his shirt rose to reveal a large fancy silver watch with many dials – a genuine Rolex thought Amber. He leant forward to retrieve his drink and downed the remnants in one gulp. 'Almost, ten o'clock and I must get you home.'

Amber's heart sank. She reached down to the floor for her handbag and withdrew a large silver purse that was crammed full of twenty-pound notes. 'It's not that late. Let me buy you a drink and I mean a real one, not fizzy pop.'

'I'm happy with just the one, thanks.' Staring at the wad of notes he quickly added, 'Heavens, you look loaded. You haven't robbed a bank, have you?'

On the defensive, Amber swiftly replied, 'No, I haven't! I've just been to a cash till. Don't you carry cash?'

Kane ignored the hardened voice and replied, 'Yes, but I don't carry that much money.' He checked his watch and smiled. 'It's been fun but I'm up early tomorrow so let's get going. I'm driving to sunny Luton to spend the weekend with friends and to see my mum.'

Feeling disappointed, Amber had wished for more time with him. Her solitary glass of gin had lasted the entire evening and normally she would have downed a further one, if not more.

They left the bar to step out into the cold air of the street. To Amber's delight, an arrangement was made to meet up the following Wednesday for a meal. As they turned into the high street, Kane linked arms with her and mentioned that he would ring for a taxi.

'I'm in no rush,' said Amber. Her pace slowed as she guided him into the doorway of a department store and kissed him hard on the lips. Reaching down for his hand she placed it squarely on the front of her coat. She squeezed the cold fingers around the fabric that covered her breast.

He pulled away and was clearly cross with her. 'Now

you have spoilt things doing that. I would never expect anything more on such an early date. We hardly know each other, do we? I wish you hadn't done that. Our understanding of a good evening obviously differs.'

Unsure what to say, Amber simply muttered a feeble sorry that she wasn't sure he even heard. Past boyfriends had made an early move and, to be fair, a little light petting had been fun. Kane was different; he was a gentleman and someone she had upset.

Moving back onto the pavement he ran fingers through his hair and frowned. 'Let's go and get that taxi.'

Taking a chance, Amber still managed to say, 'Are we still on for that meal?'

Walking slowly but not together, Kane harshly said, 'Yes, I invited you, didn't I?'

Saddened by the tone of his voice, she regretted her behaviour. Here was this incredible man treating her to an evening in a wine bar and she had acted like a loose and desperate woman. It wasn't as if she was drunk, simply flirtatious behaviour that could now thwart her chances of forming a relationship.

Kane tapped the app on his mobile screen for his local taxi company and it wasn't long before the car arrived. As they climbed in, he promised to text her with the arrangements for their dinner date. He also added that he wouldn't be attending the next Spanish class.

Amber became irritated with the driver, a middle-aged woman, who was throwing out questions and mostly ignoring their answers. Sitting in the back of the vehicle she was thrilled as Kane grasped her hand. He muttered something incoherent and she asked him to repeat what he had said. Above the noisy gear changes, he spoke directly into her ear. 'I'm sorry for snapping at you. I just want things to be perfect between us.'

A tear dribbled down Amber's cheek. 'I don't know

what came over me back there, I was a total idiot. Please give me another chance.'

Chapter 5

True to his word, Kane had not only texted Amber but had also spoken to her on the phone to confirm their date. The next few days were difficult for Kane who feared their meeting would have to be cancelled. With the way his week was panning out he was not in the right frame of mind for entertaining.

The disturbing news that a tenant had died in one of his properties hit him badly. A neighbour had contacted the police, concerned that he had not seen the young man for some time. The curtains had remained closed and the continuous sound of loud music could be heard in the next flat. The police made a forced entry into the property, where heroin and syringes were found close to the body. The family had been contacted and as expected, there was much sadness.

On top of this tragedy, his week had not improved. His agent was attempting to recover rent arrears from his other property. Solicitor and court costs were escalating. A decision was made that after the dust had settled both his rental properties would be put up for sale. It would free up monies and support his lifestyle, which no longer involved having to work.

His thoughts turned to Amber. Although he had only known her for a short time, there was no denying that he felt a special magic existed each time he saw her. The catch-22 that kept buzzing away in his mind was that he had set his sights on moving to Spain. Where was this going to leave them?

Swiping the screen of his new 5G mobile, he made the call to Amber. He suggested they took a rain check on Wednesday and could sense her disappointment. They rescheduled their dinner date for the end of the week.

***

Friday nights in the Indian Springs Restaurant, off Hanger Lane, were always lively and Kane was convinced Amber was going to enjoy the evening. The entertainment was to include a singer who wowed diners with his zany take on Beatles songs in a Bengali style. Kane had been lucky to get a booking at short notice.

As they approached the building, Amber's body stiffened and she felt she had to say something. To her mind, being seated in an Indian restaurant could hardly be classed as a romantic meal munching poppadoms and spicy chutney dips. She regretted not telling him sooner that she disliked this type of food. It was all those onions and highly spiced sauces that upset her stomach.

Hanging back on the pavement she tried to let him down easy. 'Sorry, I can't eat curries without feeling ill.' She could sense his annoyance and repeated the 'sorry' word again.

Amber was shocked by Kane's sarcastic reply, 'So we stay hungry, do we? Why didn't you tell me?'

'I didn't know we were going for an Indian, did I?'

His gaze remained fixed on the restaurant window and the diners who were enjoying their meals. He turned to face her. 'It's an expensive place and we were lucky to get a table.'

Unhappy with the tone of his voice, she muttered, 'It's not my fault I don't like the food.'

Echoing in her head were the words: *rude man – tell him you are going home.* She was saddened and confused by his behaviour. Normally he was so polite and considerate, but tonight was an insight into his character that had shocked her. He was acting like a tetchy child. What had changed?

Before she had a chance to tell him the date was over,

he launched in with, 'Do you still want something to eat?'

This time she was not holding back. 'Don't be so rude.'

Amber was fuming with his question, of course she wanted dinner, she was hungry. She debated whether to tell him where to get off, but chose to give him another chance.

'We could try an Italian restaurant in Wembley Park that I know.'

'Yes, that is more to my liking. Just don't talk to me like that again.'

There was no reply.

As they set off for the tube station, Kane accelerated his pace leaving Amber traipsing behind in his wake. Her heart was thumping away and felt like it was going to burst out of her chest. He was acting like a complete jerk; this wasn't the adorable Kane she thought she knew. She still wasn't going to give up. He was in a bad mood and just had to calm down.

It wasn't her fault her choice of food wasn't the same as his. How was she going to react if she eventually had an invitation to visit his home and the smell of Indian food was overpowering? She just knew that cuddling up to him with whiffs of heaven knows what would be a real turn off. She acknowledged that some of the ready meals she consumed didn't smell that appetising. Really their date had been a non-starter. Unbeknown to Amber, her host for the evening had gone through a troubling week and he was taking it out on her, but that was no excuse for subjecting her to all this agony.

After a short ride on the tube, they arrived at their destination. It was a busy Friday night at the Italian restaurant and they were unable to secure a table. After trying two other bistros that were also full, Kane went quiet on her. When he did join in with the conversation, it was in words of one syllable. He refused to be drawn on what the matter was or if she had upset him. His sulking was to continue for some time.

Trying to placate him Amber said, 'I'm sorry I threw a wobbly.'

Her remark appeared to do the trick and thankfully his upbeat voice returned. 'No, it was me who has ruined everything and I was so bad mannered. I've had the week from hell and shouldn't have taken it out on you – I'm really sorry. I was so looking forward to seeing you.'

He linked arms with Amber and said, 'We could try the Red Lion.'

On reaching the pub her heart dropped as they spotted the place was cloaked in darkness. The sign that hung crookedly in one of the windows read: Closed for Refurbishment.

Kane nervously laughed. 'It really hasn't been the evening we wanted, has it? I just hope you want to see me again.'

Amber reached for Kane's hand and slipped her fingers around his. 'Of course, I do.'

***

That night as Amber slipped into bed she sniffed the duvet cover that hadn't been washed for at least a month and sighed. Why would Kane be interested in her with her lazy lifestyle? The skeletons in her cupboard held stories of burglaries and heaven knows what else. She was a train wreck and, in her mind, not a good person to date someone like Kane.

She listened to the sploshing sound of the dripping tap in the bathroom, not that it was broken, she just couldn't be bothered to turn it off.

As she tossed and turned in bed, she remembered her hospital appointment that was scheduled for the next class day. She would have to attend the urology clinic as recently things had got worse requiring more frequent visits to the bathroom. Another worrying thought was that the half term for her Spanish course would then kick in and she wouldn't see Kane for three weeks. She questioned how little she knew about him, not even his surname.

Chapter 6

Amber's eyes lit up at the incoming call on her mobile and to Kane's name that was flashing on the screen. 'Hope you have your passport ready – we fly out of Heathrow on Friday after work to Lisbon for two nights.'

Amber gasped, 'Lisbon.'

'Yep, Club Europe with British Airways and you'll even get a glass of the bubbly stuff. The lounge facilities are awesome, it beats all that hanging around with the crowds in the departure lounge, we also get priority boarding.'

'But we can't go. I hardly know you.'

She heard Kane take a deep breath and his happy voice switched to serious. 'Separate bedrooms, of course. You didn't think I meant …'

The lie that tripped from her lips was delivered with a cheery voice, 'No, that never crossed my mind. Of course, I would love to come and I'll be able to practise my Portuguese.'

'I didn't know you spoke Portuguese.'

'Oh, I did an online course some years ago.'

'I'm impressed.'

'Will the weather still be warm at this time of year?'

'Warmer than here, but bring a coat. Last year I was there and had a great day out visiting Sintra in the mountains, but there won't be enough time for us to go up there.' He paused and then quickly added, 'And just for the record I was on my own and on business.'

Amber nervously laughed.

'Your passport is up to date, isn't it?'

Amber nodded and forgot to reply. Her mind was doing somersaults with the thought of visiting Portugal with Kane. If he had booked a trip to Glasgow, the same excitement would still be raging through her body. The prospect of spending time with him was like a dream come true and there was a real chance of cementing their relationship. This time, she would not ruin things by trying to kiss him or saying something stupid.

'Are you still there?'

'Sorry, yes, my passport is up to date. The last time I had a holiday was to Thassos in Greece with a friend but that was four years ago.' Amber left out the fact that on her trip she accompanied a boyfriend.

'Not somewhere I've been, but a lot of people book the Greek islands with my old company. So, that's us sorted. I'll print off the boarding passes and mail you with the itinerary. Meet me by the Costa Coffee in Terminal Five and don't be late. I tend to veer on the side of caution and arrive an extra hour early. I'll be wearing a rose in my lapel – just kidding.'

***

Breakfast in the first-floor dining room of the hotel afforded incredible views down to the tree-lined Avenida da Liberdade that could very well have been in Paris with its boulevards and pedestrian walkways. Amber gazed at the wonderfully blue sky, the sun that was lighting up the buildings and she listened to the city sounds of an early Saturday morning. It was warm and the window next to their table was partially open. The sound of the slow-moving traffic competed with the construction work of an office block on the corner of the street. She gazed across the road to a traditional tobacco and newspaper kiosk with locals coming and going. The elegant restaurants and bars with outside seating would be a good place to watch the world go by. Her attention turned back to the superb buffet of continental and cooked foods and the smart young waiters in starched aprons serving coffee from tall silver pots.

Kane smiled at her and muttered, 'I love being abroad and especially with you.'

Amber paused eating her wonderful selection of fresh fruit and returned the compliment. 'Me too.'

***

As they left the hotel, Kane took delight in pointing out the bullet-spattered buildings that had taken the brunt of the fighting in the Portuguese civil war. With his fold-up map at the ready, he navigated the route to the Clube de Fado where they were booked for dinner that evening. Grasping his guidebook, he took delight in relaying fact after fact and Amber kept replying, 'Fancy that.'

Despite it being the end of the summer, the jacaranda trees still had their leaves and many of the restaurants and bars displayed hanging baskets with magnificent trailing petunias and calibrachoa bringing colour and warmth to the city.

Stopping to window shop in a pasteleria on the Rua da Adica, the choice of delicious cakes and pastries on offer was amazing. Amber stared at the pirâmide de chocolate and pastel de nata and resisted the temptation to enter the store. Slimming down to a reasonable size was imperative to keep her man interested. Kane kept urging her to go in and said, 'Good chance to use your Portuguese.'

They rode on the ancient looking trams to an area with museums and a covered crafts market where Kane treated Amber to a new handbag and scarf. They took lunch in a bar in the glass pavilion of a shopping centre known as the Centro Colombo. It was there that Kane reached for her hand sending a shot of electricity around her body.

She tensed her fingers as he loosened his. When he let go, neither said a word and returned to eating the mouth-watering sardines and tomato side dish.

Throughout the meal they chatted about their pasts and found they had more in common than they had first thought. They both enjoyed watching films and streamed not only the latest releases but classics too. A favourite actor from long gone decades was James Stewart and both religiously watched *It's a Wonderful Life* in the week before Christmas. They also loved Marmite, peanut butter and Maltesers.

Kane supported various charities and was thrilled to learn of Amber's own efforts to support the homeless. He mentioned the loss of a sum of money he had raised as a donation but refused to be drawn on the circumstances. Judging by the sadness in his face this was a sore episode in his life. Little did he know that the charity money had indeed been stolen by Amber.

Back out in the streets they crossed over to Rosso Square where Kane took photos on his mobile of Amber under the arches. Why he needed so many pictures of her was a mystery. Continuing up the steep streets where shops petered out into low-rise apartment blocks, they paused for breath and looked down on the city. On reaching the São Jorge Castle, further photos were snapped up of the 25 de Abril Bridge and the Belém Tower that guarded the Lisbon waterfront.

Exhausted with their sightseeing, the couple walked down to the city centre and headed for their hotel. As they waited to cross the main avenue, Kane linked arms with Amber who slid her hand into his. They both must have been wondering where all this was leading.

That night they took a taxi to dine at the fado club and, seated in the cavern of a nightclub, they joined other tourists on long benches at oak tables.

Disappointingly, the pre-show meal was about as far away from sampling traditional Portuguese food as dining in a London fast food restaurant. The undercooked steak with a sad offering of chips had to be sent back and returned in much the same state. When the musicians and singers performed, Kane pulled out a pen from his jacket and scribbled on a paper napkin: *It sounds awful, they are all singing out of key and have frowns stitched to their faces.*

Amber laughed and decided against enlightening him on the nature of fado that was a style of music based on deep feelings and the disappointments of love.

After leaving the nightclub they walked the streets and both were in fits of hysterics as Kane imitated the body movements and voice of the wafer-thin fado singer in the long dress. He joked that he wished he had purchased the CD that the staff were pushing from table to table.

Back at the hotel they took the shiny aluminium lift to the third floor and, as Amber watched the illuminated floor numbers change, she secretly hoped they would continue the evening in Kane's bedroom. On reaching the door to her room he leant forward and kissed her full on the lips. She responded by placing her arms around him. It was a wonderful embrace that lasted less than thirty seconds and left her wanting more.

Kane gently pulled away and smiled. 'What a day we have had. I really think we have something special going on here and can't deny I have feelings for you.'

Before Amber had a chance to reply he turned to leave, then swung around to face her. 'When I said separate bedrooms, I meant it. Good night Amber.'

She watched him walk up the corridor with his room key at the ready. He turned and waved before entering. With a noisy click the door shut. Amber was the only person left in the hallway and she sighed.

***

Shortly after another feast of a breakfast on the Sunday morning they took a taxi to the airport for the flight back home. Back in the baggage control hall in Heathrow they waited for their luggage to be delivered on the screechy conveyor belt.

Amber turned to Kane and said, 'I can't wait to meet up again and thanks for an incredible weekend.'

'The pleasure was all mine. I'll give you a ring when I know how I'm fixed for next weekend. How about we head up west.'

Amber was elated with the prospect of spending more time with him.

Chapter 7

It came as a surprise to learn that Kane, who had lived in the London area for much of his life, had never visited the iconic Harrods department store in Knightsbridge. Today he had the whole day planned out to the finest of detail and the last of his treats was the sixty-five pounds per person afternoon tea experience. He read up on the dress code and advised Amber to don smart shoes as trainers were banned. She had no intention of entering the famous store looking like a tramp and wore smart casual clothes under a damp raincoat that had taken a bashing from the heavy rain. What a contrast to under a week ago when it was cool in Lisbon but the sun still shone.

After the splendid and costly tea, with the tiny fancy sandwiches and three bite-size miniature cakes, they took the elevator to the music department. Kane selected a fado CD from the European music collection. He asked the assistant to play the first track and Amber burst into laughter. Listening through headphones he pulled a face and shouted above the music, 'I thought it was just that woman in Lisbon who sang badly, but they all sound the same on this disc.'

Visiting the various floors in the store and clutching her Harrods carrier bag with an overpriced tiny teddy bear, Amber was aware of Kane's anxiety over the price of goods on sale. 'What they are charging is daylight robbery. No doubt it's the Sloane Rangers crowd with more money than sense that buys this stuff.'

Embarrassed by his loud voice, she told him to quieten down.

Kane's outburst caught the attention of a man, with more hair on his face than his head, who was queuing to pay. With an armful of expensive jumpers escaping like snakes on the run, he turned to face Kane and tutted.

Amber shrank further into her damp coat and frowned at her partner. She moved a few steps forward to face the disgruntled shopper and apologised for her boyfriend's behaviour.

'How dare you embarrass me by saying sorry to him.'

'Just calm down.'

Kane still irritated her by adding, 'And, don't tell me to calm down!' He reached out a hand and felt the plastic of her racing green carrier bag and in a moderately lower voice said, 'I bet you paid through the nose for that. Everything in this store sells at crazy prices.'

Tired from her shuffling around the store and annoyance with Kane, Amber carelessly chose her words and came out with, 'Oh, for heaven's sake, you can afford it.'

Kane's face hardened as he bit back. 'How dare you, I've worked my socks off to get where I am. It wasn't always like this and I thought from what I told you about my past you would understand.'

With tears welling up in her eyes, Amber was cross with herself for upsetting him further. 'I didn't mean it to sound like that, I just meant that …' Her voice trailed off as she realised he had turned away from her.

Aware that other shoppers were getting an earful of his tantrum, Kane suggested it was time to head off for the tube station to go home.

Waiting on a crowded platform with the stale air of the Victorian tunnel increasing with every rumble of an approaching train, Kane said, 'I didn't like the way you went for me back there.'

'I've already said, you embarrassed me and it all came out wrong.'

Kane sniffed loudly. 'I'm going to be busy this week so let's take a rain check on meeting up again.'

'What do you mean?' stuttered Amber. 'What's wrong

with you? We've just had a great weekend away and now you have gone cold on me.'

The train came to a halt with a screech of brakes and the doors glided open. It became obvious there was no room for any more passengers.

Waiting for the next train to arrive, Kane casually said, 'I won't be able to see you for a while as I'm off to Spain. It's probably a good thing as we obviously need a break if I annoy you all the time.'

Amber watched him with wide eyes. She was horrified to think they might be breaking up and grabbed his arm. 'You didn't say you were going away. Can't we put all of this behind us? Didn't last weekend mean anything to you?'

There was no reply as the man who was acting like a petulant child turned away to check his phone.

***

When Amber arrived home, a storm of poor reasoning rattled away in her troubled mind. She was losing Kane and her world felt like it was falling apart. Feeling bruised and rejected, depression became the enemy at the door as, once again, her thoughts were spiked with the voices from the past. The teenage girls in the group with their sinister undertones, were willing her to walk on the dark side. Recalling the bullying and indoctrination into their cruel ways, the minutest of details started to download into Amber's tortured head. Every successful shoplifting outing she had chalked up left her body tingling with excitement and ready for the next dare. She had earned their friendship and acceptance, or so she thought.

Later in life, she longed to be the one in control pulling the strings and every so often, at her lowest point, burgling homes was the adrenalin booster she craved for. The money accrued from her ill-gotten ways had always been put to good use, but deep down the feeling of regret stung hard. Feeling so low today, she told herself that she would have one more crack at pulling off the perfect robbery. Similar to an alcoholic or gambler, she promised herself this would be her last act of felony knowing full well that she would probably slip again. Interrupting her thought processes and in unison, the girls again called out to her, *'That's a good girl Amber, this is just what you need.'* The BUZZ had returned.

Chapter 8

Swathes of green shot past the window as the train gathered speed on its way to Ruislip. Amber gazed at the backs of houses with conservatories and gardens with trampolines; it brought back happy memories of the home she was raised in, living with elderly grandparents. She worshipped her Grandma and Pa.

With the clackety-clack sound in her ears, the train shuddered as it reached the station and glided to a stop with an almighty screech of brakes. With a chorus of slamming doors, passengers hurried past Amber along the crowded platform. Making her way out of the station into strong sunlight, she clutched one of her infamous *bags for life* and hung on tightly to her handbag. She crossed the road, walked towards the high street and took a left into a tree-lined avenue known as Riverside.

She told herself that this morning's escapade was going to be a walk in the park. It was also going to be her last. She just needed a bit more cash and then she would be done with walking on the wrong side of the law.

With a headful of voices questioning why she was carrying out this last raid, she still decided to press on. Her plan was to observe the house from as many angles as possible. Sometimes the absence of an alarm on the front of the property sent out the wrong message. The devices were often placed on the rear or side walls. The protected properties had interior sensors to catch intruders. She would ring the doorbell then try the rear of the property before reaching a decision on whether to gain access that way. Face covering and gloves now pulled on to avoid camera recognition, the time to enter the back door had arrived. It would be easy pickings and known in her dark trade as an in and out job.

Inside the 1930's semi-detached house, her eyes focused on the obvious signs of the occupants' attempts to secure their home. Time switch, curtains half drawn in the lounge – all clues for a burglar like Amber. Opening the fridge, it was devoid of any fresh meat, vegetables and dairy products. She convinced herself that this family must be away on holiday. They were probably sunning themselves on a Spanish beach unaware of the intruder in their home. An Xbox with games was quickly transferred to her fold-up holdall.

In her usual way Amber headed for the bathroom. She was impressed with the walk-in shower then shuddered as she caught sight of a fold-up wheelchair propped against the tiled wall. She stood completely still as she cursed herself for breaking into this home. There was a disabled person living here who didn't need all this grief – it was time to go.

Before she had a chance to leave, the clicking sound of the lock on the front door being opened became her worst nightmare. How many times had she gone over what to do in an emergency? Scared rigid, she remained in the bathroom behind the closed door. She was desperate to pass water and feared there would be an accident if she ignored the urge. She crept over to the toilet. Unhappy with not applying the flush or washing of hands, she prayed the person down below would soon leave allowing her to get out of the house as quickly as possible.

The sound of humming in the hallway unsettled Amber. Should she rush out of the room and barge past whoever was out there? The unsuspecting person coming in to water the plants was in for a fright. It was only a matter of moments before they would spot the damaged back door.

Amber took a deep breath and moved forward. She

stopped in her tracks on hearing the screechy voice of a woman who was using her mobile phone.

'Hi Sue, I'm here now. I can see where you left it, so stop panicking. I'll post the letter, so get back to the pool.'

Standing rigidly still, fear was building like a dog barking incessantly in a cage. Why was it that every time she slipped into a stranger's home, the necessity to empty her bladder became an issue? She feared her upcoming appointment at the hospital would highlight worsening urinary tract problems. Perhaps, in the future she'd make a concentrated effort to slow down on the alcohol and drink more water.

A further three long minutes passed and she heard the twelve painfully loud strikes of the clock she had seen on the living room wall. The sound of a kettle being filled scared her. 'Oh God, now she's making a drink,' whispered Amber. She pondered on whether this person was going to have black coffee as she had noticed there was no milk in the fridge.

There was a fair amount of noise coming from the kitchen with the running of water and closing of cupboard doors. Any moment soon she was going to notice the damaged door had been drilled and the game would be up. Fortunately, Amber had wiped the woodwork and floor clean of any dust, something she always did. Then it all went quiet. Was she sitting in the lounge sipping her drink and glancing at the family photos that adorned the walls? It was a waiting game that demanded Amber stayed silent until it was safe to leave.

The sound of a return to the kitchen came as a relief. The lady obviously had no idea that overhead just through the thin plasterboard ceiling an intruder was shaking with fear at the prospect of being discovered. A thought entered Amber's head: what if the person down below needed the toilet?

Amber knew that the thieving had to stop – it wasn't as if she used any of the money for herself. Why was it necessary to carry out the stealing? Irrefutably, it was the buzz, the wretched buzz, and the power over others that fuelled her obsession. Convinced she had lost Kane – what was to stop her wrecking her life?

The welcome sound of the front door slamming signified that Amber was once again alone in the house. She waited for what seemed an age (two minutes to be precise) before flushing the toilet and washing her hands. Scooping up her bags with the stolen items, she glanced at the wheelchair and a tear dribbled down her cheek. How low had she sunk?

With anxiety running at breaking point, she descended the staircase with the intention of returning the possessions. Everything was restored to the exact locations she had found them. No mess had been created, nothing stolen but the back-door lock had been damaged. She pulled out her purse from her coat pocket and extracted all her money. Three twenty-pound notes and sixty-five pence were placed on the kitchen table. It would never be enough to pay for a replacement lock but it was all she had on her.

With the adrenalin pumping, it was imperative to leave in a slow and calm fashion so as not to arouse suspicion from neighbours or the many dog walkers she had noticed in the street.

Out in the back garden she left by the gate and made her way to the front of the house. In her haste to leave, she tripped on a raised paving stone on the path and ended up lying on the edge of the lawn. Unable to move her leg, and in immense pain, she lay on the newly cut grass. She was convinced she had broken her leg.

A tall woman, whose face was laced with hate, placed

a somewhat muddy trainer on her hand.

'Ow, get off me.'

With an increasing ferocity building in her voice, the barrel of a woman screamed, 'What the hell were you doing in my niece's house? I forgot my glasses and came back and saw you coming out of the back garden. What have you nicked?'

'Nothing – let me go. You are hurting me.'

'Stay still or I'll do more than break your fingers.'

Amber's captor extracted a mobile phone from her handbag and pumped stubby fingers on three of the keys and waited to be connected. She answered the many questions and became irritated with the delay in the operator confirming the police would be along shortly.

Remaining perfectly still, Amber took in the smell of the cut grass and pictured the husband of the household duly mowing it ready for going away. The police would soon be on the scene. What was the point of denying her crime?

In a terrified whisper of a voice that eventually grew in volume, Amber said, 'I haven't stolen anything. Look my bag is empty!'

'You must have been in the house when I went in and that freaks me out.'

'I'm sorry, I didn't intend to hurt anyone.' Amber paused for breath and the bending of the truth continued. 'This was my first time doing anything like this. I couldn't afford the rent and owed big time to friends. Please let me go.'

The woman increased her pressure on Amber's hand and laughed. 'Behave won't you. Some years ago, a low-life like you broke into my place and I know what it feels like to be robbed. I'm puzzled that you are well-spoken and am sure you are not short of a bob or two.'

'I told you, I've got myself in trouble and this was to

be a temporary fix.'

Amber's head was working overtime as she recalled her online savings accounts that totalled over seven thousand pounds. With so much money, the question that begged an answer was why she felt the need to break the law? It was difficult to comprehend how the career-minded individual who was on track had blown her chances. What a fool she had been and now she was definitely on the bumpy road out of town.

Her reveries were interrupted as her captor applied greater pressure on her hand. Amber yelped in pain. 'You are going to break my fingers. I have left some money for the lock on the kitchen door I broke. Give me a second chance and I promise I will never do this again. You can say I got away.'

'Nope, people like you make me sick. The police will soon be here and will cart you away. How would you feel if your place was trashed?'

'It wasn't trashed.' Amber sheepishly then added, 'I need the loo.'

'You will have to cross your legs then as I'm not taking my eyes off you. I learnt judo for many years so don't get any ideas about trying to get away. If I have to hurt you whilst making a citizen's arrest, I will.'

The leg was definitely badly hurt and the urgency to use the bathroom would soon become embarrassing. 'Please, I need the toil...'

'You can go when the police arrive.'

'But I need it now, please help me up. I'm not going to run away with this injury. I'm sorry for what I have done and haven't taken anything.'

The woman turned to the crowd that had assembled and lessened her hold on Amber.

A middle-aged lady, possibly a neighbour, with a worried look on her face leant down to talk to Amber.

'Are you alright dear, did you slip?' There was no reply and she looked up and quizzed the onlookers, 'Has anyone called an ambulance?'

'No, just the police – she's a thief and has vandalised my niece's place.'

'No, I didn't.'

'You do know she's disabled and didn't deserve any of this.'

The word disabled thundered through Amber's head like the sound of heavy steel crashing to the ground. She turned her head to stare at the white car and two policewomen who were already on the front path. There was no doubt the ramifications of her actions would result in her being arrested and facing a jail sentence.

Chapter 9

'Has anyone seen Amber?' asked Kane.

A hush came over the crowded classroom as the Spanish tutor tutted, 'I asked her to always mail me if she wasn't coming, not that she ever does. She's missed the last three weeks.' She turned her attention to one of the students, a woman in her mid-fifties with short-cropped hair who was scrolling through pictures of her grandchildren on her mobile phone. 'Sandra, the rule is phones off. Please switch it off now.'

Kane panicked, not only had Amber been absent from class, but there had also been no response to his calls and texts. On their last date he had treated her badly and regretted hurting her. He just wished he could turn back the clock.

One of the students addressed the tutor, 'I don't want to gossip but I've heard something about Amber.'

A chorus of voices rang out with: 'Tell us.'

All eyes were on the woman who was nodding her head. 'I read in the paper about her pleading guilty to housebreaking – I was really shocked.'

There was a hush as everyone took in the news – the air was electric with chatter as the words: *Oh, my God!* echoed through the high-ceilinged room.

Kane bit his lip, leant back in the uncomfortable wooden chair and sighed. He was shocked with the revelation that the girl he thought he knew was up on a burglary charge. There had to be an explanation. She must have been wrongly accused. Amber was an intelligent individual who held down a reasonable job. Yes, she was laid back and had her moments, but surely not this. His mind was made up; he had to offer his support.

Restoring calm to her class, the Spanish tutor reminded everyone that she acknowledged their concern for Amber but a return to their studies was required. Kane nervously fiddled with the top of his highlighter pen and sighed on discovering his forefinger and thumb were coated in fluorescent green. His annoyance quickly shifted to one of panic – in two days' time he was due to return to Spain to visit his holiday home, there was no way he could cancel the trip. With the timing of the news about Amber he was going to have to make contact with her before he set off on his travels.

During the coffee break he made his excuses to leave early. Sitting in his car, he thought back to the last few weeks when he was in Spain, he had attempted to contact her and she blocked his calls. The only logical thing to do was to visit where she lived. This would be a first visiting her home – that was if she would allow him to enter. It was essential to hear her side of the story, only then could he decide on the best course of action.

***

The next morning Kane made the journey by foot to Amber's block of flats. It was a low-rise seventies building with a selection of satellite dishes bolted to the pitted brickwork and miniscule balconies with views up to Harrow on the Hill. He was pleasantly surprised to observe the welcoming entrance lobby with a vase of flowers positioned on an antique table. The light flooded in through the windows brightening up the much-faded photographs of bygone days of Sudbury Hill on the walls. Once inside the interior of the mirrored lift, he tapped the button for the third floor and his mobile rang. Normally in lifts and on tube trains he got no signal. Swiping the screen, he was shocked to discover Amber was calling.

Kane spoke first. 'I've been trying to get in touch with you. I'm in your lift and will be with you in a minute. I'll hang up.'

As he walked along the corridor, he was greeted by Amber who, to his surprise, was walking with a stick. She was shifting from one foot to another.

He touched her on the arm and said, 'Oh, my God, what's happened to you?'

'My leg got twisted when I fell over.'

'You've had a fall – does it hurt a lot?'

'Never mind my leg. Look, I only wanted to speak to you on the phone, not see you. It's not a good time for me. I've just returned from the office.'

Kane glanced at his watch – ten-thirty in the morning was an odd time to be going home. The day had only just begun.

It was a slow walk as he followed her through the narrow hallway that was littered with two black bags waiting to be taken out to the bins.

On entering the lounge, he took in the chaotic and dirty room and tried to ignore the remnants of a takeaway meal. The spare ribs with a disgusting brown sauce smelt awful.

'I haven't had a chance to clear up this morning.'

Kane lied when he told her that it didn't bother him. The place was a tip. In contrast to the disorderly flat, her books were stacked neatly in a free-standing pine bookcase. The titles included: *American Independence at what price? Quantum Physics Level Three* and various travel books. He always knew she was a bright girl but why was she living in this squalor and, more importantly, adopting the life of a thief?

'You must have gone into work early.'

Amber ignored his question and nervously coughed before stabbing a finger in the direction of the sofa that was cluttered with newspapers.

As he cleared the mess from the cushion he said, 'How's the job going?'

She shrugged her shoulders. 'I just got sacked.'

'What.'

'Yeah, I'm in big trouble and they let me go.'

Pretending not to know the bigger picture, the words tumbled from his mouth. 'What sort of trouble? Look I'll try and help. Just tell me.'

Amber leant forward and quietly mouthed, 'You really don't want to know.'

'Try me.'

To his surprise she readily caved in and his hopes of it all being a terrible misunderstanding were dashed.

'I burgled a house and was arrested. A woman caught me and that's how I hurt my leg and my hand.' There was a pause as her lip started to quiver. 'I … I've been to court and am waiting to learn when the hearing will be. I'm so ashamed and just know I'll go to prison.'

'Oh, my God. Is this your first offence?'

'Yes, but it's complicated.'

'You shouldn't serve time for a first offence but then I'm not a legal man. I'm having trouble taking in all of this. It feels like I don't know you. Why would you do such a thing? You didn't mention anything about struggling financially. On the contrary, you said you were reasonably well off and owned this place.' Kane shook his head and added, 'What I can't get my head around is after our incredible weekend away, you do this.'

'You were so horrible to me in Harrods and told me we were over, so I went off the rails again. Something triggered inside me when you broke off our relationship. I reached an all-time low and did this crazy thing.'

'What do you mean, off the rails again? For heaven's sake you are a grown woman, not some off-the-wall teenager. You are not on drugs, are you?' Kane stared into Amber's eyes searching for clues.

'No, definitely not. It was down to getting a buzz. It was a feeling of power.'

'But stealing is wrong, and I didn't have you down as a law breaker. Why, with your intelligence, did you do such a thing? Does this go back to years gone by – I still can't grasp why you would do this now?'

The lie that spilled from Amber's lips was fast in its delivery. 'It was just the once and I didn't take anything. I got caught and won't be doing that again. I regret my actions and feel woefully inadequate. My confidence has gone and I can't stop crying.'

'I don't know what to think.'

Amber lowered her voice to barely audible and calmly said, 'Would you like a cup of tea; I'm going to have one?'

'No, I don't, and I won't pretend I'm not disappointed in you. None of this makes sense and it feels like you are not telling me the whole story. It's not as if you needed the money. Do you have a solicitor?'

'No, I assumed as I was guilty, I didn't need one.'

'Come on Amber, of course you need one. Are you on bail?'

'Nope, no bail, only that I can't leave the area. I don't want to go to prison.' Barely containing the sob which threatened to erupt, Amber closed her eyes and waited for his reply.

Kane sighed. 'Let's hope not. You now have a criminal record and getting a new job will be hard. I'll get you some legal help and try to recover some lost ground.'

'Are you sure you want to help me?'

'We all deserve a second chance.'

Now on her feet, she buried her head into his shoulder and wept uncontrollably. This was the moment he desperately wished he hadn't given her such a hard time back in the department store. The build up to seeing her had been laced with his own problems and his flare-up may well have been the catalyst for her doing the things she did. With his feelings riding high he comforted the woman who was turning his life upside down.

An agreement was made that he would push for a legal meeting the next day and let her know the details. His thoughts were bubbling like peas on the boil. Why had a wonderful girl like Amber slipped down life's greasy pole? There had to be more to her odd behaviour than the enjoyment of the so-called buzz she described. There was a chance she may slip again and where would this leave her, or him for that matter? This was without doubt the biggest punt he'd ever taken – he'd ride the waves with Amber and see where the journey took him.

***

That night Kane slept badly as he tossed and turned in his king-size bed. His thoughts harboured on Amber being arrested and the difficulties that lay ahead. With a criminal record, how was she to seek employment as well as cope with her name being plastered all over the internet?

He struggled to comprehend how anyone with her intelligence could stoop so low as to break into another person's home. His own experience of being robbed still left a nasty taste in the mouth. He'd lost an iPad, a few possessions and all that charity money he had raised, but the intrusion into his personal space hurt the most. Oddly, the offender had left the place tidy and had even replaced the toilet roll – this he found disturbing. Thankfully the insurance claim had been settled swiftly.

Thinking back to the mess in Amber's flat he

wondered if he could cope with taking their relationship further. When he thought of his tidy living space and how hectic her unhygienic home was, he shuddered. He would be forever tidying up after her and this would inevitably lead to arguments.

Contrary to her seemingly chaotic lifestyle, he remembered her books that had been in pristine condition. Each of the literary treasures was standing to attention and looked as if they had been handled with gloves. Her choice of reading matter clearly fell into the category of serious factual literature. One of the titles, *Canadian Hydroelectric Innovation,* confirmed that she was some reader. His interest lay in light fiction along with his favourite *Tintin* and *Marvel* annuals.

Amber was a complicated person, someone who needed his help. His mind sprinted to an exciting scenario as he pictured holding her tight in bed and never wanting to let go. What was happening to him – where were all these feelings coming from? They had attended the same Spanish lessons and, so far, had enjoyed relatively few dates. There were things about her that worried him but there was much more that he adored. There could be no denying he was falling in love with her.

When he finally drifted off to sleep, he dreamt of Amber but everything was totally different. Meeting her wealthy parents had been difficult as they cross-examined him on his suitability to wed their only daughter. In his dream, his home was the untidy one whilst hers resembled a palace with an army of cleaners who obeyed her every command. Throughout the fantasy they returned to bed to make love and on one such occasion, she broke the news that she was pregnant.

Chapter 10

Two days can seem a long time, especially when all Amber could think about was the man who had thrown her a lifeline. She was so grateful for his intervention, offering legal representation and the assurance that everything was going to be alright. The word *alright* was probably an overstatement as the label of criminal would haunt her for the rest of her life.

Being dismissed from the job she excelled at was unquestionably going to decrease her chances of finding new employment. She recalled the meeting with her boss who told her that he had no choice but to let her go. As she left the offices, it felt like a million eyes were burning the word thief onto her back.

Amber was wishing away the days of the week until she met up with Kane again. She smartened herself up with a new hairstyle that she hoped would make her look prettier. From an up-market clothes shop in Harrow High Street, she bought a skirt and top in an effort to look better and rebuild her confidence.

***

Kane's solicitor had been in touch and they met up in his cramped office that had no window and a ridiculously low ceiling. An enormous radiator was pumping out heat that left Amber feeling too hot. As she sat waiting for him to speak, she struggled to remove her coat.

Jason Boulter, a man in his early forties, was casually dressed in jeans and a floral-patterned shirt that could easily have been mistaken for a woman's blouse. She questioned whether he should have worn a suit. As Amber accepted the outstretched hand to shake, she kept staring at his enormous Adam's apple that continued to move even though he had stopped speaking. His long, dark hair held a fringe that flopped around as this quirky man straightened files on the massive mahogany desk. A large computer screen accompanied a silver keyboard that was tucked neatly into the stand.

The solicitor looked up and explained that today was his day off and apologised for his casual attire. Amber waved a dismissive hand in the air and moved around on the hard chair to avoid hurting her leg and groaned as the pain returned. She sipped her scorching hot drink as her eyes scanned the room, taking in the numerous documents and files. The coffee she had reluctantly accepted was bitter and too hot to drink so she placed the cup on the carpet next to her handbag. Extra care was taken to ensure the mug with the hideous Christmas theme was far enough away from her feet to avoid a spill. At home she couldn't have cared less but, in this office, it was another matter.

The solicitor checked through his inbox to locate a message from Kane. 'I have it somewhere here – ah, yes, here it is. Kane has brought me up to date with your case.'

His forced smile worried Amber. He drew in breath and said, 'Have to see how we can proceed on this matter.' He then turned his attention to Amber who was holding her leg. 'Are you in a lot of pain and how did you do it?'

'The hospital said it was a bad sprain and I can hardly put any weight on it. When I was arrested, I fell over and…'

'Oh, I see. There was nothing in my report of an injury.'

Amber looked over to the door and quietly said, 'Would you mind if I use your toilet?'

'No, of course not, second door on the left in the hallway.'

When Amber returned, she carefully lowered herself onto the chair to avoid hurting her leg and observed the solicitor's face that was turning from a frown to an air of puzzlement.

Holding a file with her name printed in large black type, he withdrew a single sheet of paper and carefully laid it on the highly polished desk. He straightened the document a couple of times before moving a hand to adjust the blue glasses on the bridge of his nose.

'I spoke with Kane yesterday and he's concerned that you have full representation at any cost. He will be covering all the legal fees. I see you are pleading guilty but one area that will be addressed at the hearing is whether this was an isolated incident.'

Amber fidgeted with the buttons on her sleeves. The expression on her face was vacant and her eyes held a cloudiness that must have concerned the legal man. Her head was spinning as she rehearsed the lines that she hoped would be convincing. The question that was about to rear its head was her reason for crossing the line. She stuck to her story that it was a one-off that she now regretted. It was of course wrong flouting the law and she hoped during her court case that her remorse would be acknowledged.

Jason Boulter broke Amber's chain of thought when he leant forward and offered her a tissue. 'Are you alright Miss …? No need to get upset. Let me fetch you some water.'

Embarrassed and momentarily unable to reply, Amber dabbed her eyes. When she did speak it was in a low voice that gradually grew in volume.

'I … I'm so sorry. I haven't been feeling too well these last few days with all this hanging over me. It's so hot in here.'

The solicitor stretched out a hand to open a small fridge to the side of his desk. He passed over a bottle of chilled water. 'Here, this should cool you down. Sorry about the heat, the thermostat is knackered – I'll prop the door open to give you some air. We can reschedule for another day if you like.'

'Thanks, but no, let's press on.'

'Returning to the matter in question, would you like to expand on why you chose to…'

Leaning forward and interrupting, the harsh reply that slipped from Amber's lips made the solicitor sit up in his chair and frown. 'Breaking into someone's home was like I was high on drugs. I got a kick, a great rush of adrenalin that lifted my spirit. I already told you it was a one-off and I got caught. I won't be doing it again.'

'Are there any mitigating circumstances that you would like to divulge that may have a bearing on your case?'

Amber stared steadfastly at the ground and muttered, 'Like what?'

'Anything that may persuade the judge not to rule with a custodial sentence?'

There was no response from Amber who was now staring at a spider weaving an enormous web between the filing cabinet and the wall. Extending a hand to wipe away all the hard work, her reveries were disturbed as she heard the cough from Mr Boulter who was shaking his head.

'Kane informed me you held down a decent job and earned reasonable money and with your…'

'I no longer have a job.'

'I am aware of that, only I struggle to believe that financially you needed to set out on the road to thievery. There was always the chance you would be apprehended.

Furthermore, the items of property you removed – may I ask what you have done with the monies you amassed?'

'I didn't take anything – I changed my mind and put things back.'

Amber bit her lip. Her head was spinning as the events of the robbery played over, only on this occasion a new scenario frightened her. It was seeing that fold-up wheelchair and a vision of a disabled person, possibly a young child struggling to lead a normal life. Enough was enough; it was time to come clean. Living with the shame was something she knew she couldn't cope with any longer.

Her words were slow in coming. 'It was more than once. I stole on many occasions.'

The solicitor looked shocked. 'Oh, I see, this places a different perspective on your case. You will need to make a new statement to the police and also clarify a number of factual inaccuracies for me to adjust your plea. For the record, exactly how many times are we talking about?'

A hand crept up to Amber's forehead as she replied, 'Three years, that's how long it has been going on. Eleven times – but there were more occasions when I decided against going in when I spotted alarms or people around. I never benefitted from any of the stolen items. All proceeds were turned into funds for supporting a charity.'

'With respect, whilst donating to charity is an admirable thing to do, nevertheless these monies were secured illegally.'

'Yes, I know all that and I'm changing my plea to guilty on multiple counts. My reputation is broken irrevocably. I have lost everything.'

The lawyer shuffled his heavy body on the wooden chair with a floral cushion and removed his glasses to bend the arms backwards and forwards. 'This will be more difficult than I first thought. Are you able to recall the dates and addresses of the said burglaries?'

'Yes, I remember things easily.'

'That will be helpful. The enormity of your actions will undoubtedly have consequences.'

'Just level with me – in plain English and not any of your legal banter – am I going to prison?'

The man awkwardly leant back in his chair and sarcastically replied, 'In my very best English, I can only confirm that I will do everything in my power to help you. Any information like you suffering from stress and having recently visited a doctor may have a bearing on the case.'

'Only that my mind for the last few years has been in a mess – I only wish I'd sought help.'

Deep in thought, Amber was reliving some of the recent burglaries and, at that time, she had been convinced that by donating monies from the sale of the stolen goods it would exonerate her actions.

The solicitor waited to attract her attention. 'Your case would be helped by you visiting a doctor to highlight the presence of your fragile mental health. Are you happy to go private to see a counsellor as delays waiting for the NHS could take months?' He paused and noisily sucked in breath before continuing. 'I have to ask if you are on any medication or use recreational drugs.'

'No, I don't!' she said emphatically.

'I just wish you had sought representation earlier. We need to build a good defence pinpointing your slip into crime as something you deeply regret. You do regret your actions, don't you?'

'Of course, I do.'

Her eyes homed in on the man who was typing at speed. She observed his frantic fingers racing along the keyboard. There was hardly a sound from the keys as he hurriedly recorded details of the meeting. She wondered if Kane and Mr Boulter were friends. He looked up and paused typing and then returned to his report.

'Kane said you were his solicitor – do you also know him as a friend?'

There was a pause. The reply that followed shocked Amber. 'You could say that, I'm his brother.'

Amber reflected on Kane's offer to help. The words he had used were to arrange legal help. There was no mention of his brother's profession; then again, she had never enquired on Kane's surname so did not make the connection.

'Miss McCarthy, as you are a friend of my brother, I think you should relay to him your change of plea to guilty for multiple thefts. I also feel, with you knowing my sibling, I should hand over this case to a colleague here, as it is a bit too close to home for me. That's all for today and I hope your leg recovers soon.'

As Amber reached for her stick and pulled herself up to leave, the cruellest of voices in her head was hammering home the obvious: *You are going to jail and when Kane learns about your thirst for thievery, he will disappear just as quickly as he entered your life.*

Chapter 11

Kane ignored Amber's untidy apartment and reluctantly sat on the sofa with the pile of clean clothes that awaited ironing. There was a smell of bacon and he craned his head in the direction of the kitchen whilst speculating on the other rooms and their condition. His head was still spinning with the conversation he had had on the phone with his brother who suggested things were more complicated than first expected. Jason also relayed his concern over the mental state of Amber and the necessity for a doctor's visit and psychiatrist's report.

Today Amber was well dressed and ready to chat. 'Jason said he is your brother and won't be handling my case and will assign another colleague to take it over.'

Labouring his words, Kane replied in a disinterested voice, 'Yes, that's right, we are related but don't get on that well. I've told you this before. That's another story. Putting family politics to one side, he's ace with legal matters but I can understand his reluctance to represent you.'

'You should have told me you were related.'

'I would have thought with the same surname as mine you would have worked that out. Boulter is not a particularly common name. When I made my introduction in the Spanish class, I told you my name.'

'No, you didn't.'

'Let's just agree to disagree.'

'Look Kane, I've been thinking and there is no way I can accept your help financially – I have some savings and …'

'Behave, won't you. That's what friends are for and I'm flush with selling my share in the business. Now, tell me more about what happened. I have this feeling that if anyone can get you off with community service and a fine, it has to be Jason's colleague. Let's face it, this is your one and only offence.'

Amber looked anywhere but into his eyes. 'That's just it, it's not my first time. I'm changing my plea to multiple burglaries. Eleven to be precise. I could go down for a long stretch.'

Her revelation hit him hard. This was the woman who kept him awake at night, the person he wanted to spend the rest of his life with. He wasn't sure he could cope with all the stress she was unloading on him. When he heard she had been arrested he was shocked but wanted to give her another chance. Multiple burglaries, that was a whole new ball game. When his brother rang him, he warned Kane that Amber had a few screws loose and did he really want to carry on a relationship with her.

When Kane had composed himself, he spoke with a tremble in his voice. 'E... e... eleven times you say. You are telling me that the Amber I was getting to know is not only a compulsive liar but also a thief. How do you think those poor guys felt on discovering you had trashed their home and stolen valuables?'

'That's not how it was, if anything I left their places in a better state than when I arrived. I picked up things off the floor and left the bathroom cleaner than I found it.'

Now on his feet, Kane was waving his hands around like he was controlling traffic in Piccadilly Circus. Glancing around the untidy room, he spat out his words, 'Another lie. Don't you ever stop to think before you open your mouth? Do you take me for a fool? Look at the state of this place, it looks like a tip and you say you tidied up other people's mess when you broke into their homes. You are a compulsive liar and must be sick in the head.'

'You don't understand – I stole to finance my gifting

to a charity. I'm finished with breaking the law and will pay a big price for my mistakes, without a doubt.'

'Oh, just listen to yourself, a right little Robin Hood, I don't think. Next you will be telling me that all tigers have become vegetarians.'

'Oh, why don't you go to hell. I said I gave the money to a good cause.'

'Why didn't you fund the charity with your own money?'

'Not sure,' came back the pathetic reply.

With eyes focused on Amber's sad face, Kane didn't know what to think. 'I thought we had something special going here – I was obviously wrong. As I said before, I will finance all your legal costs. I am a man who keeps his word. But there is no more you and me. You also need to know I will soon be living abroad permanently.'

Amber tried to grab his arm. He pulled sharply away and raised his eyes to the ceiling on hearing her say, 'Please don't break up our friendship, I'm sure we can work it out.'

The voice in Kane's head was set to screeching, insisting that he saw the woman for what she was and to leave all future contact solely to the legal representation.

Out in the street Kane pulled up the collar of his blue coat for warmth. Today his heart felt like it had been ripped in two. He had to let her go.

***

Over the next few weeks Kane attended his Spanish classes and concentrated on soaking up as much of the language as possible. Amber was absent from the lessons. This fuelled speculation from fellow students as to how she was getting on and when her court appearance would take place. Someone even insisted that if it was her first offence she would get off with a fine. Only one person in that room knew the truth. Amber was in deep trouble and even with his intervention, her chances of avoiding prison were slim.

***

The day that Kane arrived late for class, he was shocked to see Amber sitting there and amazingly her desk space was the tidiest in the room. She looked smartly dressed and had a shorter hairstyle that suited her well. If he wasn't mistaken, she had lost weight, much thinner in the face – not surprising with all that was going on. She was wearing an attractive long-sleeved, pale green blouse and smart jeans. She smiled sweetly at him and then turned her attention to the straightening of books and pens that were laid out neatly in a line next to her mobile phone. The symmetry and precision of her actions concerned him. Amber didn't do tidy – what was going on?

He panicked as he realised there was only one place to sit and that was next to Amber. How could she possibly maintain such a calm and confident manner with all the troubles she was carrying. Here she was acting like nothing had occurred as she waited for her trial date to arrive.

Surely the reception she received from the others must have been difficult. Everyone wanting to know the details and speculating on the outcome of the court case. Sandra with the unruly red hair and crazy owl-shaped glasses would have given her a hard time and later enjoyed dining out on the story with her coterie of friends. It was strange that Amber chose to attend the class, possibly her built-in survival mode had kicked in demanding she face up to her demons.

Kane stammered as he addressed the class. 'I... I... I'm sorry, I got delayed and...'

Drumming gnarled fingers on her desk, the Spanish teacher's impatience was obvious. '*Por favor*, sit down – we only have thirty minutes left to complete the exercise on what we all did last week. Everyone will be reading their work.'

All eyes were on Kane as he pulled out the chair which made a grating sound on the wooden floor. Amber smiled at him and added to the disruption of the class with a further scraping noise as she shifted her own seat to make room. He felt massively awkward at being the centre of attention.

There were only inches between Amber and himself and he was sweating profusely leaving him wishing the ground would swallow him up. His earlier plan to keep a distance from her had failed miserably. How was he to know she would suddenly come back to class?

Amber mouthed a silent 'Hi' and touched his hand that electrified the sinews in his entire body. His arm jerked as he pulled away sharply.

'What the hell are you doing here?' whispered Kane.

'Charming!'

A raft of laughter from fellow students was quickly suppressed as their tutor rose from her chair.

Kane nervously extracted a hardback notebook containing his homework with the title *Spain in October* and placed it on the desk and managed to knock off his pen which rolled along the floor. It came to a stop close to the tutor who bent down to retrieve it. His face blushed bright red as she handed it back and he cringed as she said, 'Perhaps you should read first.'

Unusually for Kane, who normally had no problem airing his homework, he struggled to complete the first sentence. He failed to control the shaking of his hand as he grasped his notebook. He was so embarrassed. Somehow, he got through the ordeal with a number of mis-pronunciations and pauses that were shared with the audience.

His nervousness hadn't stemmed from arriving late or the teacher unsettling him, it was being in the presence of Amber. He took in her wonderful perfume that reminded him of his second home in Spain and the aroma of exotic flowers that adorned the walled garden. Judging by the look on her face, she was relaxed and getting on with her life.

At the close of the lesson Kane stood up and informed Amber he had to leave.

'Just hang on a bit, I need to talk to you.'

'Can we catch up another time as I'm up against a deadline?'

She frowned and commenced packing up her books and pens. Everything was placed neatly in the red leather bag and she swept a hand across the fabric to remove a scuff mark. 'I just want a word with you in the corridor – I won't hold you up.'

Out in the busy reception area they managed to stand in the entrance to the kitchen and Kane nervously clutched his work bag. Shaking his head, he was determined to speak first. 'What I don't understand is how you come back to class as if nothing has happened.'

'Staying at home worrying won't help. I need to move on as I wait for news of my trial.'

'Mmm …'

Amber frowned. 'I only wanted to bring you up to date with what your brother's legal team has been doing for me.'

'There's no need as he keeps me informed. Now, I really must go.'

It was obvious that Amber was dismayed by the

coldness in his voice and felt the need to ask, 'Have I upset you?'

Kane shrugged his shoulders. His resigned disapproval unsettled her. 'Now what makes you think that?'

Amber waved a hand in the air. 'This is crazy. We were getting on so well and I thought you wanted to help but now you shun me. I can't ignore your generosity in helping with the legal side but I just wanted to thank you properly and say I can manage to pay my way.'

'No, you hang onto your money. You will need it if you end up inside.'

Amber was clearly shocked and fluttered her eyelids a number of times before replying. 'I'm hoping I don't get a prison sentence. You don't think I will, do you?'

'Yes, I do! It sounds to me as if you are in denial.'

'Of course, I'm not. I'll take my punishment and move on.' Amber then switched the conversation to Kane's forthcoming birthday and the voucher she had for him.

'How did you know when my birthday was?'

'Facebook. I sent you a friend request and you never accepted. I could see from your profile when it was.'

Kane failed to notice the expression on her face and shrugged his shoulders. 'So, you've been checking up on me. If I wanted you as friend on Facebook, I would have accepted your request.'

'That's not fair. We were going out together. I thought we might at least stay friends.'

'Three dates and a weekend away, that's all it was. Since then there's been a lot of water under the bridge and, to be totally honest, I've had enough.'

Their raised voices attracted disapproving looks from passers-by.

Amber thrust an envelope into his hand. She turned away without saying goodbye and scuttled down the corridor. Kane's mind was literally doing somersaults as he watched her leave by the main entrance.

Grasping the envelope, he extracted a green card with the wording 'twenty-five pounds' emblazoned on the front in large gold type. He read further down to the company name of the off-licence group and the special offers for Chilean wines. His heart sank. What was she doing giving him a gift for alcohol?

Out in the car park Kane stood by his silver Porsche and stared up at the dirty black clouds that were moving around like dragons playing in the sky. The drizzle was turning to persistent rain, soaking his coat. As people hurried by to jump into their cars to avoid the worst of the downpour, he remained glued to the spot clutching the voucher Amber had given him.

The cruellest of voices was replaying the conversation he had had with his brother on the phone the previous evening. The update on Amber's case had upset him as Jason advised that she would undoubtedly serve a prison sentence. Jason expanded on his news with a revelation that shocked and confused him to the core. His exact words were: *She wants to distance herself from you and mentioned she could never fancy you. It appears that you unsettle her with your staring as if you are undressing her. She appreciates your help financially but will pay her way and will backpedal on seeing you again. The odd thing she said was she thought you were a recovering alcoholic – you didn't tell her, did you?*

The word 'alcoholic' resonated as the past came thundering back to Kane. Confiding in Amber about his past addiction was not something he had chosen to do. If Jason had told her, why had she given him a voucher to buy alcohol? What he couldn't comprehend was his brother's assertion that Amber felt unsettled each time they met. Jason must have been bending the truth.

Kane opened the door of his car and fell heavily onto

the newly-restored, grey leather seat. The rain splattered the shiny walnut dashboard and a lone leaf skipped through into the interior and lodged on the passenger seat. Normally he would have ejected any foreign bodies from the car but he just kept staring out at the rain. He kept going over his brother's comment that Amber wanted nothing more to do with him. Wasn't it her who had just said she had thought their relationship mattered?

As for her attending the lessons, he was confident Amber would have stayed away if she disliked him that much. Jason was wrong. Putting things into perspective, Kane still felt she was history and he had to make a fresh start. Booze definitely wasn't the path he was going to revisit. Tearing her gift voucher into tiny fragments, he lowered the window and watched the fragments of card pirouette down like crashing helicopters into a puddle of water.

Switching his thoughts to Spain and new friends, he was determined to enjoy life instead of fretting about Amber and her complicated existence. The problem was his head was making all the right decisions yet his heart was saying something entirely different. Enough was enough, today would be his last visit to the community centre to study Spanish.

With the windscreen wipers scraping madly on the glass that had steamed up with his warm breath, he manoeuvred the car out of the space for the journey home. He caught sight of his tutor who was desperately attempting to pick up the contents of her bag that had fallen into one of the puddles. He pulled the car to a stop and climbed out to help. Much of her paperwork was soaked and the woman was crying. Kane's heart went out to her.

'Let me help you – what a day to drop your bag.'

'Oh, thank you. It seems everything has gone wrong

today.'

He retrieved the wet items that included a relatively new looking iPhone and placed them back in the bag. Normally this lady was so hard and unfriendly, but not today. He felt sorry for her and carried the heavy holdall the short distance to her car.

As she thanked him, her words warmed his soul. 'That was a kind thing stopping to help me. I always knew you were a gentleman.'

She then lent forward to kiss his rain-soaked cheek and whispered a further *gracias*. With a click of the key fob, the bodywork on her Range Rover momentarily glowed orange as the lights flashed. Kane was saddened he would not see her again, but his weekly visits to master another language had come to a close. Still, he would soon be living in Spain and learning more Spanish every day.

Chapter 12

The late November sunshine lit up the Andalusian whitewashed houses with sandy coloured tiled roofs. Jacaranda trees towering over the buildings cast shadows on the main square prompting a Labrador dog to keep moving to harness any remaining warmth. The locals took pride in maintaining their painted wall pots that were as brightly coloured as the flowers that cascaded down from them. Massive geraniums and small white star treasures adorned the walls of the dwellings and there were drifts of bougainvillea at every turn.

Today the sky was a glorious blue with wisps of puffy white cloud crumpling the tops of the mountains. Small delivery vehicles struggled to navigate the bumpy, narrow, cobbled streets and avoiding the pedestrians was always tricky. More often than not there was a degree of impatience with beeping of horns and raised voices, only to return moments later to a wonderful stillness.

Even at this time of year there were plenty of holidaymakers all vying to be heard as the familiar words were aired: *Isn't this beautiful*? The views from every vantage point still thrilled Kane, even more so now he lived there.

Frigiliana was such a popular place to live and there were now over three thousand residents in the area. With all the new housing developments, this charming location had adjusted well to massive changes. People settling in the region from foreign countries outnumbered the Spanish locals bringing wealth and a boost to the economy. A wave of new restaurants offering culinary delights boasted mind-blowing panoramic views. In essence, whilst Frigiliana enjoyed the benefits associated with tourism, the region was struggling with the modern world as it concreted over the foothills of its mountains.

On a daily basis, visitors alighted from the buses and, within no time, hideous ceramic gifts were purchased as retailers secured maximum euros to their keeping.

Tourists continued to photograph the amazing views that had already been captured millions of times over. The heavy slog up the steep steps, past terraces of houses, was rewarded with gift shops and galleries. An abundance of potted and hanging plants complimented the brightly coloured front doors with confusing numbering. It always amused Kane to observe the ceramic house plates. Villa fourteen was situated in a terrace of ten. The adjoining building was known as thirty-one.

On this particular morning, Kane was seated in the main square. He observed a young workman taking a break from painting the wrought iron railings on the steps of the Church of San Antonio. The man with long hair was bare chested and drank from a bottle of water, slurping noisily before devouring a bag of crisps. On returning to his duties, a woman appeared on the scene pushing a buggy containing a baby. The man kissed her briefly on the cheek and she pulled away sharply. No words were spoken, only a frown on both faces as she turned to leave.

Kane waited patiently to be served his coffee. It had been over ten minutes and he wondered if the order had been forgotten. He stared at the obligatory trio of old men seated on a concrete bench opposite and waved. There was no reaction only a return to their people watching, nodding of heads and waving of walking sticks. More than likely, in their eyes, he was another tourist or, worse still, a newcomer to the hamlet of houses that was practically attached to their village. There was a price to pay with the onslaught of overseas residents settling or securing second homes.

He turned his attention to an elderly man who was leaving his home, who may well have been a hundred years old. Clutching his stick for support, it took two attempts to shut the wooden door with peeling varnish and cracks to the woodwork. The house number in blue spidery lettering read: 100. Kane wished he hadn't left his phone at home – it would have made a great post on Facebook. How many times had his friends, including his new young lady, insisted he left it on? If truth be known, his reluctance to stay in contact was to avoid taking calls from Amber as she kept on trying to reach him. A visit to the phone shop in town to purchase a new SIM card would soon put a stop to her calling.

Hadn't his brother said that Amber was not interested in him and how unsettled she felt in his company? If this was the case, why was she still trying to make contact? It just didn't make sense. He deliberated on whether Jason was trying to keep them apart – it wouldn't be the first time he'd interfered in his relationships with women.

Kane shuddered, not with the breeze that was whistling through the streets, but with the thought of the past being dragged up again. He certainly wanted to avoid the nightmares returning that mostly slipped seamlessly into daymares. The two people he treasured more than anything in the world were doing his head in. In truth he needed a break from both Jason and Amber.

Concentrating on his new life in mainland Spain had to be the way forward for him.

Chapter 13

Three days before Easter, Amber slipped off her blouse and, as instructed, folded it before placing it in the grey bag with her name emblazoned in capitals, followed by A4633 HMP Fairfield Kent. The women's prison administration manager, a mean-spirited woman with bare arms like tree trunks and a frown cemented on her face, kept tutting as the new prisoner reluctantly undressed. Amber's eyes strayed to the large, high-waisted, black trousers and dangling chain of keys that swung like pendulums and rattled continuously. A much-scuffed mobile phone clipped to a belt kept bleeping and was ignored by the woman whose attention was reserved for Amber.

Standing in the small room in just her white bra, the embarrassment became too much for Amber. Warden Kathleen Dorfee 2991 was showing signs of impatience and muttered under her breath the instruction to hurry up. She kept turning to her colleague to discuss films they had been streaming and which new ones to watch.

Amber's back stiffened and she felt the sensation of sweat forming under her armpits as the humiliation of being naked heightened. The tiled floor was cold and she curled up her toes in an effort to keep warm. Determined not to cry, she told herself the ordeal would soon be over and possibly there would be no further contact with the bully with the scraped-back brown and purple-streaked hair.

The business of stripping off for the intimate inspection was cruel as the door had been left open for the prying eyes of prison staff passing by. At one stage a lady from the administration team came in to hand over documents and to chat with her colleagues. Amber covered her modesty, placing her hands in front of her. She gazed down at her much thinner body and recalled the crazy diet she had forced on herself. Over the period of six months she had lost so much weight, the stones and pounds had dropped away resulting in a trimmer figure and narrower face. Eating the minimum along with all that exercising had paid off. She took pride in walking ten thousand steps a day and checking the counts on her smart watch.

The humiliation of standing almost completely naked was freaking her out. It felt like the two sets of eyes were monitoring her every move.

Warden 2991 impatiently raised her eyes to the concrete ceiling. 'That includes the bra – speed up, won't you?'

'Can't I have some privacy while I get undressed. Why is it necessary for you to watch me?'

'Stop being paranoid – I'm not looking at you; I conduct as many as two of these procedures a day and for your information I have just missed my tea break. During your induction we have to check you are not bringing anything into the prison like drugs or a sim card. As soon as you are ready for your shower I will wait outside.' She paused and then begrudgingly added the word *please*.

Struggling with the clasp of her bra, Amber's hands failed to undo the garment and it took a few attempts before it was dropped onto the wooden bench that smelt of bleach.

'Okay, now you can see I'm not carrying anything, leave me to have a shower.'

This brought about a reaction from the woman who yawned loudly exposing a mouthful of discoloured and buckled front teeth. 'Stand with your legs apart.'

Both guards gave a cursory glance to the stark-naked woman who was now beginning to cry.

'Pull yourself together, it's all over now. Make sure you thoroughly wash your hair. I will leave a towel on this chair with your clean clothes. Give me your belt, watch and rings. I will issue a receipt for them. They will be returned when you have completed your stretch. Ring the bell when you are ready.'

The two unfriendly wardens strode out of the bathroom and sat on chairs in the corridor. Their gaze never shifted from the room.

The wet room was larger than expected with an enormous metal shower head that could have been used as a prop for the latest *Star Wars* movie. Activating the power button with a thump of her wrist, it was pleasing to feel the hot water cascade down her body. She squeezed the unbranded body wash bottle that emitted a rude noise. The soap shot out and coated the wall tiles with a cloying racing green. After the brief shower, Amber attempted to dry off the tiles with a flannel ready for the next person. She gave up and stepped out of the cubicle onto the cold floor. Aware that she had been asked to get a move on, she tried to hurry but the far from adequate, worn towel proved useless.

She caught sight of her anxious face in the partly steamed up mirror on the wall and groaned. The dreaded day had arrived and the fourteen months of imprisonment had begun. The lady judge had been firm in her summing up but fair. The consequences for multiple burglaries carried a penalty and had Amber not shown deep regret and cooperated with the police, the punishment would have been much longer. Amber insisted all along that she would make funds available to recompense the victims.

Within thirty seconds of ringing the bell, a different woman entered the room. Thankfully this warden was more friendly and told Amber not to be frightened and that for her first night she wouldn't have to share a cell.

Tomorrow the process of settling into prison life would begin. She would be sharing with a woman called Liz Simmons.

***

After passing through various security doors a new guard was assigned to escort Amber to her cell. With a heavy heart, Amber trudged the corridors of the modern women's prison with a young, impatient warden of no more than thirty years of age, who urged her to walk faster. The rattle of keys on the thick brown belt brought home the scariness of being locked in a cell. Would one of those keys secure the heavy grey door, or would this modern prison have electronic locking devices? It would not be opened until the next morning when the bell sounded and the guards activated the doors. How was she going to cope being confined in such a small space with the sound of others shouting or attempting to communicate with her.

Through the final heavy security doors Amber stepped into Block A and the fear of being incarcerated became reality with the sound of prisoners' voices and the clatter of shoes on the hard floors.

Carrying the heavy holdall, minus her belt that had been confiscated, she briefly muttered a weak hello to the inmates that greeted her. She shivered with fear as one of the prisoners, a middle-aged woman with long, silver hair, stretched out a tattooed hand and stroked her face. 'Isn't she pretty.'

Momentarily Amber observed the furrowed brow and absence of any smile on the creased face. She was determined not to encourage further contact with this prisoner. The scratchy sounding voice, that echoed heavy nicotine usage, continued with the request to reveal her name. The warden gently pushed away the woman and prodded Amber to move on.

Amber stared at the black iron staircases and high hand rails with wells that held enormous safety nets to deter jumpers and limit injury. Prisoners attempting to end their lives was commonplace in such institutions. Daily incidents of attacks and poor behaviour were rife, something Amber would soon discover. She would have to be on her guard to avoid the troublemakers who were intent on disrupting others' lives.

All the time Amber was taking in the soulless surroundings that were to become her home for a very long time. Bereft of any windows, the grey walls and masses of cell doors equally spaced and numbered were heavily lit by overhead lighting. Concrete flooring lined with drain strips to remove excess water smelled heavily of disinfectant prompting Amber to cover her nose. The noise from some of the cells was a mixture of loud voices and banging on the toughened glass viewing hatch in the centre of the doors. Hearing this brought home the horrors of being held in prison. It was unpleasantly hot as the overhead heating drove a rush of warm, stale air around the narrow walkway. In the distance an alarm was sounding and Amber instinctively knew an incident had sparked off. She pictured the guards running to the scene to sort out the disturbance.

Then without any warning the warden came to a sudden halt in front of cell 311 and punched in a code. The heavy door shot open effortlessly as it would, no doubt, close in much the same way. Amber stared into the small grey painted room with the oblong high window and vertical bars that ruled out any thoughts of escape. It became obvious that by dark the chamber of horrors would look no better than by day.

A concrete toilet with a moulded seat and screen close

by afforded little privacy for the occupants. The thought of having the primitive bathroom facilities so close to the beds shocked Amber. Stacked high on a wooden shelf was a half-full bottle of shower wash with a sticky run down the front. A tablet of soap accompanied a new sponge in its transparent wrapper.

Focusing on the uninviting bunk bed with thin mattresses, tired blue duvets and pillows, Amber shuddered at the thought of sleeping in the institutional bedding. She wondered if the previous tenant had been violent? In the far corner of the six by eight-foot room was a concrete tray with a large overhead shower head. Graffiti adorned the walls, most of the scribblings related to statements of unfairness in the prison.

There were no pictures or homely features, just the reminder that you had no rights and were paying for your crime. A small screen television was bolted to the far wall with a printed metal sign that drove home the message that the power would be turned off at ten pm. On a wooden table with two chairs, was a small bottle of water, a bag of crisps and an uninviting cheese sandwich encapsulated in plastic. The warden mentioned this was Amber's dinner. The following morning, breakfast would be in the main dining room on level two and that's when the true initiation would commence.

A hurried explanation followed on keeping the cell tidy and the grim reminder that tomorrow she would share with another prisoner who would show her around the facilities of the relatively new building. The advice given was to keep her head down and the short sentence would soon be over. Amber had ignored the legal advice on not surfing the internet which held frightening accounts of those who thrived on initiating new inmates into their keeping. There existed a core of women offenders who befriended weaker victims to manipulate them to obey their every command. More often than not, the ringleaders exposed the rawer elements of survival in the prison jungle that would inevitably leave emotional and physical scars.

As the guard backed out of the cell, she caught the look of abject terror on Amber's face and said, 'Stand back from the door.'

'I don't want to be locked in this tiny space – I'm really scared. Can you talk to me for a bit longer?'

With a shaking of her head and no change in expression, the warden said, 'I'm going off duty in fifteen minutes and still have to file a report on your induction. Have your meal and turn in for the night. One bit of advice is to ignore any banging on the walls – best not to respond to other inmates. You have to develop a tougher skin while you are in here. Make friends but watch out for the ones who will trip you up.'

With tiredness bringing on the tears, Amber thanked the woman but couldn't help saying, 'Who had this cell last night?'

'Just someone like you, a low-risk jailbird. Don't worry about things like that. I will check on you tomorrow to see how you are settling in. Goodnight Amber.'

The sound of the heavy door locating into the iron frame cast the cell into unbearable silence which was shortly to be shattered by a thumping and a muffled female voice. 'What's your name and what are you in for?'

Amber froze on the spot and obeyed the advice about not entering into any discussion. The questions kept coming but eventually the inquisitor became bored and gave up. Much swearing followed and then it all went quiet.

Seated on the smoothly polished concrete toilet rim,

Amber desperately tried to pass water and struggled. She knew that if she did manage to sleep it would be interrupted by the urgency to reach the not so pleasant bathroom area. There was no toilet roll close by and she stared at the shelf that held the supplies and frowned. Gone were the basic comforts and she wondered how much of an ordeal the remainder of her stay in prison would prove to be.

A quick wash of hands, face and a shorter than usual brushing of her super white teeth took place before undressing. She climbed the steel ladder to the top bunk bed and, to her relief, the duvet smelt clean. With a flick of the light switch the cell was thrown into the blackest of black. With her eyes closed she prayed that her new cellmate would be a normal human being and not a twisted individual content on scoring points over others. Exhausted and close to tears, she managed to ignore shouting from one of the cells and unusually for her, said her prayers and asked for forgiveness.

The deep sleep that ensued mercifully held no memories of the prison. She dreamt of Kane's villa with the late afternoon sunlight pouring through the bedroom window casting shadows on the white walls. He was gently kissing the side of her neck and muttering words of love. In the distance, a tuneless church bell was sounding in the village calling in the congregation for the late afternoon service.

Earlier the pair had swum in the pool and sunbathed in the heat before retiring to bed. And now, their clothes lay on the floor and Kane was satisfying her beyond levels ever experienced before. The man was a love machine intent on making her body tingle with excitement, but it was just a dream. A dream that ended as quickly as it started.

Amber was awakened by screaming that reverberated

through the brick walls of the cell. Who was getting themselves into such a state at this time of the morning? Her body shook as she peeped out from the duvet to the small window that was encased with metal bars and shuddered with fear of what the day would bring.

Instead of rising from the uncomfortable bed, she lay on her front and wept desperately. How had she come to this point in her life? Not so long ago her future was bright with a man she thought was falling in love with her. All her problems were self-inflicted and now she was paying the price. Jason had told her that his brother, Kane, no longer wished to see or hear from her. He emphasised the point that he held no feelings for her, only disappointment.

Her deliberations were disrupted by the seven o'clock jail bird chorus. Hammering on walls and pipes, the noise increased to a steady clatter with shouting between cells. Then the sound of music commenced. Noisy pop songs, Radio One if she wasn't mistaken, echoed through the corridors. A scary voice from a neighbouring wall competed with the racket going on. 'What's your name?' Amber did not wish to reply, so the question was repeated only in a harsher tone and included a plethora of swear words. Amber hated vulgarisms and, when she worked for the insurance company, she was forever reprimanding the youngsters in the office.

Swinging her legs onto the cold floor, she sat on the edge of the bed wondering what to do next. There had been no instructions on where to go for breakfast or anything else for that matter. A heavy thud on the wall made her body shake with fear. Panic swept through her head as the reality sank in of so many other people around her. With a grating sound that switched to a screech, the door swung open and there stood a warden dressed in blue trousers and white top. There was much activity in the walkway as prisoners headed in the direction of the breakfast room.

'My name is Jones and you should be fully dressed by now.'

Amber offered a limp apology and reached for the holdall to retrieve her clothes.

'I'll give you some privacy to get ready and wait outside.'

'I'll be quick but I do need the toilet.'

'You should have gone earlier. You'll have to adapt to the timings and workings of prison life.'

The cell door was left partly open leaving Amber to use the toilet and drag on underclothes, skirt and jumper in record time. The noise in the corridor was worrying and it became apparent that two women were arguing. A five-second face wash followed and with the feeling of grubbiness still present she gazed through the scratched toughened glass of the door and said, 'I'm ready.'

Out in the corridor there was much chatter from other prisoners and Amber was aware that many were staring at her. One of the women smiled and then turned abruptly away to laugh. The warden explained that when they reached the breakfast room, she would introduce her to her cellmate, Liz Simmons, who had been transferred from the west wing. Her new mentor would bring her up to date with the layout and rules of prison life.

***

The scene that unrolled, as Amber entered an enormous oblong room with hideous tangerine painted walls and a food counter serving breakfast, was overwhelming. It felt like a thousand eyes were staring at her. There was an orderly queue with varying shapes of people – obese, skeletal and many with extensive tattoos that covered their necks and arms. Some held terrifying stares whilst others had fear glued to their faces. Drug addicts with hollowed faces and decaying teeth silently shuffled from foot to foot holding their plastic trays.

The noise of inmates chatting was to last throughout the meal time as did the staring that unsettled Amber. The clatter of prison regulation shoes continued up to the counter as the friendly kitchen staff served the food. A sausage shrunk to the size of a chipolata accompanied a bright rubbery fried egg and a single slice of toast were slopped onto the tray. There must have been at least forty people in that room with only four wardens present. Amber was later to learn that this was the first of two sittings for the block she was assigned to.

Before she went up to collect her food, the warden singled out a young woman with a razor short haircut, cheeky smile and a sea of freckles on her face. She readily made room for Amber to slide along the bench to join her.

'Okay, you ladies get to know each other. Liz this is Amber and I'll check back later on your progress.'

Amber stared at Liz and had to raise her voice to compete with the noise that filled the room. The girl looked so thin and her bony face showed signs of anxiety. Prisoner A4591 was first to speak, 'Pleased to meet you. How long are you in for and what did you do?'

'Oh, fourteen months for burglary, I was lucky it wasn't longer. I want to go home.'

Amber speculated on Liz's age being no more than twenty-five and watched her cut up the toast and dip it into the eggy offering. 'I'm in for shoplifting and this is my second offence.' She quickly added in a triumphant voice that her sentence only had another nine months to run.

Amber gulped. Nine months was a massive amount of

time still to serve and the thought of her own longer stretch seemed never-ending.

Liz studied Amber's sorrowful face and said, 'Do you have family or someone special waiting for you?'

'No family, but there was a guy who no longer wants me and he lives in Spain.'

'That's rough, since being in here I lost my fella to another woman.'

'Oh, that couldn't have been easy coming to terms with.'

Liz shrugged her shoulders and muttered, 'That's life. Doors open and close and we just have to keep going, don't we?'

Amber nodded her head and took a chance hoping no one would hear her say, 'Aren't there some odd people in this place?'

Liz's eyes strayed over to a group of women. She placed her head close to Amber's ear. 'You mean like that lot over there. Most of them are repeat offenders. Some are right nutters – you want to stay clear of them. There are also loads of people like you and me who don't want trouble.' Her attention switched to the queue for the food counter that was thinning out. 'Come on, let's get you something to eat and I'll see if I can get another piece of toast for me.'

Whilst Amber was hungry, the thought of greasy food at seven o'clock in the morning was ruled out. Her usual breakfast was a banana and a café latte from her coffee maker. Eating from trays with hollowed out areas for a puddle of baked beans and scrambled egg was not her idea of breakfast. She would stick to just toast and coffee.

As they were queuing, there was an almighty crash as a tray ended up on the ground. Punches were flying and bright red blood oozed from a skeletal-looking girl's face. A cheer from the diners went up and a small group of women were encouraging the fight to go on. Two wardens were on the scene in seconds and broke up the disagreement. The offenders were put to work on cleaning up the mess on the floor before being marched out of the room to face disciplinary action. Out in the corridor there was a further disturbance as a few of the younger inmates were joking around. Their childish behaviour involved breaking wind and shouting obscenities at people as they passed.

Amber was to learn that incidents of this nature were common and to be ignored. Her cell mate would later reveal details of a riot five weeks ago when a fire in the west wing had to be put out. For many of the less disruptive and non-violent prisoners, who just wished to serve their time peacefully, it must have felt like they were in the house of hell. Amber couldn't help noticing the number of people grasping their vaping gear in preparation for use in the day room. It appeared that whilst smoking tobacco was prohibited, the electronic cigarette was very much in use.

Amber corrected her staring for fear of drawing trouble and dropped the remnants of the lightly toasted bread into an enormous black plastic bag that smelled horrible. She quickly turned away to follow Liz who was keen to collect her personal items from the duty manager's office. As they trudged along the corridor, there was yet another obstacle to avoid. A prisoner, no older than mid-twenties, was kicking off. Her screams were silenced by one of the guards who led her away.

The sadness in Liz's eyes was evident as she said, 'Alcohol and mental problems, she shouldn't be here. I feel sorry for her but we can't get involved. In here you have to look after yourself.'

A moment of panic surged around Amber's head as the reality of her own crime hit home and where it had landed her. She accompanied Liz along the corridor. First impressions of her were acceptable, possibly a little rough around the edges but she was caring as well.

Having collected her case from the duty officer, Liz followed Amber to the cell that the two women were to share. Whilst hanging her clothes in the small locker she explained they would be working in the laundry for two hours every morning and then transfer for cleaning duties. There would be an hour of leisure time for games or a visit to the library. Amber's ears pricked up at the prospect of borrowing books. Liz then mentioned that their evening meal had to be collected and brought back to the cell to eat. The dreaded plastic tray and bottle of water would have to be returned the next morning before breakfast. Amber would be initiated into the delights of slopping out and the dreadful smells of discarded food and possibly worse.

Late afternoon, everyone returned to their cells for the long session of being locked in and then the boredom would set in. The living space was tiny and, for anyone suffering from claustrophobia, the consequences could be truly harrowing.

As they sat on the uncomfortable padded chairs, Amber offered her new friend her one and only small bar of milk chocolate. Liz thanked her profusely and said, 'You keep it, things like that can be swapped for fags and other things. I keep getting offered an old mobile but won't stray from my ruling. I'm staying clean to avoid trouble. The other thing is, quite often, they want something more in return.'

Amber threw a dismissive hand into the air. 'I don't smoke, certainly not those vape things and I'm going to be careful not to get sucked into any dealing. Some of those women look menacing. I read on the internet that in prisons there are runners, women who establish who wants what, and leaders that move in with their supplies. You wouldn't want to get on the wrong side of them.'

'Yeah, it's a bit like an internal mafia and difficult to keep your nose clean. The ones you need to watch are the over-friendly ones who prey on pretty girls like you.'

'What do you mean – are they bullies or control freaks?'

'Not really, all I'm saying is, be on your guard as some of the ladies can get a bit frustrated being banged up in here.'

Amber crossed over to window and gazed through the bars at the cloudless sky with birds flying from tree to tree. She could hear the sound of traffic and acknowledged that there were people out there getting on with their lives while this was her first full day in jail. Turning to face Liz she said, 'Not sure what you're implying.'

Liz threw a sympathetic glance at Amber who suddenly understood and shuddered as she replied, 'Oh, I see what you mean.'

Chapter 14

Fourteen hundred miles from Kent, the contrast between Kane and Amber's surroundings couldn't have been greater. It was mid-day in the quaint village of Frigiliana with the temperatures topping the high thirties, the necessity to cool down in the pool was paramount.

Kane's new lady friend, Sue, was fuming with anger. 'You need to stop calling me Amber!'

'And I said I was sorry, it just slipped out. She means nothing to me.'

'Oh, yeah, that's what you said before – it happened the other day when we made love.' She forcefully moved his hand away from her arm and sadly said, 'How do you think that makes me feel?'

Kane wasn't going to apologise again but could understand how she felt. What was he playing at mentioning Amber, especially when they were in bed?

Now on her feet, Sue sorted through her handbag and held a black key fob in the air. How many times had Kane worried about his girlfriend driving after drinking so much wine? He stretched out a hand to take the key and pleaded with her, 'It's not safe, stay and have a coffee.'

'Why don't you stop telling me what to do? I'm not drunk so leave me alone.'

The last thing she shouted back before slamming the door was that she wasn't prepared to share him with another woman.

Kane reluctantly said goodbye and watched her light green Fiat 500 disappear out of sight on the mountain road that led to the coastal town of Nerja. He had begged her not to drive and she had declined his offer of something to eat. Now he feared for her safety. The twisty roads were dangerous at the best of times, especially as she drove far too fast. Refusing to take a taxi home, Sue always did what Sue wanted to do, saying she was an excellent driver.

***

Kane returned indoors and glanced down from his bedroom window to the steep slopes with the vibrant green terraces and small olive grove that was all part of his land. Normally, the view delivered a calmness to his life but today his thoughts were anchored on girlfriend, Sue. He didn't want to lose her as most of the time they got on well, bar the occasional disagreement. They both had their lives to lead and this mutual arrangement suited them.

Sue was considerably younger than Kane and lived in one of the local villages. She was a regular visitor to the villa and thought nothing of swimming naked. The lovemaking that followed was breathtaking, only today, like the time before, he had called her by Amber's name which understandably annoyed her. He was shocked and embarrassed to be mentioning the girl from back home, the person he had tried to help. He still thought of her but hadn't brother Jason repeatedly said that she wasn't interested in him? The exact words he had used were: 'Forget Amber, she'll pull you down'.

The distraction with his new lady friend in Spain would never measure up to his brief encounter with Amber. She had inspired special feelings in him. Whilst he knew the past had no place in his life, it didn't stop him thinking about her. There was no turning back of the clock. Amber was one hell of a mixed-up individual serving time in one of Her Majesty's hotels and would be there for some time. Her lawyer had done his best representing her but it wasn't enough to stop her serving a custodial sentence. Kane had felt unsettled to learn that Jason himself was going to visit Amber in prison saying she needed a friend. What was Jason thinking, it could only stir up more heartache for him?

Then another possibility crept into his head – what if Amber befriended Jason, or worse still, his brother became attracted to her?

He switched back to thinking of Sue arriving home and going straight to the beach. She would probably stretch out on a sunbed with the scorching hot sun streaming down on her already tanned, slim body. The ridiculous, vibrant yellow, baseball cap with lank hair peeping through the slit in the back would be cast to one side as she made her way down to the sea. Twice a week, Kane accompanied her to the beach for a swim or to take coffee close to the Balcón de Europa. This ancient landmark was the perfect place to spend an hour before moving on for a snack or another ice cream.

Drifting off to sleep in the hot sun on a comfortable sun lounger, he listened to the cicadas clicking loudly then pausing for a few moments. Kane's reveries were interrupted by his mobile and the hideous new ring tone that Sue had installed. Swiping the screen, his heart raced on realising she was calling on Facetime.

'It's only me. I want to say sorry.'

'You have nothing to apologise for, it's me who's at fault. What was I doing calling you by the wrong name? That girl was a friend for a while and I still feel concerned for her. Believe me, there's no love or anything like that going on. I promise I will get things into perspective.'

'That's what I want to hear – you need to let go.' There was a pause and Sue added, 'Anyway, she's banged up and not available, whereas I am.'

Kane hoped that, on the small iPhone screen, Sue wouldn't detect the runaway tear that had reached his chin. He so desperately wished to eradicate memories of Amber and return to having fun with Sue.

Forcing a smile, he said, 'I'm going to concentrate on the here and now and that includes us. We are good together.'

Sue was grinning and cheekily said, 'I was thinking of having a siesta and, only if you want to, you could come over here right now.'

Chapter 15

The first few days are always the worst, at least that's what the prison library supervisor said, but Amber wasn't so sure. With everything that was going on in her first week, all the warnings and tips on surviving in this concrete jungle, she felt it could only get tougher, not easier. Without Liz looking out for her it would have been even harder to navigate the pitfalls and complexities of sharing with one hundred and ninety-seven women. Whilst Liz was proving to be a good cellmate, in truth she didn't really know her. Hadn't she stressed that the ones to watch were the friendly individuals and here was Amber revealing her weaknesses and history to a stranger. She would have to be on her guard.

Amber longed for her daily visit to the exercise yard and tended to stay close to Liz as there was always something going on. The cluster of women who boasted they were reoffenders were out in force and they appeared to be up to something. Amber sneaked glances as they squirrelled away cigarettes, sim cards and drugs. In contrast, on the tarmacked area, plenty of sport was being played and Amber longed to join in with the football. People were having fun and laughing which brought home the fact that not everyone in prison was on a mission of deceit. It wasn't long before the two hours of relative freedom came to a close as the shrill of the electric bell sounded. There were always a few prisoners who the guards had to remind that it was time to clear the yard. It was then back to work in the laundry, kitchen or washing floors.

The days turned slowly and, after a month, Amber began to get a measure of her surroundings. She was intent on taking advantage of the educational classes on offer. It wasn't long before she was mentoring less educated prisoners in basic arithmetic and reading. Many had never read a book in their life. Her request to work in the library was granted and she enjoyed her general admin duties and helping inmates find a good book to read. There was one other person working in the cubby hole of a room that was described as a library. Whilst Beth was friendly, Amber remained wary of the woman with the stooped shoulders who had the annoying habit of finishing off one's sentences. Avoiding her foul-smelling breath was not that easy in the cramped environment. Strangely, this inmate had not enquired about her criminal record or probed for skeletons in the proverbial cupboard. In return Amber spoke only of her love of books and encouraged the conversation towards happier times. The small department housed six racks of paperbacks, many in poor condition with torn or bent covers, and a small number of large print editions. The diversity of literature fell into general fiction, romance, biographies, religious, educational and a smattering of self-help books.

A steady stream of women used the library, many possibly new readers who desperately required a distraction from the reality of being locked up for hours on end. Clasping their identity cards that had to be scanned, most were friendly and sought not only reading material but the chance to chat. The ruling on borrowing was a limit of two books and Amber soon learnt how to input the information on the relatively new laptop that was clamped firmly to the metal worksurface. With the latest version of Windows installed, the touchscreen worked a treat. A combination of scanning bar codes and guiding people in their search for the perfect read was a great way to pass time. The rota gave her two mornings a week which was preferable to the hour after lunch when she returned to washing down corridor floors and walls.

Greeting the ladies, the most common question was what Amber could recommend for them to read. A gentle quizzing about favourite genres soon enabled her to direct the reader to the relevant book shelf. There was an autobiography of an international best-selling author that appealed to her. This author fell foul of the law and ended up in prison. The incredible storyteller still managed to build up his sales of books despite having a criminal record. The publicity that evolved from being held in prison worked well for him.

It wasn't long before two women started to hang around the library area unsettling Amber as she heard snatches of their tense conversation. She was also concerned as the rule was no vaping. Both kept taking sneaky puffs on their hideous, purple-coloured tubes and releasing clouds of vapour into the cramped room. Where were the wardens when you needed them? Reprimanding these people would only result in uncomfortable consequences.

Much of the women's interest hinged on the newcomer to the library and what floor of Block A she was on. Their scraped-back hair that exposed huge foreheads and permanent frowns sent out a message of 'don't mess with me'. Amber stepped back behind the desk. Unpleasant language fell heavily from their mouths. The queue of people borrowing books soon dissipated leaving her alone with the obnoxious ladies.

'Are you wanting a book?'

A forced smile from the taller of the women revealed badly decayed teeth with many gaps. 'I don't do romantic, girly stuff; got any books on escape tunnels?'

Amber laughed, not because she found the request funny, more out of nervousness and boldly replied, 'Sorry, the last person who borrowed that book didn't return it.'

Both women giggled and moved close to Amber before scooping up a pile of books from the counter which they dropped on the floor. A loud clattering sound echoed through the corridor. Within a short while, a guard was on the scene enquiring about the mess. Amber promptly explained that she had been clumsy. She caught the look on the women's faces who were both nodding and enjoying every moment of their troublemaking. One of the prisoners stretched out a clenched fist and unrolled stubby fingers with the word power tattooed in large, royal blue letters. 'Hope to see you again. If you get bored, I'm in 189 and always in. The doorbell is not working so just come in. What did you say you name was?'

'I didn't.'

'Well, what is it?'

Not wishing to reveal her identity Amber remained quiet. To her relief there was no reaction. As the women left the library, in unison they blew a kiss in her direction before shuffling out of sight. She wondered about their turbulent past and what had brought about such sour and empty lives. She would have to be careful not to enter into discussion with them again, but knew that was nigh on impossible. Being holed up with so many people there were always going to be stirrers and meddlers content to trigger trouble. She acknowledged that this would be the pattern of things to follow. The only solace was in believing that these individuals were outnumbered by moderate and kind prisoners with whom she felt safe.

***

Coming to terms with being in prison was testing as Amber reflected on the agony she had inflicted upon others during her robberies. The self-destruct button had well and truly been pressed resulting in her custodial sentence and an uncertain future. The seeds of her obsession for breaking the law stemmed back to her early days as a teenager when she joined in with older girls stealing makeup from department stores. It had all started as a bit of fun and steadily grew as the challenges and pressures from the bullies increased. With each episode the sensation of excitement heightened, leaving her keen to see how far she could push the boundaries. Any thoughts of being caught had been dismissed; she had no misgivings.

At the time, she never gave a thought to reducing retailers' profits – they could afford it. In essence, Amber was hooked on pleasing the ringleader and eager for inclusion in the next contest. During and after each encounter, she felt invigorated with an infusion of confidence that lasted for a long time. It felt good being part of a group who maintained that she was a key player and being adored by everyone; whereas her mother had regularly told her she would never amount to anything. There is much truth in the old saying that if you tell someone enough times they are ineffectual, eventually they will believe it – and that's exactly what happened to Amber. Her teenage years were laced with sadness even before her parents died in a car crash.

Bizarrely, her desire to steal again had lain dormant until she reached her early thirties. After a period of depression, it had come back with a number of robberies being planned and executed.

Amber held down a perfectly good job, but she never forgot the powerful chemistry that whirled around her body and head each time a burglary took place. Her explanation that all proceeds from the robberies had been donated to charity would never be understood by anyone, least of all Kane. Deep down she knew her savings should have been substituted to help the homeless charity she supported, but that wasn't the path she had chosen.

***

Sharing a cell with Liz had its moments and whilst Amber enjoyed her company, she still remained suspicious of her cellmate's quizzing regarding her life. The question that buzzed around her busy head was whether Liz was trying to play with her mind?

During the last few weeks, one particular woman had been overly pleasant towards her. The fifty-something year old prisoner, with a short haircut, had always been too ready to slip next to her at mealtimes. On one occasion she physically pushed another diner away to make room. Suggestive comments were made followed by a squeezing of Amber's leg. Amber was infuriated and told the woman to back off. She appeared to know a fair bit about Amber's conviction details, then again, the grapevine worked to perfection. The question that needed answering was had Liz provided the information that kept this prisoner so interested in her?

Prison was a dangerous place to be and the only way to survive was to stand up to the intimidator which is just what Amber did. Telling the woman to keep her greasy hands off her and to get lost could have resulted in an aftermath of terror. Oddly, the opposite happened with an apology and mercifully no further harassment followed.

During lunch one day, in the noisy oblong and windowless room with six guards present, everyone was chattering and appeared to be more excitable than ever. Amber leant forward on the wooden bench and scooped mash potato and burnt fishfingers from the plastic tray that served as a plate. The peach yoghurt for afters was so tiny as was the banana with the bruised skin. Liz was on a high and kept talking about counting down the months to her release. She had finished her meal and was already clearing away the tray and urged Amber to hurry up. Someone was kicking off and an argument was firing up. A small group of prisoners chivvied others to join in the chanting as the guards controlled the situation.

Hungry and frightened it was time to devour what remained of the unappetising meal in record time and leave the disturbance of the dining room for the relative calm of their cell. There would be just under two hours before locking up time and there was a matter that required clarification.

Entering their small, grim-looking grey box that served as a living space, bedroom and toilet, Liz sighed as she reached for the remote on the television and muttered, 'Won't be anything on the box tonight and even if there is, when lights go off so does our watching.'

Amber ignored the comment and said, 'Look Liz, I'm going to ask you just the once and I want you to level with me.'

A look of worry enveloped the face that was normally reserved for smiles. 'Oh, I hope I haven't upset you.'

'Not sure. You know that woman with the razor-sharp haircut and all those tattoos, well she keeps …'

'You mean Joanne, she's harmless. I often pass the time of day with her.'

'I thought it was you.'

Liz looked shocked and anxiously raised her hand to her mouth. 'What do you mean?'

'She's been hitting on me and the thought of what she was implying disgusts me. She seemed to know a fair bit about me and it appears you have been dishing the dirt.'

Liz steadied herself against the flimsy locker door. 'Oh, my God, she was friendly and sounded concerned for you. I only mentioned you were serving time for burglary and were finding it tough settling in. Please believe me, I had no idea she would become a nuisance. I'm sure she's okay and not a skirt chaser.'

Amber still gave Liz a hard time. 'Well, I don't go for people touching up my leg so I beg to disagree. I'm just trying to keep my head down and get out of here and you really haven't helped. Wasn't it you who warned me about the ones that are too friendly?'

'Yep, and I slipped up big time – sorry.'

Amber playfully punched her friend's arm and offered, 'Let's forget it. Did I tell you I have my first visitor tomorrow?'

Liz's smile was back again. 'Is it Kane, is he coming to see you?'

The mention of Kane's name sent a shiver up Amber's spine. How she wished it was him. 'No, it's his brother and he's a decent bloke, terribly old fashioned in his ways but he's okay. I agreed to the visit as I'm hoping he will pass a message to Kane for me.'

Liz was amused with the revelation and giggled. 'Brother, you say. Is he a looker – you know fit?'

***

The visitors' room was full of people and Amber recognised a number of her fellow inmates seated opposite their loved ones. There were fifteen tables and two guards who kept scrutinising everyone in the room and then switching to checking their mobile phones. The clock on the wall with the juddering minute hand would bring the meeting to a close in a relatively short space of time.

Jason sat upright in the chair and reached for Amber's hand and momentarily squeezed her fingers. Feeling unsettled she pulled away and wondered if agreeing to seeing him had been a good idea. Since she had only met him on that one occasion, he shouldn't be so familiar with her. Wiping her palm on the top of her jeans, she sat nervously and said the first thing that entered her mind. 'I imagine in the legal profession you've made plenty of visits like this.'

'No, probably hard to believe but this is a first for me. A lot of the cases are divorce settlements or property transactions. I've never been in a prison before and couldn't believe the checks I had to undergo.'

'The difference is you get to go home.'

Jason frowned. 'I've had to leave my coat and things with the admin office. Enough about me, how are you coping?' He looked around the room at the prisoners and their visitors and added words of solace, 'You'll soon be out. All you need to do is keep your head down.'

Amber observed the well-spoken man in his dated clothes and recalled Liz's enquiry on whether Jason was good looking. Definitely not. She giggled and held a hand to her mouth.

'What's so funny?'

'Oh nothing. It's just that I've still time to serve and can't see an end to it all. But I know I deserve to be in here for hurting so many people. I want you to believe me that I never kept any of the stuff I stole – all the proceeds went to charity. I'm turning over a new leaf, only I'm scared about my future. Who is going to give me another chance to secure a job?'

'Well, I'm going to help you. I've been thinking a lot about you. I'm hoping we can remain friends and see where it goes from there.'

Amber needed friends but worried this man's understanding of the word differed greatly to hers. 'Look, the last thing I need is a new man in my life, and if I was looking for someone, it wouldn't be you.'

Jason looked disappointed and tried again. 'See how you feel when your parole comes around.'

'You must know that I'm still carrying a torch for your brother. I want him to know I'm really sorry. Can you tell him I'm improving my life and want to see him when I get out? Mention that I would love to hear from him. You will do this for me, won't you?'

Amber could sense his reluctance but he still replied, 'I'll ring him later. Look I'm sorry for any confusion only I thought the coast was clear as Kane said he didn't want anything to do with you. He's got a new lady in Spain and they seem to be hitting it off. He speaks highly of her.'

Amber sighed. 'Oh, I see. I'd still like you to pass on my message.'

Ten minutes later the electronic buzzer sounded bringing an end to their conversation. She watched Jason rise to leave and thanked him for visiting, then held up the red security pass and was escorted out of the room.

As she underwent the two separate security checks and gained access through the various steel doors, her mind was doing somersaults. She was taking a chance trying to edge her way back into Kane's life again. She briefly pictured a young woman at Kane's side, or more likely in his bed, but dismissed the thought instantly.

Chapter 16

Swivelling the laptop on the kitchen table to block out the penetrating sunlight, Kane swiped the Facetime app and it took a while for Jason to pick up. When his face appeared on the screen, he looked flustered and was anxiously rubbing away sleepy dust from his eyes. He was bare-chested and, for all Kane knew, could have been naked.

With a smile on his face and a laugh begging to be supressed, Kane was first to speak. 'Haven't rung at a bad time, have I? You look like you've just got out of the shower.'

Jason frowned and raised his wrist to look at the huge silver watch with multiple dials and muttered, 'It's only ten o'clock on a Saturday morning – what do you want?'

Moving his face closer to the screen, Kane delivered the line that had been rehearsed so many times before calling Jason. 'When you visited Amber this week, did you give her my message about me wanting to keep in touch?'

'Of course, I did.'

'And what did she say?'

Shaking his head Jason lowered his voice to a whisper. 'I'm afraid it's bad news. She reiterated what she said before – in short, she doesn't want any contact and wants to draw a line under the whole episode. She's trying to move on and you are not part of her plan.'

'Oh, that's not what I thought she would say. You do know she has tried to contact me and it has been me who has been back-peddling up until now.'

Jason interjected with, 'How do you expect the girl to feel? One minute you are showing interest in her and the next you don't want to know. As if she hasn't enough on her plate coping with being in prison, you keep dangling the bait and pulling it away.'

'That's not fair, it's complicated and my feelings have been torn apart too. I was just trying to stay friends and see what developed. I'm thinking of writing to her.'

Kane heard his brother sigh. 'Oh, for heaven's sake. Why don't you just accept it is over. Let's not forget you already have a girlfriend in Spain. I met her when I visited the villa and she looks gorgeous.'

Glancing out to the swimming pool with the backdrop of the mountains, Kane broke into a cold sweat. His brother was of course right, there was another woman in his life. A mutually beneficial relationship that was fun, but there was no love.

'She's more of a friend. We have an arrangement that suits us both, that's all.'

Jason laughed. 'Sex you mean.'

'Don't be vulgar.'

Jason snapped back. 'Amber is not someone to be treated in this way and I intend to look out for her. You just get on with your life in the sun and your bit of stuff.'

'She's not my bit of stuff.'

Kane questioned why Jason was being so unfriendly this morning. It was the glazed look he'd seen before and knew it wouldn't be long before he made his excuse to end the call.

However, the bombshell Jason unloaded shook Kane to the core. His heartbeat rose as the words were amplified on the laptop speaker. 'You may as well know that I've quite taken to Amber and the path is clear with you off the scene – let's see what happens. I may even end up with a reciprocal arrangement like you and your girl.'

'What do you mean?'

'You know, a no-ties relationship with plenty of sex

just like you and Sue, if I get lucky with Amber.'

Kane was fuming and ringing his hands in an attempt to control his anger. 'Hold on there, you can't get involved with a client and anyway I still have feelings for her.'

'Just for the record, she was never my client and has settled her account with my colleague before going into prison.'

'I think it is about time that I applied for a visit to see her,' said Kane angrily.

'Calm down brother or you will end up with a heart attack. Amber has to want to see you to grant the visit and she's made it perfectly clear she is not interested.'

'But, I…'

The tone in Jason's voice was electric. 'I haven't time for all of this and it is probably best we end the call as the broadband is poor here and I can hardly hear you.'

'Mine's working normally.'

Kane stared in disbelief at the screen that now only displayed his contact list. He was fuming with anger and banged his hand hard down on the kitchen worktop. Whenever they argued, his brother blamed the broadband and terminated their session.

Kane slipped from the bar stool and wandered out to the pool area, gazing up at a jet aeroplane cutting through the paint-box blue sky leaving a white puffy trail. The plane full of passengers was possibly returning to the UK. How he wished he was on that flight. What if Jason was right and she didn't want to see him? The logical step was to Google the prison and view the online application for visiting. It would take a while to complete the security searches and then it was up to her whether or not she saw him.

The mid-day heat was boiling and a theatre of cicadas with their loud clickety clack sound filled the air. Up on the foothills of the mountains his eyes focused on a group of horse riders who were winding their way into a small forestry area. The heat was bearing down and Kane looked to the neighbouring villa to check if anyone was around. Within seconds he removed his miniscule white shorts and dived into the cool water of the magnificent pool. Swimming underwater he remained there for longer than usual and swam a length. With lungs desperate for a refill, he still stayed in the deep end. It was like he was punishing himself for treating Amber so harshly. When he finally came up for air, he was shocked to see his current lady friend standing by the edge of the pool.

Hanging onto the ladder, Kane gasped for breath and managed to say, 'Sue, what are you doing here?' His eyes strayed to her friend Macy, an American girl who had come to live in Spain at the start of the summer.

'Had a good swim? You sound out of breath, are you okay?'

Feeling naked in the water and hoping the two girls hadn't noticed his dilemma in not being able to climb out, he moved away from the ladder to the tiled edge of the pool.

'We just called in to see if you are still going to the fiesta in Nerja next week. There's a crowd of us meeting in Calle Carabeo by the side of my favourite tapas restaurant. The crowds will be manic. You are coming, aren't you?'

Kane nodded his head. 'That's a week away and yes, I'll be there. I may have to fly back home for a few days to see an old friend but that shouldn't stop me attending. Why don't you take Macy indoors and get a drink and I'll pull the sunbeds into the shade?'

'No, you get out of the pool and we will get the chairs ready.' Sue patted her beach bag and proudly said, 'I've brought some cold beers with me and…' She stopped in full sentence as her eyes homed in on Kane's shorts lying on the scorching-hot paving stones. A solitary flip flop lay in a flower bed.

Sue giggled and Kane felt even more uncomfortable as he asked for a towel from inside the villa and muttered, 'It's not funny.'

Encouraging her American friend to accompany her to collect a towel, Sue guided her to the patio door leaving her boyfriend to jump out of the pool like a demented frog with a new set of hind legs.

Chapter 17

Back in the UK, the rain hammered on the metal roof of the prison making it difficult to decipher the warden's words as she informed Amber of a change in meal times. The annoying thing was that her cellmate, Liz, was consigned to a later sitting. Shadowing Liz always felt the right thing to do but today she would be on her own. Safety in numbers remained the main priority as one of the prisoners who had caused trouble in the library was on the scene again.

Two weeks ago, Carol Roberts, entered their cell and told Liz to butt out, or words to that effect. The woman extracted from her jogging trousers a small clear bag which contained white powder and whispered in Amber's ear that if she had no money then an arrangement could be struck. Her response was to inform the woman with the frown that rarely tripped into a smile, that she was not into drugs. As for the reference to an arrangement being struck, it didn't bear thinking about.

Amber was relieved when the package was returned to the keeping of the folds of fat that hung over the frayed waistband. Mercifully the woman made no fuss and left the cell. Amber had considered informing the charitable warden who looked out for her, that she was experiencing problems with another prisoner. Liz insisted the trouble would escalate if she grassed on a fellow inmate. Her advice was to distance herself from the woman who would hopefully move on to bothering someone else.

Today was Thursday and Jason had booked another visiting slot. Amber had agreed to see him again in the hope he would have news of Kane. It would soon be time to present herself to the officer in the admin office to undergo security checks before being admitted to the visitor's room. She readied herself for the inevitable body scan that would confirm nothing had been passed to her prior to entering the final check point. Amber put on smarter clothes, black trousers, red jumper and tidied up her hair. She desperately needed a haircut as the black, curly mop looked a mess. How she missed the ease of booking a cut and blow dry with her favourite stylist, Jamie. She wondered if he had mentioned to his colleagues that Amber had stopped using their salon.

On the way through the ground floor that led to the three-stage security of the visitor's lounge, she caught sight of the woman who had pestered her with the offer of drugs.

'In a hurry Amber, where's the fire? Fancy a coffee, I'll treat you.'

Amber, slightly out of breath, politely refused saying she had a visitor and was already late.

'That's a shame. Let's say this time tomorrow then.'

'Sorry, I'll be working my laundry shift.'

Gripping Amber's arm really tightly the reply was accompanied by a bitter smile. 'Not a problem. Before we go out into the yard tomorrow, you will meet me for one of those fancy coffees with the frothy milk. After we can go back to my place.'

Removing the woman's arm with as much force as it had been applied, Amber pumped up all her strength and let out a shout that everyone in the area heard. 'Let's get one thing straight – if you are looking for a fight you picked the wrong person, so stop haranguing me.' She delivered her lie with a menacing threat. 'I got done once for beating a woman so hard her eyes nearly shot out of her head. Now push off.'

The bully was visibly shaking and stood back from Amber. For the remaining part of Amber's prison sentence, she was never to be bothered again. The grapevine worked wonders and her status climbed to 'don't meddle with Amber'.

***

On reaching the last of the checking stations, Amber frowned at the guard she knew would carry out the examination. This would be repeated after leaving the visitor's suite. Inside the room with cameras suspended over the tables there was much chatter as prisoners leant forward to talk with their guests. Many of the women were responding to questions on how they were coping and if parole was on the cards. Seated at table six was Jason, who looked as if he had gone through some sort of transformation process. His hair was smart and he no longer sported glasses; he later revealed he was wearing contact lenses. He was well dressed and there was no sign of the hideous flower power shirts or red wrist strap. A slightly more attractive man greeted her, a man who was on a mission. Amber accepted the outstretched hand and felt the tightness of fingers that willed her to pause the moment.

Jason gazed around the room of fourteen jailbirds, taking in their hollow faces and tattoos. Each one of these people had a story to tell, a revelation that had left broken hearts and families to pick up the pieces.

'So, how is it going? You do realise that you have completed seven months. We will soon have you out of here.'

Rolling her eyes in the direction of a security camera and to a prisoner who was staring at a photograph that had been passed to her, Amber casually said, 'Nothing prepared me for being holed up in here. If it hadn't been for Liz, I would have gone out of my mind.'

'Who's Liz?'

'We share a cell and get on well. She's teaching me

chess and I'm enjoying it. We will probably keep in touch when I'm out. The only problem is she is due to be released before me and I'm petrified I could get some awful person to share with.'

'You will be okay,' Jason said unconvincingly.

Amber wasn't so sure she would be okay. The prison or, as she commonly referred to it, the jungle, was a terrifying place. She forced away the negative thoughts and said, 'Did you give Kane my message about keeping in touch?'

Jason nodded his head and tapped the dial glass on his slim gold watch. 'I wasn't looking forward to you asking that question.'

'What do you mean?'

Labouring his words, Jason offered, 'Well, well, not so long ago, I Facetimed him and his unusually morose mood concerned me. I could tell from his face he was annoyed when I passed on your request. I'm sorry but his response was not good. He said you needed to leave him alone and to tell you he has a girlfriend called Sue. It sounds serious to me, but I did tell you all this.'

Close to tears Amber said, 'No, that can't be right, she's probably just a friend.'

'I saw a picture of them on the beach and she was in a bikini. They looked pretty close.' Jason looked deep in thought and eventually added, 'She is quite a looker, but you don't want to know about that, do you?'

What Jason said about Kane's unusually morose mood didn't ring true. In the short time she knew him this description sounded totally alien. The odd frown, but never morose. Then again, there had been a few cases of his sulking that annoyed her.

Amber tried a different tack. 'Possibly you caught him on a bad day when you rang.'

The vigorous shaking of his head went on for a while.

'No, I don't think so. He said if you asked after him again, I was to tell you to stop pestering him. He really doesn't like you. You just need to accept that my brother never settles down with his women.'

Jason then reached for her hand again. She physically shook but felt unable to move. Then the bombshell was delivered with a toothy smile. 'I wouldn't treat you like that. Perhaps when you get out and are more settled, we can go out to dinner. No pressure, just as friends.'

Retrieving her hand into the safety of the metal rim of the table, Amber's head was spinning. Kane would never have said those things, she just knew he was too much of a gentleman. Her heart was breaking and she was certainly not on the rebound looking to find another man. She put a hand up in the air to attract the attention of one of the wardens. The visit was over.

Jason's face went bright red as Amber told him not to visit again.

Chapter 18

The May fiesta in Nerja always drew large crowds around the Balcón de Europa, a rocky promontory with spectacular panoramic views out over the Mediterranean towards North Africa. The backdrop of the mountainous terrain held steep terraces dotted with white-washed homes that glistened in the sunlight.

Waiting for the main event to begin, there was much excitement amongst the crowds of people who lined the streets.

'Hey, I think there are more people than ever before. I hope we'll be able to get some lunch,' shouted Kane.

Sue frowned and prodded Kane in the ribs. 'Don't you ever stop thinking about your stomach. I've got an apple in my bag if you need it.'

'I don't like apples. I want some *churros* followed by a late lunch. There is so much to try on those food stalls.'

The sun was bearing down on the town and there was no shortage of vendors selling hats, sunglasses, drinks and snacks.

The theme of the festival was land and agriculture, mainstays of the local economy along with tourism. The highlight of the event was a procession of local residents in colourful costumes, dancers, musicians and horse riders. This year farming implements and tractors were to be a main feature.

Kane impatiently checked his watch for the third time and it was then that they heard the roar of the crowd as the procession started.

Tall men, dressed in giant tomato and pepper costumes ran the length of the Balcón screaming at the top of their voices. Chased by farmers, the vegetables were encouraged to jump into an enormous frying pan. Farm labourers with gigantic ladles and wooden spoons stirred in further ingredients for the feast. The contrast couldn't have been more different to the following parades with bathers in their swimming costumes dancing to pop music and townspeople pulling carts loaded with local produce. The parade switched to the more traditional women in vibrant flamenco dresses and men riding beautiful Andalusian horses, wowing the onlookers.

Close to Kane's viewing point, the delicious smell of grilled meats from the wood burning grills wafted through the air. The *tortilla Española* and *croquetas* were always a favourite as were the *churros* coated in sugar and chocolate sauce. Sue laughed, 'Here we go, you can stock up on your *churros* now.'

The festival organisers and police were continually encouraging street performers and musicians to return to the safety of the paved areas. With all the theatre that accompanies a festival, the danger of crowds amongst vehicles and horses was always an issue. Safety announcements were regularly being played and the fun of the carnival continued without incident.

There was a lull before the next procession that led to an exodus of people anxious to be fed as they battled with the crowds for the meal tents and stalls selling local olives.

In the back of his mind, Kane was still worrying about yesterday's phone call with his brother who had insisted that Amber wanted no further contact. He wondered if Jason had misunderstood what she was saying but quickly ruled this out. Maybe Jason was meddling again in his affairs. Rushing back to the UK and expecting her to see him was a big ask. He would stick to his original plan and not look to revive his friendship with the girl from Harrow.

The sound of another band approaching brought him back to the festivities. The view of the church of El

Salvador was where all the activity was taking place with a large crowd lining the square. The enormous wooden doors were fully open and the congregation followed the procession of the cross that would be carried through the main streets of the town. The statue of San Isidro, the patron saint of farmers, was being moved slowly on the shoulders of young men. It came to a stop every so often as the process of blessing the streets and releasing of incense took place. Young and old priests with stern faces orchestrated the safe journey for their treasured icon. The religious party would wind its way through narrow streets of gift shops and restaurants before turning back towards the coast for the sanctuary of the church.

After an early lunch of pizza slices, cold beers and a move to a shaded area closer to a hotel on the Balcón, Kane and his friends waited for the afternoon events to commence.

Kane shouted above the noise of the crowd. 'The horses are next. Do you remember last year how good those riders were?'

'Keep your voice down,' said Sue who seemed more interested in devouring more of the incredible olives that she kept handing around to her friends.

The crowd hushed with the explosive sound of thundering hooves as six excitable horses came to an abrupt halt. Riders in bright yellow costumes proudly took their beasts through their dance steps that involved the horses raising their legs high. There was a rhythmic clatter of hooves on the road. The horses' elegant walking and sideways moves brought about an enthusiastic reaction from the onlookers as loud applause echoed through the narrow streets. A vigorous shaking of the animals' heads went on for a few moments and golden bells on their platted manes rang out in the main square. The arrival of the police on grey scooters brought an end to the display. The noisy popping of exhaust pipes went on for some time as the law enforcers casually chatted and checked their mobile phones.

With the show now over, Kane, along with others, moved away from the barrier for a photo opportunity. Walking slowly towards the riders, he was impressed with the automatic focus on his new camera and made a slight adjustment to the lens. It looked and felt like he was actually standing next to the horses. He thought of Sue who was still back in the shade and her generosity in buying him the camera for his birthday. Keen to post photos on Facebook, he was already composing the text for the prompt that would read: *What's on your mind Kane?*

Pressing the shutter a number of times, he continued to edge forward. Moving his eye momentarily away from the viewfinder, his whole world literally slipped in those few seconds. Skidding on the wet surface of the square, where the animals had been sprayed with cold water, he frantically tried to stay upright to limit the ferocity of the fall. He heard the screams from the crowd but it was too late as his body thumped into the hind quarters of one of the horses.

The scared creature pulled violently away from its owner. Frantically kicking and standing on its hind legs, the startled horse was out of control. Under the knife-sharp hooves that cut deep, Kane's feeble body was tossed from side to side like a rag doll. Screaming with pain and attempting to cover his face, the stamping continued. Bright red blood quickly formed a pool under the man who now lay motionless on the ground.

The overexcited animal was manoeuvred away and led towards the old town. Chaos broke out as people moved in to help, many backing off accepting they were probably too late to be of assistance. The square was pitched into silence as people looked on in horror. The only sounds to be heard were the parrots in the palm trees and the bathers on the beach below who knew nothing of the accident back on the Balcón.

Across from the square, girlfriend Sue covered her eyes fearing the worst for the unfortunate person who couldn't possibly have survived such an ordeal. She craned her head searching for Kane but he was nowhere to be seen. Had he gone off to buy some more of his favourite *churros*?

Gripping the safety barrier, Sue glanced over to the man on the ground and the remaining horses that were being led away. A first aider and three police women formed a circle around Kane's body in an attempt to hide the horrendous scene. The injuries were so severe that those helping were initially unsure whether it was one of the riders or someone from the crowd. The broken body and destroyed face belonged to a man whose wallet lay on the blood-stained concrete.

A much-creased photo of Amber was carried by the wind along the Balcón de Europa to eventually become wedged behind the bronze sculpture of King Alfonso XII. The lonely royal who camps out by the railings was frequently photographed by the tourists, only today their attention was focused on an incident further along the walkway.

***

Reaching speeds of 120 km on the fast road to Malaga, the strident wail of the ambulance was heard in the surrounding areas of Nerja. The traffic was manic and there was much changing of lanes as the driver battled to reach the hospital some 40 km along the coast road. The ETA should have been a further thirty-five minutes, only roadworks on the approach road to the city were delaying journeys. Their patient had life-threatening injuries and the paramedic who fought to save Kane's life kept telling him to stay awake. Attempting to stem the flow of blood from Kane's face, arms and chest, the young woman shook her head vigorously and shouted over the roar of the engine to her colleague that things weren't looking good.

The broken face was massively disfigured and bloody and it was evident that there were broken ribs. Despite the paramedics' efforts, they were losing the battle. Hooked up to a respirator the shallow rise and fall of the ribcage was causing concern. The man's vitals were checked and a larger dose of morphine was administered. Drips and monitors that bleeped were continually checked and still the man on the trolley remained perfectly still.

Unable to move a muscle Kane could feel immense pain but was unable to call out. Locked down on the stretcher he heard every word of the paramedic and desperately wanted to shout out, 'Don't stop trying, I can hear you. I'm not ready to die.'

With images ramping up in his head, the sensation of sliding and falling into the horse continuously played; the beating he had endured was so vivid as every kick of the beast increased in strength. The morphine raced around his veins and dulled his senses but he still knew his chances of surviving were limited. They say when you are close to the edge, the events of your life flash through the mind, only for Kane, he felt like he was stepping off a stage for the last time. Thoughts of Amber in prison and his regret for not visiting her moved swiftly to his brother who thrived on lying. The two most important people in his life were slipping away. There were to be no second chances only a dull sadness relating to lost opportunities.

***

With a screech of tyres, the ambulance came to stop outside the accident and emergency entrance of the hospital. The stretcher slid from the rear of the vehicle, its wheels making contact with the concrete with a slight bump. Medics and nurses in green shirts and trousers transported the blood-stained body into the emergency unit. Kane's clothes were cut from his body with enormous scissors and fell to the floor. An assessment of his injuries took place. All the time instructions were being given on vitals, drugs and procedures that were required to save the man from Nerja who fell under a horse.

A newly trained nurse with only three days experience of working in casualty rushed away from the horrific sight of the torn and bloody face with broken teeth hanging from the half open jaw. Standing in the corner of the emergency room she held a hand to her mouth but never took her eyes off the patient. Nothing had prepared her for viewing horrific injuries of this nature.

As the drips and a respirator were hurriedly set up, a senior medic in a green tunic, managed to stem the flow of blood and turned his attention to the damage to the ribcage and organs. The ECG readings indicated a low heart rate and it was established that without breathing assistance, life could not be sustained. There was much bleeping of monitors and the trolley with all the accompanying equipment was hurriedly pushed into the scanning suite.

A call took place to theatre seven to admit the patient for surgery. The duty manager was instructed to inform the next of kin. Jason's name was retrieved from Kane's mobile phone. On receiving the call, Jason listened to the hospital employee, who spoke relatively good English, as he relayed the terrible news.

***

Sixteen hours had passed before the two passengers settled into their seats for the flight to Malaga. They willed the safety checks to finish quickly as the Boeing 727 still remained parked on the tarmac connected to an airbridge with the main door fully open. A woman in a fluorescent yellow plastic coat and clutching a clipboard kept going in and out of the cockpit. She eventually stood outside the cramped area by the toilet to address the main air stewardess. The shaking of her head was a clear indication to Jason that the flight from Gatwick was not leaving the ground anytime soon.

An announcement was made without any trace of compassion which informed the passengers that, due to a technical issue, the flight was cancelled. There was no apology only that passengers should disembark and make their way to the transit lounge. Details of a flight the next morning would be advised shortly. Jason casually glanced out to the starboard wing and said loudly, 'At least it hasn't fallen off.' He sarcastically added, 'I knew we shouldn't have booked with a budget airline.'

His mother was clearly embarrassed and raised her eyes to the panel above their heads and muttered, 'Zip it Jason – people are listening.'

Her son shrugged his shoulders before issuing a weak apology.

As they waited for people to vacate their seats, images of his brother in intensive care shot through his mind. All that he had been told was that Kane had been in an accident with a horse and was badly injured but out of immediate danger. And now with the delay there was the worry of not reaching the hospital until the next day.

His mother, a slim woman with a birthmark on her left cheek and short silver hair, who was showing signs of severe panic, turned to her son and whispered, 'Tell me again what the doctor said about Kane and how the accident happened?'

Jason once again replied to the same question that she had already asked a number of times in the departure lounge. 'Mum, it wasn't a doctor I spoke to, it was a hospital coordinator who told me to come over as quickly as possible. All I know is there was an incident with a horse and he is out of danger but in a bad way.'

A puzzled look grew on the mother's face. 'But we know that Kane isn't a rider, so what was he doing on a horse?'

'I don't know; he probably went trekking in the mountains with friends. I can only think he has multiple injuries that include fractures. Until we get there, we have to stay calm as he is going to need our help in the weeks ahead. It could be a long job and will involve us staying in his villa.'

'What about your work?'

'I have no client meetings scheduled and if necessary, can work from out there in Spain. Saying that, his broadband is not that brilliant. I just hope Kane isn't too badly hurt.'

'Your brother has always been accident prone. Do you remember when he fell off his motorbike and broke his wrist?'

Jason raised a hand to his face and stifled a laugh. 'You are thinking of his friend Colin who had the crash. You remember, Colin, he was Kane's best man at his wedding. Kane had a scooter, not a motorbike.'

'Of course, I do,' came back the matter-of-fact reply.

She folded her glasses and placed them in a grey case and then took them out again.

Grasping his small travel bag, Jason extracted the euros he had hurriedly purchased at an extortionate rate from the departure lounge and counted the notes. He shuffled in his seat and attempted to stand up. 'I think we ought to leave now. I'll get the coats down – have you got your handbag?'

Mary Boulter frantically searched the cramped area by her feet and lifted up an inflight magazine and said, 'Can you have a look please?'

Her son reached down and effortlessly retrieved the bag and handed it over. He then lowered his head as he attempted to stand up to enter the aisle. There were so many people in the cabin all anxious to retrieve their onboard luggage from the overhead lockers. Many were moaning that the flight had been cancelled. The queue in the aisle was hellish and a young woman smiled at Jason and casually said, 'Let's just hope we get an early Malaga flight in the morning. Do you think they will put us up in a hotel?'

Not wishing to engage in conversation Jason nodded. As they shuffled forward, she addressed him again. 'Oh, well, on the bright side Spain will still be there tomorrow. Hope you have a great holiday. Where did you say you were staying?'

Jason yanked their coats and hand luggage from the compartment and snapped at the traveller. 'I didn't. Now if you don't mind moving forward, we want to get off this plane.'

***

The early morning replacement flight took off on time and, on reaching thirty thousand feet, the cheery pilot's voice informed his passengers that the weather was good with no turbulence reported. Onboard refreshments would be served shortly and he went on to painfully introduce each of the cabin crew by name and length of employment with the airline. Jason nervously played with the fabric on the edge of his seat and observed his mother who was staring out of the window. He was aware she had not slept well, not that he had either, and chose not to engage in conversation.

He noted the food trolley being wheeled out by an attractive airhostess who looked just like Amber. It was her gorgeous face and the hint of a smile creasing her cheeks that reminded him of the girl back home in prison. His mind cast back to his last visit and his pathetic attempt to show her some affection. What was he playing at making out he had feelings for her? This was his brother's ex-girlfriend and, whilst he hadn't represented her in the build-up to the court appearance, he had initially interviewed her. He wondered if she was still coping with being incarcerated with so many tough women, some of whom were capable of derailing her chances of a respectable life. With the strange things she had revealed about getting a kick from breaking the law and not getting caught, surely an individual with her hang-ups could easily slip back into crime on being released. He would make no further contact with her and, as for brother Kane getting in touch with her, he would do everything in his power to thwart the rekindling of that relationship.

When the trolley reached their seats, Jason smiled at the young woman. As he scanned the flight attendant's face, the resemblance to Amber was uncanny. His eyes travelled down to her stomach and that's where any similarity ended, this girl carried far too much weight. He was now aware his staring was unsettling the lady who was unscrewing the top of a carton of milk. 'Tea or coffee, sir?'

He feigned a smile and politely replied, 'No thanks.'

***

It was a short flight and touching down in Malaga brought back the reality of having to visit the El Angel Hospital to discover the extent of Kane's injuries. Clearing customs, Jason wheeled their two cases and urged his mother to speed up her walking.

Out in the bright sunshine the temperature was already soaring into the high seventies and would be even hotter by mid-day. As they settled into the hard seats of the yellow Chevrolet taxi, the Spanish driver engaged first gear and the vehicle lurched forward leaving his passengers feeling unsettled and gripping their seat belts. The complex of airport roads and roundabouts gradually gave way to a dual carriageway and the speed increased. The customary worry beads hanging from the driver's mirror swung at all angles and made a clattering sound like nails in a tin.

'Do you think Kane will be OK?' asked Mrs Boulter for the umpteenth time.

'We just have to wait and see,' replied Jason impatiently.

Thankfully, the ride was short and as they entered the busy hospital, Jason's mother informed her son that she had left her phone in the taxi. He groaned as she asked him to go back and retrieve it. Jason swore under his breath knowing that it had taken a few minutes to reach the main desk and the vehicle would have long gone. Telling her to sit on one of the benches, he stored the cases next to her and set off for the exit point. Glancing down to the many yellow Chevrolet taxis, he turned to leave. Why was everything turning out to be so difficult? Obstacles thrown in their way to reach the hospital, first the delayed flight and now mother losing her enormous press button pay-as-you go phone.

Returning to the reception area his mother had left her seat and was talking to a man on the desk. They were to take the lift to level seven and follow the signs for the critical ward offices. The floor in question was busy with doctors and nurses moving around the corridors that led to the wards and their designated work stations.

On reaching the desk, Jason was impressed with the young man who tapped away on his computer and confirmed that he had their names as next of kin. He pointed the way to the visitor's lounge. Upbeat and determined to support his mother in this worrying time, Jason reached for her bony hand that was cold despite the heat. 'I'm sure it is going to be ok. Kane is a fighter and the hospital will do everything possible to make him better.'

The reply that shot back bore no connection to her son. 'Colin, the lad who fell off his motorbike, did he break any bones?'

Jason stopped himself from muttering: *What's that got to do with all of this?* He gently guided her along the highly polished blue floor and was surprised to see Kane's girlfriend, Sue, coming out of the waiting room.

Dressed in a summery blue cotton dress and brown slip-on shoes she looked stunning. Jason's eyes strayed to the trim figure, tanned arms and legs. He instantly recognised her from his last visit to the villa and stretched out a welcoming hand. He was impressed with the beautiful woman with the long blonde hair that cascaded down to her shoulders. Despite all the stress she must have been going through, her face still held the cheery girlish smile. The composure of this woman shone like a bright light and Jason told himself that his brother was a lucky man to have found her.

He grasped her thin fingers, she pulled away and he said, 'Hi Sue, good to see you again. We got here as quickly as we could. This is my Mum.'

With a trace of a Birmingham accent, she greeted them. She smiled kindly at her boyfriend's mother, and said, 'Pleased to meet you Mrs Boulter. I am sure you must be exhausted from travelling and all the worry of the accident.'

'How is he?' came back the desperate voice.

'Stable now but it has been awful seeing him so badly injured. I think we are past the worst. He will need various operations and then…'

Jason's voice rose as he interrupted her, 'When the hospital rang they said it was serious but under control. We haven't been told the extent of his injuries and with all the flights booked solid it's been a game trying to get here. All they said was he had fallen off a horse. He could have been at death's door for all we knew.'

The expression on Sue's face changed to fraught. She took her time to answer. 'The doctor said he was satisfied that the broken bones would heal. The massive bruising was expected after such an accident.' Labouring her words her glance switched between the two worried faces. 'It wasn't a fall from a horse, he actually fell under one.'

Jason nestled his mother's head into his shoulder and both were shaking from the shock. 'You say he was trampled, that's awful. Just how bad is he? Can we see him?'

'He has two broken ribs and twisted his leg when he fell.'

Simultaneously, both took a deep breath and Jason said, 'Thank God it is no worse. Have they said how long he will be in here?'

Competing with the noise in the corridor, Sue raised her voice. 'He's out of critical care and just been transferred to a private room. He doesn't say much but certainly knows I'm there.'

Jason nodded and smiled at his mother. 'That's good. His body has taken a real beating and it's going to take a while before he can move around; possibly on crutches at first.'

Sue frowned and levelled with them. 'It's his face that's a mess. I need to prepare you before going in that it's not a pretty sight. It's been beaten up something awful.'

Mrs Boulter was trembling and trying not to cry. 'Face, oh, my God – what was he doing so near to a horse?'

'I honestly don't know. We were at the festival and I had gone off with some friends to buy snacks. It's all a bit sketchy but someone said he was taking photographs and got too close and tripped.'

The frightened woman found her voice and muttered. 'Is he in a lot of pain?'

'I'd say moderately comfortable and the medication is helping. He is lucid and responds to conversation but needs to rest. I am waiting for an update as there will have to be operations for facial reconstruction. A few of his front teeth were knocked out. I was due to return to London to start a new job but obviously I'm taking each day as it comes.'

Struggling to take in the news, they all mulled over what to do next.

***

Lying totally flat and staring at the ceiling, Kane

remained silent as his family stood by the bedside. They stared at a face they could barely recognise and visibly shook. The horrific sight of the partly bandaged head and black puffed-up eyes brought tears to their eyes. Indentations of the horse's hooves had left massive ruts that were ruddy red with spongy purple bruising. It was a miracle his eyes hadn't been ripped from their sockets with the intensity of injuries inflicted. He was naked from the waist up with bandaging to the rib cage and arms. From under the blue sheet a solitary catheter tube ran down to a bag clipped to the side of the bed. It was bulging with urine and needed emptying. Kane's arms had cuts and his chest was frightening shades of red and purple. The poor man was in a terrible state and, whilst awake, was mercifully drowsy. He had survived the ordeal.

They tried to talk to him but there was no response, only a raising of his right hand to acknowledge them. A nurse came in to check his vitals and Sue asked for an update. Jason pointed to the catheter bag, the woman raised her shoulders and put a thumb up. The draining of the bag into a large jug took about thirty seconds. She disposed of the blue surgical gloves in the bin and left the room.

'I hope they are not all like her in this hospital?' said Jason as he turned back to his brother.

Sue leant over the bed and whispered in Kane's ear, 'Say hello to your Mum and brother, Kane.'

As the battered man slowly moved his head, he struggled to speak. Eventually, a gravelly voice laced with sadness rang out, 'My face and mouth are hurting.'

Kane's mother gently caressed her son's hand. 'We're here now son. You are going to be alright.'

'My face, my face is bad, isn't it?'

Sucking in breath the woman in her late sixties turned

to her younger son and then back to Kane. 'The doctors say it can be sorted. One day at a time.'

With eyes focused on his mother, Kane attempted to raise one of the arms that had been used to shield his face from the horse. He pleaded with her, 'Did they really say that?'

***

During the long days that ensued, the family and Sue supported Kane by taking turns to sit by the bedside. He rarely spoke and when he did it was usually in words of one syllable which were difficult to comprehend. His mental health was particularly low. In essence, the life had been sucked out of him. The injuries to the face were horrific and although the medics had promised the bruising would subside, the wounds would still be prominent. Surgery on his destroyed face would be scheduled later that week. There were no guarantees for restoring his attractive looks but every effort would be made to bring about a satisfactory outcome. The biggest problem was stopping him touching his face which was slowing down the healing process. He kept pulling off the white cotton gloves. Drifting in and out of sleep, it was distressing to hear him cry out Amber's name. Sue flinched each time he did this.

Sue was incredible but there was no denying that she would eventually have to reduce her time spent at the hospital in order to take up the new job. Her relationship with Kane was mainly just friendly with no ties. Her only solace lay in knowing Kane's mother and brother were committed to looking after him.

Two weeks had flown by since they had arrived and at the end of a harrowing day, the fifty-minute drive to Frigiliana took its toll as tiredness crept in. In normal times, staying at the villa would have been a perfect holiday break, taking in the sun and swimming in the large pool, but not on this trip. On happier occasions, Kane had been a good host and often drove his guests to the thriving coastal town of Nerja for dinner. The stroll on the Balcón was restful with views of the sea and craggy outcrops that held the explosion of white new-build houses. The small Spanish town delivered sun, sea, shops and incredible restaurants. Who would ever have envisaged that the most recent fiesta would have resulted in a man tragically falling beneath a mighty five hundred kilo beast and surviving?

Chapter 19

Two hundred and sixty-eight days into her prison stretch, Amber was oblivious to Kane's misfortune, let alone that his brother and mother were still in Spain looking after him. Had she been informed she would have been devastated, but Jason hadn't contacted her. With the seriousness of the accident she would have wanted to fly out to be with him, only in her present circumstances this would not have been possible. When Jason had last visited her, they hadn't exactly parted on good terms. He had chosen to flirt with her and was just out for himself. Little did she know that this channel of communication with Kane had been totally unreliable.

Coping with life in prison had become marginally easier for Amber, mainly due to her standing up to the bullies and understanding the pitfalls of being inside. It also helped sharing with Liz with whom she planned to keep in contact after her release.

Her positive stance on adjusting to whatever life inside the jungle threw at her helped with focusing on the future. Acknowledging her wrongdoings, her goal was set on achieving redemption and upholding her status as a caring individual. The past would never be wiped out but she could do something about her future. Deception and thievery would no longer have a hold on her life. The catalyst for moving on had come from a meeting with the prison chaplain. Amber was no church-goer but on talking to the incredible woman of the cloth, something clicked inside. In essence the words: learning to love yourself, opened her eyes and heart to aspire to a fresh start. Each time Amber saw Reverend Lewis, the two women simply nodded at each other; there was no necessity for words as it was obvious the healing process had begun.

Prior to her court case, an area of improvement for Amber had been to move away from her slovenly ways. She had worked hard on losing weight and tidying up her apartment. On arriving at HMP Fairfield, the lockup that prisoners A4633 and A4591 shared was kept spotlessly clean. Orderly and clean became the new rule and Liz, who wasn't the tidiest of individuals, struggled at first with the constant spring-cleaning. There was no denying the camaraderie that existed between them helped with the boredom of being locked up for so many hours a day.

There wasn't a day that Amber didn't think of Kane, but with all her plans for the future, it was easier to block out emotional feelings. There were no more tearful episodes as she gradually came to terms with the fact they had both moved on. Yet deep inside the corners of her mind a file with his name on it lay dormant. It was a reminder that the show wasn't over yet. For now, they were on different roads that she hoped might eventually merge. Memories of Kane could never be wiped away. She liked to picture him sunbathing by his villa pool in the Spanish mountain village and hoped he was happy and occasionally thought of her. Her separation from him was the price she was paying for breaking the law. On her release she wondered if she should contact Jason to enquire about Kane's address in Spain but dismissed the thought. Her dislike for his brother fought against asking him for a favour.

With a fierce determination to make the best of her time in prison, Amber volunteered for extra duties to keep her mind and body active. She thrived on befriending other prisoners who were struggling to come to terms with their lot. Whilst everyone in her wing had been allocated duties, she went that step further. Adding to her busy workload, two hours a week were dedicated to assisting with educational support. Amber was intent on bringing out the best in others.

Prior to losing her job and freedom, there were occasions when she had encouraged and nurtured co-workers at the company where she was employed into growing their skills. Whilst people who came into contact with her knew nothing of her secret pastimes, an empathy had existed. Most accepted the poorly dressed worker, who always arrived early for work, for who she was. There were times she said weird things but outweighing all her failings, underneath the outer façade, a beautiful butterfly lay waiting to emerge.

***

Staring through the cold, steel-barred window, Amber gazed down to the exercise yard and the women, mostly in groups, walking around the perimeter walls. She could make out a few of the faces from her wing and made a mental note of those to stay clear of. This morning most women looked as if they were behaving, but you could never tell what some of them were up to.

Normally, on being allowed outside there were raised voices, but not today. It brought home the sadness of the incident earlier that morning when one of the women who was refused early release had been found dead in her cell. The police were on site. The woman in question was someone who had been inordinately kind to Amber and just a few days ago had sat next to her at breakfast. There was no suggestion of Alice being desperate; on the contrary, she was upbeat and readily accepted Amber's offer to share her toast. This tragic incident indicated yet another of the scary happenings that resulted from being holed up in jail. There had been fights, bullying and even a small riot that was quashed before it snowballed out of control. Even though HMP Fairfield was a relatively new correction unit, Alice's death was just another to be added to the list of people who lost the will to live.

Much of Block A on level two had been cordoned off whilst the forensic teams investigated. Someone at breakfast claimed they overheard a warden say that two inmates had been transferred to the governor's office for questioning. Chinese whispers soon shot around the prison of the suicide and the disturbances that had ensued.

Amber had chosen to remain in the cell and was struggling to get her head around the fact that Liz would soon be due for parole. The consequences of being landed with a new cellmate were too scary to consider. What if she ended up sharing with one of those creepy women who roamed the corridors befriending the vulnerable, the sort who loved to dominate? She would have to be on her guard and pray the days and nights zoomed by leaving her able to cope with any problems that might occur.

Her weighing up of scenarios was halted as Liz came into the cell after completing her corridor cleaning duties, and plonked herself down on the narrow bed. In a quizzical voice she asked, 'Wasn't that the girl you got on well with. The one who topped herself?'

'Don't talk like that. She must have been so distressed to have ended her life. I know she didn't get early release but there were only four months left to run. I just wish I could have helped her.'

Liz nodded her head and sighed. 'It's the quiet ones that end up doing it. Didn't you say she had a partner?'

'Yes, an older man living in Ealing. He will be devastated to hear the news. Life just isn't fair, is it? I should have been there for her.'

Lifting an arm into the air and resting a hand on Amber's shoulder, Liz smiled. 'And that's what I like about you, you care.'

'Thanks, that means a lot to me.'

Amber's eyes took in a quick tour of the small cell and focused on the walls where both women had attempted to make their surroundings more bearable. Each had pinned images to the cork board above the chest of drawers in an effort to stay connected with happier times. Liz had displayed a magazine page of a wonderful Spanish seaside picture with families enjoying the warm weather and sunshine, whilst Amber plastered loveable cats and a bottle of red wine that begged to be opened.

Amber switched the conversation to Liz's imminent release date. 'Not sure what I'm going to do when you leave here. It's only just over two weeks to the big day.'

'You'll cope and, in no time, it will be your turn to go home. Have you thought any more about going back to work?'

Amber looked up to the cell window and down to her friend's face. 'I don't have any option as bills need to be paid. I still have some savings but not much after I paid everyone back. As for finding a job, I'm not sure anyone would want a criminal working for them.'

Liz sucked in breath, shook her head and tutted. 'It's usually me who's negative, not you. I am convinced you will get another chance; it may not be in the same line of work. Just focus on new horizons. I'm not going to have a heart attack over getting a job straight away.'

'Good on you but there is something that I need to discuss. I don't want you throwing a wobbly, it's just an idea. You said your only option was to go back to Durham but you would probably end up living on the streets until you got a break.'

Liz laughed and waved a finger in the air. 'I was in my dramatic mode and not seeing the whole picture. Durham is out of the question as my mum and I don't get on, so I can't go home. I'll get some help from the probation team and live in a hostel in London. There are counsellors who look out for people like me. My plan is to stay in the East London area, possibly Tottenham.' Pausing for breath she finally added, 'Handy for the football.'

'But you don't like football.' Amber smiled sweetly at her friend who had smoothed the way for her in prison. 'I'm not having you staying in a hostel. My place is big enough for the two of us and together we will be stronger. I'll speak to the admin lady and explain you need the key from my personal things.'

A look of astonishment came over Liz's face as she attempted to take in the kind offer. 'No, I couldn't possibly stay in your flat. It's not fair, I'd only cramp your style.'

'I don't do style, what you see is what you get with me.'

'It's really kind of you but I can't. Anyway, you won't be out of this place for ages. Apart from that, it's not fair to take over your pad.'

Amber sighed. 'Why don't you just remind me how long I have left to stay banged up in here?'

'You'll soon be out when you get parole.' Liz looked thoughtful and quickly added, 'Look, with me staying in your home, let's not forget I'm a thief and you hardly know me. I wouldn't want you worrying I might be weighing up things to pinch.'

Amber raised her eyes to the concrete ceiling and swiftly down to make contact with Liz. 'Never entered my mind. Nothing worth stealing and anyway, the fridge is empty.'

'I promise not to let you down as I'm going straight …' Liz's eyes lit up as she broke into laughter. 'What I meant was that I plan to stay on the right side of the law this time and not …'

'I know what you meant,' said Amber who also giggled. 'It's all about a new start for you and me. You move into my place and keep it spick and span for when I get this ball and chain removed. I'll need you to help with rent when you get your benefits.'

'Are you serious – you really are prepared to let me bed down in your place? You won't regret helping me, I promise. I should get my allowance soon and pay my way.'

Amber polished the lenses of her glasses on her green tee-shirt and muttered, 'So that's you sorted.' She paused, and with a pained look on her face added, 'Just don't forget to clean up after yourself. Nowadays, I keep a tidy ship but it wasn't always like that.'

'Don't I know it – I put something down and you move it.'

'Yep, I do go over the top – in the past I lived like a pig but not any longer.'

Liz nodded her head. 'I'll stay as long as I'm welcome and not a moment longer. If your fancy man, the guy you often speak about, walks back into your life then I'm not hanging around. What was his name?'

A sad voice echoed around the brick-built cell. 'Kane.'

***

The day that Liz walked out into the bright sunshine, Amber passed over her front door key and mentioned the name of a neighbour who had been keeping an eye on the property. It was a sad moment for Amber as she pictured Liz going through the various security points and undergoing a body search. On taking possession of the items that had been confiscated when she was admitted, the paperwork would be completed, and then with a few short steps the door to freedom would be cast open.

Later that afternoon, Amber stood in the exercise yard ignoring fellow prisoners who were particularly noisy as they hung around in groups. The governor had recently ruled that on Thursday a second exercise session would be allowed. Thrilled with being outside in the late afternoon, Amber stared at the amazing sunset and gathering dusk. A flock of chattering starlings that were lined up on the twenty-foot-high fencing became the topic of conversation. Normally it was the clumsy pigeons perched on ledges and walls that featured as wildlife around the prison.

Listening to the roar of the traffic and a car alarm that kept sounding, Amber longed to be free of her chains and venture out into the wider world, just like Liz had done some six hours earlier. Her turn for release was going to come around and, for the meantime, it was all about keeping her head above water. A newly revised plan was forming in her head that would assist her getting back on track. She acknowledged that the past would always be there but tomorrow was another day – she had to remain positive. Her parole interview was scheduled for late November which was not that far away. If successful, she could be home by January after spending Christmas in her cell.

Amber's thought process was interrupted by a group of women who were out of breath from their game of rounders. A short and stocky girl excitedly addressed her. 'Come on Amber, you are good at this – do you want to play?'

Returning a smile, Amber triumphantly said, 'Count me in.'

She joined in with the fun and ran faster than the older prisoners many of whom had piled on the weight. One of the women kept telling Amber how impressed she was with her being so trim and good looking. Rather than offend the redhead who was serving a stretch for assaulting her lover, Amber smiled and waited for her turn with the bat.

The remaining twenty minutes of their leisure time was the happiest Amber had experienced since entering the towering grey walls of HMP Fairfield.

Chapter 20

Pulling on her coat for warmth Amber shuddered as the late January cold wind did its worst. Clutching her release papers and holdall, she crossed the road from the prison and momentarily gazed back at the high walls and buildings that still held around two hundred prisoners. Some of these offenders stood little chance of improving their lives. The reality of surviving in the outside world would become too much to bear for many of them. Backsliding into reoffending would undoubtedly result in returning to live in the castle with only one exit door that rarely opened. She hurried to the local station and speculated on how many times she would have to change trains to reach her home town of Harrow.

After a long journey, Amber spotted Liz waving madly and speeded up her pace. There was no mistaking her friend but something was different. Normally she dressed in dark colours but today her coat was bright blue and accompanying her was a small Yorkshire terrier.

There were hugs and kisses and Amber looked down to the dog and said, 'You didn't say you had a …'

'Don't worry, it's a client's pet. I've got a few of your neighbours signed up for dog walking; it's an easy way to get some cash. I bet I could line up more people if I put an ad in the newsagent.'

Impressed with Liz's entrepreneurial skills, Amber congratulated her and turned her attention to the adorable terrier who was holding up a paw to shake. In a quizzical voice she said, 'When you approached the residents in my flats, did you say where you were staying?'

Confused, Liz muttered quietly, 'Well, yes. It's not a problem, is it? I said I was living in your place and available to offer my services.'

'Oh, I see. I'm amazed they took up your offer knowing I'd been found guilty of theft.'

'On the contrary, the two people who trusted me with their pets both asked after you. They were pleasant enough and jumped at the chance of someone local helping out. You need to chill out as there are people out there who are prepared to give us a second chance.'

Liz pulled on the lead and with her other hand held up the black waste bags holder. 'Shall we start walking as I've been out nearly an hour and this little madam needs to be encouraged to spend more than a penny, if you get my drift.'

Amber was elated to be out in the open with a horizon that did not feature a high wall and aerial mast protruding from the East Wing. It was wonderful seeing the shops and the streets that she had dreamt of walking along again. She found the cold air exhilarating and took deep breaths to sample the smells of a normal street. Liz helped with carrying the bag whilst reining in the inquisitive dog that was determined to sniff out every leaf and twig.

'I don't know what I would have done without you visiting me and our phone calls. I just wish you had replied to the letter I sent you.'

'I'm not that good at writing.'

'That's ok. What about the flat, is everything tidy and have you paid that bill I told you about?'

'Yep, to both questions. Your neighbour has been a gem checking up on me so I bought a bunch of flowers to thank her.'

The two women headed along the high street and into Amber's tree-lined road in the direction of the block of flats where she lived. There were many false starts as the dog walked around in circles on the grassed areas that badly needed cutting. On reaching the steps up to the lobby, Liz handed Amber her key, and set off to return Sissy, the terrier, to its owner.

Entering the building, Amber was pleased with herself as she climbed the stairs without having to stop to catch her breath. Not so long ago, carrying all that body weight, she would have been puffing away like a train. Losing the best part of three stone had enabled her to live a more comfortable life. Gone were her tent-like garments and jeans fit to burst. She gazed at her reflection in the mirror on the landing and acknowledged how trim she looked. All that dieting, prior to being sent for trial, had paid off.

Unlocking her front door and letting it glide open, the relief of being home started to build. Stepping onto the clean but worn-out hall carpet, she gazed at the pictures on the walls and favourite ornaments on a table outside the lounge doorway. A small pile of mail was neatly stacked and probably held contact details for social services to set up a meeting. Inside the lounge, it was as orderly as the day she had left it over a year ago.

Liz had kept up the housework and, judging by the smell of furniture polish, had recently gone spray crazy. The laundry basket, minus its lid, had found a new home in the small kitchen and was piled high with clothes that spilled onto the floor.

Moving around the flat, her eyes scanned the size of the rooms. After being confined for so long, it was strangely frightening to have so much space. Yes, it was good to be home but it would take some adjusting to having a free rein again. Spending so much time in a cramped cell with no horizon had blurred her sense of freedom. There had been so many rules that had to be obeyed. Life outside those walls had never been far from her thoughts but now it was laced with a scariness that she hadn't anticipated.

Hearing Liz opening the front door and call out her

name momentarily sent a shiver through her body. Just how long could her remaining savings of three thousand pounds support the two of them? Fortunately, there was no rent to pay as the property had been gifted to her when Auntie Jane died, but there were bills to pay. Oh yes, Auntie Jane, the wonderful lady who had helped her grandparents care for her after the tragic car accident that stole her parents.

Liz became excitable as she listed the jobs completed in the two-bedroom accommodation: hoovering, washing of walls, taking Amber's popcorn-coloured duvet to a local launderette and ending with an apology for breaking so many cereal bowls.

Observing the drying rack in front of the lounge radiator, Amber spied skimpy knickers and white bras and a lone sock that had made its way onto the carpet. 'Just one thing, I don't want to watch TV looking at your smalls. Also, what have you done with the remote for the TV?'

'I'll move them straight away – sorry. The remote is in my bedroom.'

'What's it doing in there?'

'I took your kitchen telly into my room and the lounge handset works on that one.'

'Oh, I see. Not the clearest of logic though.'

Liz's eyes were sparkling with excitement as she changed the subject. 'Let me show you your bedroom, it looks better now I've had a go at it.'

Once inside the room Liz pointed to the far wall. 'I moved the bed away from that damp plaster that was peeling. It keeps coming back despite me trying to dry it out. The guy in the newsagent told me to buy some blocking paint.'

'I'd forgotten about that. It never used to worry me but now things are different. Not sure I can get a builder in just yet until the finances improve. Let me see what you have done with the spare room you are sleeping in.'

Liz led the way and pleasingly the single bed had been made.

'Where are all your things?'

'Over there.'

The pathetic sight brought a lump to Amber's throat. One tiny well-used case with a small tear on the side and two Sainsbury plastic bags leant against the wardrobe door.

'Is that everything?'

A barely audible voice confirmed that this was the extent of her possessions. 'It's all I need.'

When Liz returned to the kitchen to make a cup of tea, Amber wept uncontrollably. On those lonely nights in the prison, Liz had spoken of the hardships she faced as a young woman on the streets and the derelict properties she camped out in. The dangers she faced and stories of abuse had made them dark days for this girl. Witnessing her worldly belongings that amounted to so little, Amber's heart went out to her. It strengthened her resolve to secure work and take control of their destiny.

***

That night back in her comfortable bed, with the light still on, Amber's eyes strayed around the bedroom. Over the period of her imprisonment, she had missed having her own space and personal belongings and was pleased to be home. It seemed unreal that only this morning she had been cramped up in a small cell with her new inmate. Fortunately, the middle-aged Caribbean woman from Lewisham was a gem and had made her laugh. She was in for fraud and this was her second conviction. She refused to discuss her crime and spoke mainly about the good times, some of which were hilarious. Sharing a cell with Alesha had been an eye opener as this lady's life story had been revealed. Two husbands and, surprisingly no children, her love of life centred on travelling and that's where the bending of the rules had become her undoing.

Alesha introduced Amber to the game of Monopoly and every time they landed on *Go to Jail* they burst into laughter and vowed to stick a yellow note that read: *Go Home.* Amber was saddened that she would never again meet up with this charismatic woman who had the ability to turn the darkest of days into brighter ones. Her infectious laughter was something not to be forgotten, or her snoring – boy, could she snore.

As Amber mulled over her time in jail, her thoughts moved to getting back into work and that wasn't going to be a walk in the park. Potential employers would have to think hard before engaging two women with criminal records.

***

The next morning Liz was up early making breakfast. There was much clattering of kitchen utensils and she had left the hot tap running in the sink. The smoke detector in the hallway had sounded and woke Amber from her perfect night's sleep. Mountains of blackened toast greeted her in the kitchen and Liz was holding the alarm in her hand. She looked perplexed as she attempted to replace the battery.

'You have it the wrong way around and do turn off the tap,' said Amber as she stared at the messy worksurface that was covered in crumbs from the frantic scraping of the burnt offering. 'How many slices do two girls need at this ridiculous hour?'

'I was hungry, it's eight-thirty and I need to walk the first of the two dogs. Did you sleep okay?'

'Yeah, best one for a long time. It was great waking up in my own space and seeing all my things. I wouldn't want to go back to trudging along corridors to the dining room and all those people queuing for breakfast. I certainly won't miss the rubbery scrambled egg.'

'I liked the egg.'

Draining the last drops of coffee from Amber's favourite mug that now had a chip on the edge, Liz smiled and in a quiet voice said, 'All behind us now. Look, I must get off. I'll see you at lunch time. I'm going to knock on some doors to offer my services, fingers crossed I'll get more interest.'

On hearing the front door click shut, Amber commenced restoring the kitchen to its former glory. The catalyst for shifting from her slothful ways had only come about the day after she was arrested. Her transformation from apathetic to purposefully enthusiastic could only be celebrated as a remarkable turn of events.

The morning, what was left of it, panned out with a long soak in the bath and reading two chapters of a paperback that Alesha had given her prior to leaving prison. It was a true story of a man who started a charity for the homeless and in turn ended up living on the streets. It brought home the foolishness of Amber's own attempts to raise money for charity by stealing. She could still hear Kane's sarcastic voice as he made the point about her being a right little Robin Hood. Any future efforts to attract monies would never include burglary. There would come a day when Kane would be proud of her, only that day was a long way off.

Liz returned just before mid-day and, whilst she was still upbeat, it was obvious something was bothering her.

Clutching a dog lead, tin of baked beans and loaf of bread, Amber didn't have the heart to say that she disliked the dreaded pulses with all that gooey orange sauce.

'They were half price; perhaps I can get some more if they are still on offer.'

'If you do, let's have a change from the beans. How did the dog walking go?'

Liz drew breath. 'Fine, the couple from number six and the woman with the young child in flat two, send their regards. I tried the houses along the street who have dogs and didn't get lucky. I got short thrift from that battle-axe of a woman who has a red door in the last but one townhouse.'

'Not sure who you are referring to. What was the problem?'

'She wasn't that complimentary about you saying she wouldn't trust you with her dog, that's if she had one, let alone a house key. I felt like thumping her.'

Amber shrugged her shoulders and calmly said, 'I didn't say it was going to be easy. This is day one for me and I can see the woman's point; she obviously read about me in the local press or heard it on the grapevine. I'm not that bothered as I am hoping we will be judged by what we do in the future and not the past.'

'It's just me panicking as I don't want to be homeless again. I'll have to get my arse into gear and find work, diversify away from dog walking.'

Amber raised her hand and with her knuckle tapped gently the side of Liz's head 'No need for that sort of language. Get it into that brain of yours that we *will* find employment. Just remember that there are more decent people out there than miserable ones. We'll find a way.'

A smile was now developing on Liz's face. 'You really think so.'

'Yes, but it's going to take time. I have a plan to involve us both in charity work and some of the positions are paid ones. Little steps at a time. Whilst I think of it, how did you get on with the Job Centre interview – anything of interest?'

'Oh, it was ok, I suppose. Nothing that jumped out that I could apply for. Main thing was a lady down there has helped complete the paperwork for my benefits. She did say it takes a while to get it approved and paid.'

Amber gasped. 'You've been out of prison all this time and are only just getting around to applying for benefits? What were you thinking?'

'Don't give me a hard time. It was all those forms and I missed one of my interviews with the Job Centre. If you've lived on the streets like I did, you manage on next to nothing. I did do a bit of begging recently with a cup in South Harrow and kept getting moved on but it was worth a punt.'

'You did what? Look, you and I need to stay on the right side of the law and if that means cleaning toilets then so be it. I still can't grasp your reluctance to apply for benefits.'

'I don't do form filling. I could always become a lady of the night and not pay any tax.'

'Don't even joke about things like that.'

With a positive nod of her head, Liz then reached up to open a cupboard for a saucepan. 'That's me told.'

'When I eventually get a business going, I shall be the managing director and you can be my assistant,' said Amber with a grin on her face.

'Suits me. Now, how about I warm up those beans?'

Chapter 21

Three months can seem a very long time especially when adapting to living with a horrendous face injury. An operation performed in the Malaga hospital had been successful in straightening out Kane's crushed cheek bones and reconstructing his nose. The deep rivulets inflicted by the horse's hooves had reduced marginally, as had the purple swelling. Two lower front teeth had to be extracted and a wound to the forehead finely stitched. The damaged ribs had been, in truth, the easiest to repair. Coping with the scarring and mental anxiety was undoubtedly the worst part to come to terms with.

The only saving grace was that there was no longer any physical pain. The throbbing and tenderness that had been unbearable had now mercifully subsided. Every day Kane agonised over his foolishness on the day of the festival when he had moved away from the spectator's area to take photos of the magnificent horses.

There remained only one follow up appointment at the hospital and dental work that was scheduled with a private clinic. Kane rarely left the villa and only slipped out to the local mini market when it was quiet. His face was always covered with a scarf, which attracted stares from locals and friends. More recently they had held back on enquiring how he was and offering their help. The trauma of coming to terms with living with such a mangled face was proving to be too much for Kane who, up until recently, had regarded himself as a moderately handsome man with everything to live for.

Ex-girlfriend, Sue, had been a rock during the crisis and he was grateful for her care during the early days of his recovery. She now lived in London but kept in touch. Their relationship had been fun but both knew it was a temporary fling with neither wanting any commitments.

Brother Jason and his mother had been there every step of the way for Kane and had stayed in Spain for six weeks before travelling home to England. Jason had suggested they kept in touch on Facetime and Kane insisted it would only ever be with his brother. The thought of anyone else staring at his appearance on the screen was not on the cards.

The healing process was under way and, whilst there were bad days, on the whole he remained positive about moving on from the awful circumstances that had left his face so disfigured.

When Kane ventured outside to buy food from the local shop it was always an ordeal. With the soaring temperatures that beat down on the Andalusian village, his attempt to cover up drew glances from all he came into contact with. The rumours of the accident were widespread and, even with his face partially covered, the image people viewed was shocking. Locals and neighbours had always warmed to Kane but any offers of help had been shunned. There was little doubt that, for the immediate future, the British man living in Casa Emilia wanted to be on his own.

Inside his home and around the pool Kane felt safest. Every time he caught sight of his reflection in a mirror, the empty face startled him. The outstanding dental work to rebuild the broken teeth was scheduled for the following month. He was sure there would come a day when he would leave the scarf in the villa and go out into the world. A changed face didn't have to mean the end of his life but even with this optimistic approach, it wasn't going to be easy.

Today the weather had been scorching hot but, with the threat of a storm brewing, Kane chose to sit inside the garden room to read the new book a friend had lent him. The sound of his mobile ringing made him jump.

Retrieving the phone from his pocket he was pleased to discover his mother was calling and activated the speaker function.

'Hi Mum, you are not on the mobile I bought you.'

'No, I'm calling you on my landline. Those smartie phones are too difficult to use. I just like to press buttons. Now, how are you?'

Kane drew breath and ran a finger over the uneven contours of his face and sighed. 'Still haven't grown a new head, but yes I'm fine.'

'How are you coping with seeing people?'

'Not too bad. I'm out and about but still covering up. Not for much longer, possibly a month or so more. I'm beginning to accept that I'm not the best-looking man in the village, just the ugliest man on the mountain.'

'Don't let me hear you say things like that,' replied his mother in a tearful voice.

'Sorry, it gets me down looking like this. Let's not talk about me. How about Jason, is he still as busy as last time we spoke?'

'No, he's caught up with his work and things have calmed down. He's thinking about coming over to see you. He will give you a call to arrange a date.'

Not sure if he was ready to see his brother again so soon, his mind went over the past and the times they had fallen out. Even when Jason was helping him to recover there had been moments of friction. The one thing he knew about Jason was his love of a free holiday in the villa.

Trying to sound upbeat, Kane went over the top when he replied, 'That's great, tell him to give me a bell to make the arrangements.'

'Bell, what do you mean?'

'Sorry Mum, I meant a call.'

'Well, why didn't you say call? I just remembered

your brother said he had heard that the girl you were fond of has left prison and has tried to ring him. He ignored the call and then she called again.'

Kane held the phone at arm's length and stared desperately into space. He knew Amber must have been due for release soon but had made up his mind not to enquire about her plans. He desperately wished Jason had not volunteered this bit of information. Replying to his mother Kane said, 'She was just someone in the Spanish class I got on with.'

'That's not what Jason said, anyway it's none of my business. I'm not sure you associating with a criminal is a good idea. What was she in for?'

Dismissing her question, Kane promptly moved the subject away from Amber. 'Did I tell you I'm going for the final work on my teeth implants in a couple of weeks? Not sure how I'm going to get to the clinic in Malaga as I'm not driving, probably a taxi.'

'Well, good luck with that and keep me posted. I need to go now as I've arranged to meet a friend for coffee in the new Luton shopping centre.'

After they said their goodbyes, Kane wandered aimlessly back and forth from the house to the garden despite the rain that was steadily getting heavier. It was the crack of thunder that brought him to his senses. He wished Jason hadn't stirred up his emotions again by mentioning anything to do with Amber. Coping with the effects of the accident was hard enough without a further distraction. Who was he trying to kid? The mere mention of her name left his mind bubbling with anticipation. He had to establish if she was safe and getting used to life outside the prison walls. The decision to contact his brother was made.

***

Staring at the iPad screen, the sight of his brother amused Kane. His head had been completely shaved and he was wearing new glasses. This was Jason's second attempt to smarten himself up.

Kane tried to supress his laughter but could tell Jason wasn't impressed as he joked, 'At first I thought I had Facetimed the wrong number and got a handsome man.'

'Very funny. I wanted a fresh start and have updated the clothes I wear. I was feeling like a left-over from the seventies and in truth, I was that man. My hit rate on attracting women has been practically zero and I haven't had sex in …'

Kane interjected, 'Now hold on there, far too much detail. Perhaps you are right trying out a new haircut and clothes but remember that we don't always see ourselves as others do.'

With the thought of his own horrible appearance, he wondered if he shouldn't have dismissed the hospital doctor's advice about seeking out a facial reconstruction surgeon. He was scared silly of undergoing further treatment. When he was anesthetised for his operation, he could hear every word the surgeons and staff were saying only he couldn't move a muscle. For the first part of the procedure he was awake hearing references to the patient being asleep. Surgical tools were being requested that included scalpels.

Jason stroked his cheek and smiled. 'I actually think I look quite distinguished.'

'Not sure I would go that far.' Kane put his face closer to the screen, took a deep breath and said, 'Mum said Amber has been released and I want to know if she is ok.'

'Oh, for heaven's sake, you aren't still carrying a torch for her, are you? I thought you'd got over her. With you not interested and already having a girlfriend, I suggested that she came out on a date with me. She's a right little darling that one and now she's slimmed right down she has a body to die for. She turned me down but I may have another try.'

'Y... y... you did what?' stammered Kane.

'Grow a pair brother, won't you? Sue, your girlfriend, stood by you after the accident. Greedy little sod, and now you want Amber.'

'Sue and I aren't even together any longer, just friends. I wouldn't mind chatting to Amber. If you could ring her for me, I would be grateful.'

Jason yawned. 'I don't know why you don't ring her. Okay, I'll make contact, but if she says no, this time, let's agree you have to let go.'

Kane half-heartedly nodded and stared at his image in the screen. He really looked awful. How was Amber going to react if she saw him?

'I want you to do me a favour. Promise you won't tell her about the accident or what I look like now.'

Jason was dumbfounded and raised his enormous eyebrows. 'She's going to know one day so why don't you just bite the bullet? People will accept you for who you are. Stop worrying or you'll have a heart attack.'

'No, you mustn't tell her. Do you understand what I am saying?'

'Yeah, I suppose so,' said Jason in an uninterested voice.

'So, are we agreed that you will ask her to ring me and stay quiet about my face? Tell her I don't do Facetime and give her my mobile number. You do have my number, don't you?'

'Of course, I have it – I ring you often enough. If that's what you want, then I'll do it, but I still think you are crazy.'

Kane swiped the end of call bar and Jason disappeared out of his life just as he had done so many times before.

***

Two days passed before Jason reluctantly contacted Amber whose number he still kept on her case notes. He left a message saying he would Facetime her that evening. Her response was to enquire what he wanted, but he didn't reply to the message she left. When the call finally came thorough, Liz and Amber had almost finished their dinner. With her pink iPad propped up against the fruit bowl, the two girls smiled back at Jason as he greeted them.

'God, is that really you Jason? I can hardly recognise you,' said Amber who was genuinely shocked with the new makeover.

Jason swept a hand over his shaved head and moved closer to the screen showing off his large puffy lips and far from perfect teeth. 'I wanted a change. Do you think I look younger and more handsome?'

Amber shuddered at the sight of the man who had flirted and tried for a date. She gently kicked Liz's leg under the table and tried not to laugh. She stared back and replied, 'Not sure.'

Jason had a smirk on his face and his breathing increased to panting as he smarmily said, 'Who's your friend?'

Liz held fingers to her mouth and whispered that the guy was a creep.

'This is Liz, who shares my place – we were cellmates in prison. What was so important that you needed to contact me?'

'I wanted to know how you are getting on since being released. How is the job hunting going?'

Annoyed that he was interrupting their evening, Amber put her eyes to the ceiling. 'Yeah, I'm good. I'm trying to get an interview for a job working on the bins.'

Jason looked puzzled. 'With your qualifications, surely you can aspire to greater things.'

'I have a debt to pay to society and if it means clearing rubbish or cleaning toilets so be it. You have no concept of how difficult it is to slot back into a decent job. Getting a second chance is nigh on possible, so I can't afford to be fussy.'

'Oh, I see. I did offer my help but you turned me down.'

Amber ignored his remark and pulled a silly face at Liz before returning to the screen. 'Now if you don't mind, I would like to finish my meal. I'll say goodbye and please don't contact me again.'

In an effort to stop Amber ending the call, Jason interjected, 'Kane … Kane asked me to call.'

Amber practically fell off her seat at the mention of the man she still thought about and here he was asking after her. Her quivering voice was accompanied by eyes that were closed tight. 'What did he say?'

'Just that he wants you to ring him. I'm not sure what he wants. Have you a pen and paper and I'll give you the number?'

Reaching for her mobile Amber swiped the screen, selected the contacts file and duly inputted the code. Jason had to repeat it twice and looked annoyed.

'Are you sure you couldn't give me an inkling of what is going on?' said Amber.

'Nope, I'm just the messenger.'

For the first time, Amber looked at the background of Jason's room and her gaze fixed on a picture that hung on the wall. She had seen the image before but couldn't for the life of her say when or where. It was a crazy painting, a surreal image of animals featured by the River Thames in London. It really was not to her liking.

She turned her attention back to Jason. 'Okay, thanks

for the number, it is different from the one I used to ring him on.' With this she abruptly ran a finger across the end of call prompt on the screen and the horrible man disappeared. She instinctively knew he would be fuming at being cut off.

Liz touched Amber's hand and muttered, 'I didn't like him one bit.'

'Oh, forget about him. Did you hear what he said? Kane wants to speak to me. Do you think I should ring him straight away?'

'Definitely not. Sleep on all of this. Get his skunk of a brother out of your head and you'll have a clear mind in the morning. The other thing is to make the call when I'm not around.'

As Amber flipped the lid shut on the iPad, she told herself how lucky she was to have found a wonderful friend in Liz.

***

The message that pinged into Kane's inbox pleased as well as irritated him. For a solicitor, Jason's spelling and grammar were atrocious. His brother mentioned that his call to Amber had been on his iPad and that she looked amazing. He also mentioned that Kane should not build his hopes up of getting back with her. He confirmed she would make contact with him. Her news was she was living with the girl she shared a cell with in prison. He went on to say that during the video call they looked too cosy and he wouldn't be surprised if they weren't in a relationship. He stressed the point that in prisons there were many temptations.

On reading this, Kane kicked his leg hard into the table leg and muttered, 'What right does he have making a dumb statement like that?' Even if Amber had chosen that path it was none of his business to assume either way. This was Jason in full swing shouting his mouth off. Whilst there were times when they got on well, his attitude could change instantly. It was hard to comprehend his brother's mood swings and lies. There was no denying that his frame of mind usually changed when he visited the villa in Spain and he reverted to Mr Nice guy. However, Jason was a mean-spirited person who enjoyed winding him up.

Kane counted to ten, this being something his mother always told him to do if he got cross with things. His eyes drifted back to his mobile to the last few lines of Jason's e-mail that indicated Amber was going for an interview for the position of bin operative with the council. He stressed that she could do much better than this for herself. He signed off like he was concluding a client letter: *if you need anything else, don't hesitate to contact me*.

Kane leant back in his chair and attempted to control his anger. The friction between the two siblings had to end. Over the years, how many fresh starts had there been? It was difficult being there for Jason when any chemistry between them was challenged on a regular basis.

The comment about Amber's choice of employment was understandable. Kane knew exactly what was going on in her head. She was determined to show she would do whatever it took to win back her dignity and secure a modest salary. Launching back into society after prison was going to be challenging with many rebuffs heading her way. Employers would have their own thoughts on engaging an ex-offender and Amber would have to convince them that she was worthy of a second chance.

***

The following morning Kane was up early and took his breakfast by the pool. His head was buzzing with the showdown he would eventually have with his brother in an attempt to end the friction between them. There would be harsh words on both sides and he would have to volunteer the final piece of the jigsaw. For the meantime, space was what they needed and a steering away from discussing his lady friend back in England.

Sipping black coffee from a tiny china cup, he heard the sound of the front door bell ringing. Kane shouted out that he was coming. The heavy door swung open and there stood his neighbour, who lived in the largest villa on the development, clutching an Amazon parcel addressed to Kane. The elderly man dressed in a green tee shirt and white baggy shorts over thin, hairy legs, lowered his eyes. 'I think this must be for you, they must have got the wrong villa.'

Kane smiled. 'Thanks, I was expecting something today. Do you want to come in?'

With no eye contact, the pensioner replied, 'No thanks, I'm a bit busy right now.'

Unable to comprehend Peter's strange behaviour, Kane returned indoors in search of scissors to open the massively taped up box that he knew held the two DVDs he had ordered. He questioned why they wasted so much packaging on small items. As his hands encouraged the cardboard box to split open, he momentarily looked over to the kitchen worktop and spotted his red scarf and loudly said, 'Oh, my God.'

A feeling of nakedness overwhelmed his body as it became clear that he had answered the door without covering up. No wonder neighbour Peter looked shocked. It must have been a terrible sight viewing Kane's appearance up close.

This was the turning point for facing up to venturing

into the outside world without a mask. Hiding away would no longer be an option. He was never going to be the most attractive man on the mountain, but he was going to get on with his life.

Chapter 22

When Amber rang it was late afternoon and Kane was in the pool and missed the call. The cold water had soothed his face and he floated on his back looking up at the cloudless sky. A feeling of well-being encompassed his mind. To say he wasn't nervous at the prospect of leaving the house without his scarf would have been untrue. It was a mixture of sheer panic combined with the necessity to go public that pointed the way ahead. The plan was to prewarn his friends of his decision and then invite them to the villa. There would be a few gasps followed by words of encouragement and obvious relief that he was ready to resume outings and parties.

Drying himself off with a large, blue, beach towel he went indoors leaving wet footprints on the colourful floor tiles. Retrieving his mobile from the lounge he was about to make his first call to his good friend, Katherine, who lived three doors down. The divorcee from Basildon had included him in her circle of friends right from the start and this had opened up many opportunities for Kane. He lost count of the number of gatherings and pool parties he'd been invited to. There was never a lonely moment with Katherine around as she worked her magic on everyone with whom she came into contact.

As Kane selected his neighbour's number, he noticed a missed call notification. It was not a number he recognised but it was from the UK. His heart beat raised as instinctively he knew it could only be Amber. He sat down on his favourite comfy chair and turned on the speaker function of his new Apple phone. As he prepared to return the call, his thoughts were racing. If he got through to her, this wasn't to be the moment to reveal details of his accident. He wanted her to remember him the way he had been back home. Moderately good looking and not with the goofy expression of missing teeth and a face that looked like a prune. Although she would be unable to see him during an ordinary phone call, he was ashamed of his appearance and still reached for the scarf to cover himself.

It took a time for her to pick up and, judging by the sound of her voice, she was bubbling with excitement. 'I have been looking forward to calling you. It's been ages since we last spoke. I hope Jason told you I'm so ashamed of what I did. I'm determined to make something of my life again. More to the point, how are you?'

Kane was hanging onto her every word and calmly said, 'Oh, middling and keeping myself out of trouble. I've also been thinking about you a lot and although I know we can't turn the clock back, I would still like to remain friends. How do you feel about that?'

'Well, yes. I'm just amazed you still want to know me after all I've put you through.'

'Well, that's settled,' said Kane who loosened the scarf and let it slip around his neck. It was wonderful speaking to her again and there were so many questions stacking up in his head to ask.

Amber nervously laughed. 'We should have done this on Facetime. Seeing each other would have been fun. I've lost loads of weight and now look half decent. Do you still look the same? I'm sure you won't have had a haircut like your brother. His choice of clothes doesn't do him any favours either.'

With panic building, Kane once again pulled the scarf up. 'Me, no, I'm much the same, ugly as sin. I agree my brother hasn't exactly enhanced his looks. As for me using Facetime, I can't be bothered with all that lark. Let's just stick to the good old phone call. More importantly, Jason says you survived prison and are back in the flat.'

'Yep, finally out of clink and I'll tell you sometime why I acted so foolishly. I have definitely changed and only do positive now.'

'That's what I wanted to hear. My brother said you have your cellmate living with you.'

'That's right, Liz needed somewhere to live and has been through a terrible time. We get on well living under the same roof.'

Kane had to hold the mobile away from his ear as Amber's explosive laughter burst through. 'Don't worry, she's not a lesbian or anything like that. I know which side I like my toast buttered.'

With an air of relief in his voice, Kane interposed, 'Never entered my mind. Tell me about your interview, when is it?'

'Oh, I had an e-mail and there are no vacancies at present, but they have my CV on record. I will check the website on a regular basis for updates on openings. I imagine Jason told you it was on the bins? When we spoke, he was so rude and judgemental. I don't like him one bit.'

Kane nodded his head. 'At times he drives me mad but believe me underneath there lurks a good guy. I won't say any more than he has had a troubled past, it's complicated. I want you to know I'm proud of you for applying for that job. You may even end up as CEO of the county's waste disposal service, who knows?'

'I've got to secure the job first. My ambition eventually is to start my own company but not in rubbish.'

Kane emitted a clicking sound from his mouth, something that often happened when he became excited and it was down to the missing teeth and damaged facial tissue. He experienced the occasional dribbling episode and was forever dabbing his mouth with a tissue. Even if Amber learnt of his problems how could she possibly find him attractive? The chances of them becoming closer seemed insurmountable.

'Another thing is I no longer live like a tramp. Something clicked inside me before my court case and now everything has a place. Tidy, clean and organised, that's me,' said Amber in an upbeat voice.

'Wow, that's some transformation. Your place was a mess although I never said anything to you for fear of offending.'

'That's because you are a gentleman.'

'No, I don't know about that. I remember seeing all your pictures that hung at varying angles on the wall and desperately wanted to straighten them.'

Eager to speak, Amber interrupted, 'And while we are on the subject of your brother.'

'We weren't speaking about him.'

'I know, but there's something I want to say. He can be a bit odd and creepy, can't he?'

Kane's hackles rose – it was crystal clear that she really didn't like Jason. Was he missing a vital bit of information, a disagreement or worse still, had he actually hit on her? 'Clarify odd, is there something I need to know?'

'I was referring to his home and terrible choice in pictures. When he Facetimed me, in the background on the wall was this picture. I've only seen one like it once before and I wouldn't give it space in my flat.'

'We all have different tastes Amber.'

'Yes, I know that but this one was bottom of the pile on my wish list. The painting was of a solitary unicorn racing through the sky over the River Thames with a backdrop of a forest of purple skyscrapers. Cars on the bridges were represented as sheep and hideous, coloured cow faces grinned at me. It was horrible!'

Ripping the scarf from his face, Kane thought his head was going to explode. A cruel voice confirmed the worst possible news. There was only one painting like that in the entire universe and her description was so precise. It had to be Amber who broke into his flat and stole the iPad and all that money that was intended for the charity. The picture was indeed his own attempt at art and certainly fell into the amateur category. The painting which she described with such accuracy now belonged to Jason. The thief had turned out to be the girl he secretly loved. Jason was right: the woman had a screw missing.

'Kane, are you still there? You've gone quiet on me. I haven't upset you, have I?'

Still shaking from the trauma of her revelation, Kane gazed at his reflection in a mirror on the wall and whispered to himself, 'God, with what I've been through with my bloody face and I thought nothing could upset me as much as that did. How wrong I was.'

'What was that you said?'

Struggling to control his anger he shouted, 'I said, does Flat 7 Mercer Court ring any bells? Is your photographic memory about to recall the picture you just described and the misery you inflicted on me? That picture is an original and painted by me. It now hangs in Jason's flat, but you already know that, don't you?'

Clutching his mobile Kane could hear Amber breaking down as the realisation dawned that her world was crumbling again. Her quivering voice went up in tone. 'I... I... don't know what to say. I'm so sorry. You are the last person I wanted to hurt. You didn't live in that flat when we dated, how was I to know?'

'I moved as I couldn't stand the thought of someone having invaded my space and all along it was the girl I fancied. How do you think I feel? I wish to God I'd never set eyes on you. You took the charity money and my iPad and I hate you.'

'I can't believe it was your flat. I'll pay back that money and replace the iPad.'

'And that will make things better, will it?'

Kane could hear Amber crying but felt no compassion and in a firm voice said, 'I hoped we might one day get together but now, well, you have ruined any chance we may have had. That's us done. I'll never forgive you and don't ever contact me again.'

Just as Kane went to end the call, he heard the solitary word: *please…* but he promptly swiped the screen and the line went dead.

***

It took Kane the best part of a week to leave his home as his mind drifted over how differently things might have turned out if Amber hadn't mentioned his painting on his brother's wall, he would have been no wiser. Somehow, he'd have told her about his face and she would have jumped on the first plane to Malaga. The alternative scenario switched to making love on a sunny morning with shadows falling and rising as their moments of bliss sped towards the final climax. But why did she have to spoil everything? Bitterness was all that remained and he wished Jason had never passed on his request for Amber to call him.

Chapter 23

Liz returned home to find her friend in tears and gasped as the story unfolded. It soon became clear that Amber had shattered her own dreams and was paying the price.

So close and yet so far and she had blown it with the wonderfully good-looking man who, to all intents and purposes, had been prepared to forgive her reckless ways. If only she hadn't noticed the picture hanging on Jason's wall, the future may have panned out differently. Yes, the thievery was confined to the past but thoughts of what might have been would continue to sting hard.

***

Two months into being back in the flat both girls were experiencing rejections on the job front with companies holding back on even offering interviews. Being upfront and transparent didn't always help as revealing custodial sentences resulted in a *no thank you* cross on their application forms.

In order to receive benefits, you had to prove you were looking for work. Countless visits to industrial estates and offices drew no hope of securing a job. The new Prime Minister was hell bent on boosting the economy and one would have imagined there must be an employer who would take on two ladies for minimum wage. Amber continued to check the council's website on a weekly basis for vacancies on waste collection, to no avail. She worked on the principle that there would be natural wastage of employees in this line of work. People would come and go and it was just a matter of time before new posts would be announced.

The finances were taking a beating and coping on

benefits was proving to be hard. Liz suggested they register with the local food bank and Amber flatly refused saying there were more needy cases. The worry was in meeting household bills and, with the service charges still to be paid, her predicament was whether to pay the electricity first as the red bill was long overdue.

'I could spread my wings in different areas and walk more dogs,' offered Liz.

Amber handed her a mug of coffee and sighed. 'You've done well hanging onto your three clients especially after the lady in that house posted those notes through all the doors in our street.'

'She's a miserable bitch doing that. What I can't work out is how it got out that we had done a stretch. I hope she hits bad times like us and sees how it feels.'

'Come on Liz, there is no need to be resentful. I told you we need to grow a thicker skin as this is the territory we signed up for. Yes, Mrs Berry is a curtain twitcher. Guy in the ground floor flat, told me that she lost her husband to cancer three years ago. I'm thinking we should look out for her.'

Liz shrugged her shoulders and looked anywhere except at her friend. 'Now I've heard everything.'

Looking thoughtful, Amber's mind was going over her cost-cutting plans. She was coming to the conclusion that her much reduced savings were going to be tested. It saddened her to think that not so long ago there was plenty of money in the bank and a full fridge, but not any longer. Her eyes scanned the living room that was tidy but tired. The sofa had taken a beating over the years and needed to be replaced. As for the decoration, there was no money to buy paint let alone replace furnishings. In spite of the negative things that they were encountering, she had to remain optimistic about the future. It just needed one of them to land a job and a degree of normality would return to their lives.

One way to earn a bit of money was working from home. On the internet there were no end of companies and individuals who made claims of making a good living from assembling goods. Ignoring the get rich quick advertisements, Amber narrowed it down to those not requiring deposits or purchase of start-up materials. Another area to watch was the frequency between payments for work carried out thus avoiding the tricksters who came and went in the blink of an eye. The work ranged between sewing garments, finishing off products and packaging. Accepting that this type of contract was labour-intensive and paid well below the average hourly rate, there were no other options but to give it a try.

Amber spotted a small post on her Google search from a man with an Italian name. Luca Ferriana claimed to be a trader of household items and made no promises that workers would become big earners. The post stated he currently had some orders for people in their area who would work hard and to a high standard. Payment was on collection subject to inspection of the home workers' finished product. A mobile number was listed to arrange a phone interview.

'I've got something here that we ought to consider, come and have a look,' said Amber as she made a screen print of the details on her phone.

Straining her eyes to read the small type, Liz was told off for not wearing her glasses. 'It's an Italian guy called Luca offering work.'

Liz's ears pricked up. 'I'm game but tell me more about the man with the dishy name. Would we meet him for an interview? The Italians are always good looking, even the older ones. Its ages since I've had a man in my bed, especially with a name like Luca.'

'How do I know what he looks like? He's probably

bald, old and lived all his life in Lewisham. His only claim to fame might have been a one-minute walk-on part in the TV series *Only Fools and Horses*. He's probably a wheeler dealer. These South London entrepreneurs work from lock-up garages and tout their wares in pubs. Then again, judging from the well written ad, my guess is he's the real thing. I'm normally a good judge of people and will weigh him up in the phone interview.'

'What would we have to do? I know someone who stitched knicker gussets and struggled to get paid. It can be hard work for all those hours with little to show at the end of it.'

Amber's eyes drifted above her friend's head and muttered, 'Glass half empty Liz, as negative as ever. The advertisement mentioned masks, so that can hardly be difficult or heavy work, can it? I've still got my auntie's old sewing machine.'

'Masks, who's he supplying, Ann Summers? Oh well, the job might have its perks with the odd sample we are allowed to keep.'

'Very funny, they are probably for abroad, medical, I don't know. It may be all sorts of products we would be expected to make up. We haven't even rung the guy yet.'

Liz looked up from the screen and said, 'Well let's ring. It could always just be a filler while we search for something better. You never know your job with the council may come up soon and you'll be quids in.'

***

The voice on the end of the phone, with a heavy Italian accent, was friendly and Amber guessed the man's age to be early to mid-fifties. She particularly liked the way he managed to make his product range sound interesting. The company was Puglia Creations, named after the Italian region he had grown up in. The criteria for getting involved was you had to be hard working and capable of finishing goods to a high standard. His current order was for a moderately small supply of masks for export to Turkey. He described the process of assembling the pre-cut fabric with filter pockets and elastic straps as not too demanding. Luca made the point that if the standard fell or damage was excessive, the pay would be affected. He said he was prepared to give them a chance and would deliver a small trial order. He ended the call with his singsong voice that was amplified on Amber's mobile. 'I thinka you willa get alonga fina with me.'

Liz and Amber both smiled and after the call they hoped Luca would make the delivery in person. They joked that he could be shared.

That night Amber lay in bed in the darkness and reflected on the temporary work they had secured, her mind conjured up the Italian guy whose accent amused her. She allowed herself to visualise the older, well-bronzed man in smart clothes and locks of hair that he repeatedly smoothed away from adorable brown eyes. Lips that begged to be kissed were accompanied by high cheekbones that made him irresistible.

She ruled out the possibility that the mystery Italian was married or dating someone at present or that he could be overweight with a shiny forehead that looked as if a duster had polished it. It had been ages since anyone had held her tightly and eased off her clothes one by one leaving a trail all the way to an enormous double bed. With the energy of a super human, Luca would thrill Amber with his lovemaking. How many times had previous lovers satisfied her and then promptly checked their mobiles for messages and apologised for leaving so soon? Definitely not in the case of Luca who would continue to stroke her naked body and say wonderful things that made her skin tingle.

Amber's fantasies were interrupted by the noisy couple next door who were arguing again. Activating the screen on her phone, she was shocked to see it was one-thirty in the morning. Within minutes, embarrassing yelps of gratification penetrated the thin bedroom walls. Amber rose and yanked the single bed to the middle of the room and climbed back under the duvet, covering her head with a pillow. Listening to others getting up to whatever, was maddening; perhaps she would suggest to Liz that she had the larger bedroom.

Within a short space of time all went quiet leaving Amber wide awake and unable to drift off to sleep. The buzzing sound of the fridge in the kitchen was getting worse and there was little money in the kitty to replace the twelve-year-old appliance with the blackened door seal.

Counting sheep and forced yawning denied the deep sleep she craved. Kane's name kept springing into her head. Somehow, she had to get him out of her thoughts to move to the next step of her plan. Surviving the adjustment to being out in the real world required a supreme effort and much hard work. Liz also needed to get her head around moving and shaking things. There was only so much Amber could do to help her.

***

It was just two days before Luca got in touch to say that the small order for masks was almost ready to be delivered to the flat. Payment would be by cash. She was pleased when he volunteered the phone number of another of his home workers to check out his credibility as an employer. Amber contacted a lady called Vivian Barnard who spoke highly of Luca and dropped into the conversation that he was a gentleman. Her association with him had been over a two-year period.

Things were beginning to look up as Amber's benefits, despite the red tape and delays, were now being credited to her bank. Liz had another dog to walk, an Alsatian that was muzzled and drew worrying looks from passers-by. She complained that the poop bags the owner supplied were far too small for the hound from hell. Amber went to great pains to advise her flatmate that there was a limit of fifteen hours one could work before it affected the amount paid out on benefits. Liz reminded her that all her transactions were settled with cash and the authorities would never learn of the arrangement.

That afternoon a battered, grey Ford Transit van parked up outside the flats, four eager eyes homed in on the poorly dressed man with the short beard and shaved head. Amber gauged his age to be late forties. There were shrieks of laughter as the girls acknowledged that the driver fell short of their hopes of this being their drop-dead gorgeous Italian making the delivery. Four tattered cardboard boxes, that looked like they had been used a hundred times before, accompanied an A4 white envelope which was handed to Amber.

'Sign here,' said the man with a South London accent who handed over a biro with a chewed end.

'Will you be picking up the order or will it be your boss?'

'No, Luca is too busy. It will be me and I'll check your work before handing over the cash. The instructions are all in the envelope.'

With no further communication he turned to leave and Liz tried to stem her laughter as she pointed to the two inches of blue elastic waistband of his underpants that were peeping over the half-mast jeans.

The guidelines for assembly and packing were

straightforward and the note was signed off by Luca with a reminder of his mobile number. The boxes were opened revealing the pre-cut fabric for the masks and Velcro fastening strips. The final stage only required placing the masks in cellophane wrappers.

Liz raised her shoulders and muttered, 'Easy as piss, I would say.'

'Don't say things like that. Just say this looks easy.'

Irritated with Amber's regular advice on what to say or do, Liz chanced saying that it wasn't like she had sworn or anything like that.

The entire order was completed in just under three hours. Liz's attempt to speak with a posh accent failed to impress Amber. 'Hardly a brain teaser executing the work, wouldn't you say, old girl? Let's hope further orders will be more challenging than this one.'

The man in the rusty transit van returned the following day and nodded his approval after checking for quality control. He handed over fourteen pounds in a mixture of notes and coins and left without saying another word. The money was hardly monumental but both girls worked on the principal of there being further orders in the future. The vote was unanimous to spend the money on a takeaway. Amber ruled out Indian and they settled for pizza.

Standing in a queue inside their local pizza store, Amber was weighing up what to buy while the smell coming from the wood burning oven was making her hungry. Liz asked her if they also sold chips. Amber insisted she wouldn't need fries.

It was then that Amber spotted a girl from her old office and decided to say hello. Rita Warren, who worked in billing, was a tall girl who wore short skirts and skimpy tops that kept her male colleagues buzzing around her. Amber had in the past felt sorry for her as the gossipers in the office, mainly women, branded her as the hop on and off girl. Amber knew this was totally unfounded and cruel. On seeing Rita in the pizza takeaway, Amber had to speak to her and enquire how things were going.

'Hello Rita, how are you?'

'Oh, my God, is it really you? You've lost so much weight. I didn't know you lived around here.'

'Practically next door. This is my flatmate, Liz.'

The two women acknowledged each other and then the shuffling of feet commenced as the customers in front edged closer to the counter. 'I'm sorry we lost touch; the day I left the office it was a hurried affair, as you probably remember. I hope people don't still speak badly of me.'

Rita's face switched to serious, leaving Amber petrified of the reply that was to be delivered.

'No, not in the least, you were popular and everyone was shocked to hear the news. I no longer work for Freeman Slater. I took a lower paid position managing a charity shop in Pinner High Street. I'm much happier and the people are great. How about you?'

Moving that bit closer to Rita's face in an effort to prevent others from hearing, Amber took a deep breath and went for it. 'You must know that I went to prison and I've been out some time but it is not easy adjusting to things.'

'Yes, I know what happened and I'm not judgemental. You must have had a tough time.'

'Two classic margheritas,' shouted the girl ahead of them who was extracting her purse from a large green handbag and eying up the cans of fizzy drinks behind the counter.

Rita smiled. 'We can't speak here, how about you give me a bell? Let's swap contacts and we can catch up big time.'

Amber was thrilled with the prospect of talking to someone about charity work. Coping with everything that had happened, any thoughts of getting involved again had been low on her agenda but not dismissed.

Clutching their fifteen-inch pizza boxes, the two girls headed back home and Liz was unresponsive to Amber's attempts to engage in conversation. Where had the buoyant young Liz gone?

When she did speak it was clear she was upset. 'You ignored me totally in there when you talked to that girl.'

'Oh, don't be silly. I was surprised to see her. She's had a tough life.'

'And we haven't.'

Amber bit her bottom lip and held a hand to her mouth. 'Now, don't be silly. We are not joined at the hip, just concentrate on the takeaway we bought with our earnings.'

That evening only one pizza was eaten as Liz claimed she wasn't hungry and later when her meal had cooled down it was sliced up and placed in the fridge.

As Amber undressed for bed that night her mind kept going over Liz's strange behaviour and she decided to return to the lounge where her flatmate was still watching TV. Pulling on her much-faded, blue, towelling dressing gown she strode into the room and let loose. 'I want you to level with me, what's got into you? We were on cloud nine before we went out to get our meal.'

Liz removed her feet from the sofa cushions and calmly said, 'I'm sorry, what with getting that order for the masks ready, I've been trying to tell you all day and then you seemed more interested in that girl than me and there …'

'Tell me what?'

'In the shower this morning I discovered a lump in my

breast and I don't know what to do.'

Amber crossed the room, leant down and took Liz's hand and gently squeezed the rigid fingers. 'I'm sure it's nothing but first thing tomorrow we are going to get you checked out.'

'I was putting that off because I was so scared, of course I need to make that call.'

'Still think you should have eaten your pizza,' joked Amber.

'Me too. I said I wasn't hungry but I'm starving – I think I'll microwave some of it.'

***

One week later a visit to the Middlesex General Hospital took place and Liz sat with Amber in the cramped waiting area of the breast clinic. There were women of all ages waiting to be seen. Surprisingly, a man was also present and wore the obligatory NHS dressing gown as he sat rigidly looking into space. He ignored his wife or partner's attempts to chat. It appeared men were also victims of breast cancer.

The thing everyone in that room had in common was that they were in gowns with a sole pocket that held a key for an allotted clothes locker. The receptionist was sensitive to her patients' needs as their minds must have been raw with worry. She regularly rose from her desk to inform of the inevitable delays as scans and tests were rolled out. This was a normal morning for this employee but not for the outpatients.

Most people's eyes were focused on the daytime TV screen or their mobiles. The names on the room doors all included the accreditation of consultant surgeons. Swivelling her body on the plastic chair that creaked, Liz turned to her friend and whispered, 'I don't want an operation or any of that chemo treatment.'

'You are going to be just fine. It's only a check-up and scan.'

Liz nervously thumbed through a house and garden magazine and managed to drop it on the highly polished blue concrete floor. It was retrieved by a woman who had recently entered the room. They got talking and it was revealed that she had ignored her lump and eventually told her husband. The doctor fast tracked her to the clinic. Liz observed her wringing of hands and shuffling of feet and told her she was going to be okay.

The average consultation time was in the region of fifteen minutes and as people came out, a number of them looked relieved and headed for the lockers to get dressed. Others were shown to a smaller waiting room to undergo ultrasound scans or mammograms. When Liz's turn came, she insisted Amber remained in the waiting room as the lady consultant welcomed her into the room.

Liz was one of the patients who went on to have the two scans. Within thirty minutes of having the tests she returned and sat heavily down on the seat. It took twenty minutes before she was called back to the consultant's office for the verdict.

***

Waiting for the bus home, the persistent drizzle soaked their coats but nothing was going to spoil the good news that Liz had received. The six-millimetre lump on the right-hand side of the chest was, in the consultant's opinion, non-cancerous. The mammogram results confirmed a fatty tissue that would probably remain the same size but was of no worry to the patient's long-term health. No follow up was required and the kind Indian doctor had shaken Liz's hand rather too enthusiastically before bidding her farewell.

Chapter 24

Attending the job centre appointments, it became clear that even menial work was in high demand. Job hunters waited their turn to use the screens to scroll for potential openings and made copious notes or took photos of the text on their mobiles. Both Amber and Liz had applied for cleaners' jobs to no avail. Trudging around the industrial estates with CVs to hand out would continue for some time.

Only last week the manager of an engineering company was present when Amber introduced herself to the receptionist. An impromptu interview took place in the management suite with their HR Manager. The swish room was furnished with comfy chairs and a glass table littered with sales brochures. Amber noticed a can of furniture polish and a stained duster tucked on a lower shelf of a bookcase. A wall holding block printed photos depicted their manufacturing unit in Bury and product information.

With the anxiety of the interview, Amber sat with her legs crossed and wished her choice of clothes was more suitable for their meeting. The young woman, who was marginally older than Amber, was dressed in a smart blue skirt and white blouse. Her eyes scanned the CV and she nodded her head in approval.

'You were with Freeman Slater for a number of years and held down a good job.' There was a pause as something caught her eye and the smile instantly turned to a frown. 'Just fill me in with why you left this company and the employment gap.'

Amber was aware of the office workers filing past the glass walls who momentarily stared into the room. With the inevitable drilling down of questioning, she acknowledged this was going to be a short meeting.

'I took a break for personal reasons and with the recession I am finding it hard to secure work again. You said that you have a vacancy for an accounts manager and I have the qualifications and skills to apply for this position.'

'Should we take these talks further and invite you back with the other candidates, I will still need you to fill in the missing information. Do you mind telling me the nature of the personal reasons for the break?'

Shifting anxiously on the leather covered chair it became clear that this interviewer wasn't going to give up on her probing and the sorry tale would have to be shared.

Amber stood up, much to the manager's amazement, and in a matter-of-fact voice she quickly delivered a rushed goodbye. 'I'm not sure this job is what I'm really looking for, so I'll leave it there.'

Out in the car park the tears welled up. She should have remained in the meeting and relayed the true picture of her time off work. After all, they were going to find out soon enough with the references and declarations referring to a criminal record. Finding a job and convincing the decision makers to take a chance on her was proving to be difficult. Why was she even bothering to try? The world she had entered was a cold and heartless place and she acknowledged the plight of reoffending prisoners who chose to return to the likes of HMP Fairfield rather than cope on the outside.

The process of knocking on any more company doors was brought to a halt for the day. Like many times before when things seemed so bad, Amber's optimistic approach suddenly kicked in. She marched steadily out of the estate and ignored the workers who were loading a lorry. There was no giving up. For the meantime, the state benefits were being paid and Liz had her dog walking job. The promise of extra work from Luca would certainly help.

***

On reaching home there was no sign of Liz but there was a note on the kitchen worksurface. Luca had rung and a delivery and instructions for the second order would be made the following morning. There would be no more masks, this time packaging socket sets was on the agenda and the deadline would be twenty-four hours.

When the same grumpy delivery man arrived with ten heavy bags of car socket parts and metal boxes, he made two trips up in the lift and came close to taking a lump of wood out of their front door. Viewing the amount of work involved, the expression on the girls' faces was one of bewilderment. This was going to be hard work for a relatively small amount of money. It would involve working late into the night. In essence, the payment was for one person only. It was a good job that Liz was able to help share the load. It was miniscule earnings but as things stood with bills to pay, the money would be helpful.

An old blanket was draped over the dining table to assemble the kits. Handling the various socket ends left fingers greasy and Liz complained about the sharp edges of the tins. The instructions were easy to follow and working as a team they set to work. It was simply a matter of placing the right size sockets into the correct storage slots and then packing them into the boxes provided.

The following day Luca's assistant handed over twenty pounds and asked to use the toilet. He left the seat up and dribbled on the porcelain, much to Amber's annoyance. Within a few hours a text was received thanking them for their help and indicated a further job.

Over the next two weeks Luca kept them busy with further consignments of kitchen utensils that required making into kits to be slotted into colourful packaging. The packets of screws and crayons that were damaged needed sorting for resale and took many hours to work through. Their boss unquestionably fell into the realms of wheeler-dealer but he also seemed to be a gentleman. Amber was determined to learn more about the character behind the business and suggested they met up. She would also tackle him on increasing the hourly rate.

In total there had been five orders and the money was gradually mounting up to pay the council rates and water bill. In response to Amber's recent call, Luca said he would consider meeting up the following month. He explained that there was a lull in orders but she was not to worry as he expected it to get busy shortly. True to his word, it wasn't that long before there was another job to complete.

Luca mentioned that he was increasing the hourly rate and switching to paying outworkers by direct bank transfer. Amber was used to sending and receiving money via her bank and supplied him with the account details.

Another week sped by and there were no texts or calls for further work. On checking her online bank account, Amber began to panic. No funds had been credited from Luca. There had to be a logical explanation and she made the call to his mobile. The stark message rang warning bells: *This number is not registered on the network.*

Amber glanced back to the balance on screen and the nightmare of nightmares raised its head. She thumped her fist on the kitchen worktop and began to cry.

'What the hell's wrong?' screamed Liz. 'Is this something to do with Luca?'

Between sobs Amber breached her rule on swearing and muttered the dreaded f-word. She apologised profusely.

'He's emptied my account. The money has gone.'

'Oh my God, you mean your benefits and all that dosh we earned has gone.'

'Worse than that, my remaining £1,400 savings was in a bond that expired and I had moved it across to the current account while I decided where to reinvest it. It's all disappeared. Luca fleeced me, not only the pay for that big job but all my money.'

'How can that be?' shouted Liz. 'He didn't know your security details, did he?'

'I told you he was paying us by transfer and I gave him the account and sort code, that's all. Everyone does that when they receive payments online – it's not like I revealed any passwords.'

Holding a hand to her head Liz muttered, 'Oh, bugger, that's us stuffed.'

Reaching for her mobile Amber dialled the number on the back of her debit card that was listed as: Report a Fraud.

It was a long wait before the department in question picked up and this led to many security questions. The young girl on the line listened to Amber's explanation of an Italian man who had emptied her account. The bank was helpful but informed that at this point there was no evidence to suggest Luca was the man in question. They were able to confirm that at five am the money had been moved. An investigation would be opened and the police would be informed. The point was made that banks could no longer guarantee to restore monies transferred out through fraudulent behaviour and Amber had to acknowledge that she had read and understood the ruling.

After the call they sat and sipped a cup of tea as

Amber made an effort to control her emotions that were threatening to return to the hysterical crying fit. The nagging voice inside her head was grating away: '*Now you know how it feels to be robbed.*'

With her head held low Amber was going over the events that led to the scam. Luca appeared to be one of the good guys but still managed to trick her. It was her fault for being so naive. Not only did he rip her off with those poor wages, but she actually trusted him and wanted to meet up. He realised she was desperate for cash. He paid peanuts and waited for the moment to pounce.

'Don't beat yourself up,' said Liz who was physically shaking.

Through narrowed eyes Amber sighed. 'The missing money is bad enough, especially if the bank refuses to pay up. There is something else that bothers me. I'm thinking that Luca wasn't even Italian. He was probably putting on an accent and I stupidly fell for his charms. The guy sounded really lovely and I should have been more wary of scams on the internet.'

Liz gasped. 'Not Italian, do you really think that's possible? He must have used a mobile with a sim card that couldn't be traced. Let's just hope he slips up big time.'

Amber rose from the sofa and looked over to her handbag that held a five-pound note and sixty pence in coins. This was all that was left until the end of the week when her benefit allowance would be paid.

'The thing that bugs me is the way he set us up.' Amber wrung her hands in annoyance. 'I'm even beginning to wonder if his sidekick, that horrible bloke who paid us cash, might be him.'

'Yeah, nothing would surprise me. Con man doesn't even begin to describe this man. I bet the woman who gave the reference was a fake as well,' Liz stretched out her arms, bringing her hands together simulating the wringing of Luca's neck.

Amber waved a dismissive hand in the air. 'Just calm down. One thing for sure is we aren't going to see the likes of him again. Things are going to be tough whilst I sort out this mess. We have to move on and pray something breaks on the job front.'

'I'll get more dog walking and I can earn some money begging in the streets.'

'Behave won't you, I already said you won't be doing that again. Main thing is we have a roof over our heads and receive benefit monies.'

'Don't you hate Luca? I know I do.'

Shaking her head Amber's response no longer bore any animosity towards the mystery man. 'I'm past feeling cross with him. The man was a thief, end of. Now I know how it feels to be robbed and it's not a good feeling. It is payback time for me and I honestly believe that I have finally served my time and things can't get any worse.'

Chapter 25

The charity shop in Pinner High Street, with the alluring window dressing featuring mannequins suspended at different angles robed in winter coats and hats, appealed to Amber. It brought back memories of past Saturday mornings working in her local charity shop. This was back in the days when she took no care with her appearance and the manager joked that she might like to purchase some of their clothes in an effort to smarten up. When the shop wasn't busy, she helped in the backroom sorting through donations to spot the money-making items. There were countless pictures and small worthless objects, especially household ornaments, many of which were unsaleable and destined for the skip.

For a number of years Amber used to volunteer making the trip across to Brixton after work to assist at a mobile soup kitchen. She also helped with the distribution of food to the homeless, to the ones who rarely came out from the shadows. Her anonymous contributions to the charity were financed from her efforts to raise money from thieving. The latter would never be understood by her unfortunate victims. On hearing her limp excuse for breaking and entering homes, Kane had told her there was no room in his heart for the woman who had made excuses for what she had done. At least she could now admit that there had been no real justification for her actions in the past.

Standing inside the store, Amber's eyes scanned the immaculate shelves of goods and racks of clothes that could easily have been mistaken for new garments. There was no clutter or smells from the discarded possessions. A dedicated manager and staff had obviously worked hard to change the traditional image of a charity shop to make it a busy and profitable business. A poster in the window and above the counter advertised Thursday as being their discount day. This charity was literally flying with ideas for attracting punters. A free paperback of the customer's choice was another good teaser for making a purchase.

Amber caught the attention of one of the two sales assistants, definitely volunteers, just like she had been, and asked if the manager was available. Rita appeared through a doorway clutching a cardboard box full of DVDs and her eyes lit up on seeing her visitor.

In an excited voice Amber greeted her old work colleague. 'I said I would come and have a look. It's incredible and so different to the usual drab charity stores that we are all used to.'

'Great to see you, just let me put these in the rack and I'll be with you.'

Amber watched the care she took in sorting out the movies into genres that would hopefully turn into sales. A price ticket with a smiley face offered a two for one deal that would last until the end of the month. Rita's creativity for sales and merchandising was a breath of fresh air and monies secured would benefit the homeless, a cause that was dear to Amber's heart.

'You must have known I take a break at eleven, come in the back and I'll show you around.'

Behind the scenes was just as orderly. Rita was clearly passionate about the role she played. Keen to learn more about the workings of the shop, Amber encouraged her old workmate to expand on her aims for the business.

'We are classified and registered with the Charity Commission as a small independent organisation. Touch wood, we are doing well in the current climate and there's a good team working here. As for me, I'm still learning and can't take all the credit for the sales.'

'Don't be so modest Rita, you are a natural.'

'Err, not too sure about that. I was a volunteer for a couple of years, two Saturdays a month. It's only been seven months since I became a full-time salaried manager. The man before me put in the hard work, he set the standards for me to follow.'

'It takes dedication and hard work to keep the wheels turning. If a paid job like this came up for me, I would really be on cloud nine. You are just incredible, well done.'

Rita waved a dismissive hand in the air. She then filled a large kettle and flicked on the power before frowning as the blue light on the device failed to come on. It took two further attempts to engage. 'It keeps on playing up. To be honest we are waiting for some kind person to bring one into the shop that we can use. We have overheads to meet and our ethos is all about raising money rather than spending it. We have to watch the pennies.'

'Tell me about it,' laughed Amber. 'When I worked in a charity shop, we had to bring in our own coffee and toilet rolls.'

'You never mentioned that when we had our little chats back at the office. I always saw you as the quiet one who went home after work.' Rita stopped in full flow as her eyes scanned Amber's trim figure and presentable clothes. 'Hope you don't mind me saying how much weight you have lost and how good you look. You weren't too fussy with your appearance when we worked together.'

Pleased with the compliments and thinking back to her slovenly ways, Amber smiled. 'Train wreck would be the best description and I've come out the other side. I don't suppose there are any jobs going here?'

Rita shook her head. 'Sorry, I'm the only salaried person, but I do know of another charity shop in Alperton which is looking for a Saturday manager. Are you on benefits?'

Amber nodded and was trying to control her excitement. 'Yes, and the rules are that I can work sixteen hours a week before it affects payments.' Her heart sank when the reality of attending interviews flashed through her mind – it was her duty to mention a certain matter.

'I'm obliged to inform any potential boss that I've done time and that will probably be the end for me.'

'Now, don't go worrying about that. I've met the owner of the shop and know Toni won't be judgemental as long as you level with her. She is quite a character, rather eccentric and speaks her mind.'

'That's not a problem, I prefer straight talkers. All I have to do is convince her I can do the job; please give me her number and I'll get in contact. If you could ring her later today and mention me, that would be great.'

Rita put a thumb up in the air. She then bent down to retrieve a blue, striped bath towel from the floor and placed it inside the washing machine that sat at an angle on the uneven concrete floor.

'Let's diary a date for catching up properly.' Rita looked deep in thought and proceeded to straighten the cups on the shelf above the fridge and nervously said, 'Don't answer this if you think I'm overstepping the mark, but what was it like being in prison?'

A brief silence ensued as Amber traced a finger along her lips. 'Well, it was no walk in the park and there were moments that frightened me. It's like the house of horrors but worse. Strangely, you look forward to coming out but the reality of surviving in the outside world is harder than you think. It's difficult to make ends meet and the stigma of what I did will haunt me forever.'

'Oh dear, you have had a bad time. Are you okay for money?'

'Bless you Rita, yes, I'm fine. I equate my life to a colourful rainbow, only just now I'm only seeing it in black and white.'

***

Two days later, Amber's interview in the Alperton charity shop took place in a cramped storeroom full to the ceiling with boxes of jigsaws, ornaments, suitcases and old vinyl records. Seated at a small desk covered with paint splashes, Toni Ceedar, a woman in her sixties with an enormous chest and a weathered face, cleared her throat loudly. She reached into a drawer for a bottle of water. Gulping down the entire contents she wiped her mouth with the back of her hand. She proceeded to polish the lenses of her glasses on the edge of a blouse that was pulled from a box. Her attention switched to the list of questions on her pad that were highlighted in blue felt tip pen.

In her south London voice Toni opened the meeting. 'Sorry about the state of the place, there's never enough hours in the day for clearing up and dragging the Dyson around. Its only dust and I never heard of anyone dying from a lack of cleaning.'

Amber scanned the untidiness of the room and made a quick comparison to Rita's immaculate shop. This woman was poorly dressed in clothes that could well have been selected from the rails upstairs and her shoes looked in need of a good clean. In essence not only did the owner appear dishevelled, but the place was a tip.

In Toni's storeroom, towers of paperbacks reached high against the poorly decorated walls. Three Sellotape dispensers with remnants of leftover tape stuck to the holder added to the chaos of the wobbly pine desk. A half-eaten sandwich had missed the wastepaper bin and cheese and pickle lay on the floor close to Toni's white plastic chair.

When Toni spoke again the hoarseness in her voice returned suggesting that she was a smoker. There was no smell of stale tobacco or yellowed fingers. Her open handbag revealed a mobile phone and a silver-grey electronic cigarette with a much-bitten tip. Vaping was her substitute for the burning weed.

Holding Amber's CV at chest height, Toni fired the first of her questions. 'Let's cut to the chase. How about you tell me what landed you in the clink?'

Amber was taken aback and shifted her bottom on the hard chair. She fleetingly raised her eyes to the partially painted ceiling and then back to the white sploshes of paint on the desk. Rita had warned her that this owner called a spade a spade. 'I was done for entering and removing goods from houses.'

'So, you are a thief, are you? What's to stop you nicking my gear or money if I gave you a job?'

Saddened by the query, Amber vigorously shook her head. 'Err... err... no, of course I wouldn't. What I did was inexcusable and it's now making getting a job nigh on impossible. I think I should leave as I am obviously unsettling you.'

'Behave, won't you. What turns you on, and I'm not referring to you know what?'

Amber nervously laughed. 'Well, you can see from my CV that I held down a good job for many years and in my spare time have volunteered for charities. My heart goes out to the homeless and that is where my interest in working for you stems from.'

'That helps. I see you are single, not met the right guy yet. That surprises me as you are good-looking and you were born on the seventeenth of March, St Patrick's Day – are you Irish?'

Amber saw the funny side and cheekily said, 'Would that prevent me from working here?'

'Pleased to see you have a sense of humour. It's a tick on my list knowing you held down that office job for many years, a skilled position if I'm not mistaken. Now, spill the beans, what made you throw it all away and end up with a criminal record?'

Amber felt embarrassed with the questioning and dropped her voice to barely audible. 'I went off the deep end and am still paying the price. Can we change the subject and you tell me more about the role?'

'You won't earn much here as it's only a Saturday post, but there are days I may be able to offer you extra sessions when I can't come in. Sometimes volunteers cry off work when they get a cold or become pregnant. Tell me, have you ever taken a sickie?' Toni quickly added, 'You're not pregnant, are you?'

'Definitely not,' said Amber shaking her head vigorously. This extraordinary woman's interviewing skills were unique, to say the least.

Toni kept clicking her biro on and off. 'You'll assist in grading and pricing the merchandise as well as working alongside the volunteers. The second to last job of the day is to reckon up the takings. There's next to no cash taken as everyone is into contactless which minimises the banking. As long as they keep on swiping those cards, I'm a happy woman. I will always lock up and see you off the premises. How does that all sound to you?'

'Just what I want to do. You said the counting of money was the second to last thing I would do. What's the last?'

'Hoovering and fluttering the feather duster around the place, darling.'

Amber watched Toni rub the side of her neck where a small lump protruded through the skin. She yawned loudly without covering her mouth. 'My gut feeling is to offer you the job. Now, do you think you can cope with working with an old fart like me?'

Instinctively, Amber knew the opening suited her and believed that this woman would be a good boss. 'Yes, that would be great. The only thing is I can't cover staff shortages as I'm hanging out for a full-time job with the council.'

'Not a problem. When you start this Saturday at eight o'clock, bring in your P45 and bank details for your salary. I pay monthly, not weekly. I'm assuming you do have a bank account as I don't pay by cash.'

Nodding her head Amber was overwhelmed at the prospect of securing a job and thanked her new boss.

'I will be your mentor until you get a handle on things and watch you don't nick anything. Just joking.' The nervous laugh that followed continued for some time.

'Don't say things like that. I wouldn't dream of doing such a thing.'

Amber stretched out a hand for her new employer to shake. She observed the liver-spotted skin and dirty fingernails and absence of any ring. Toni was obviously a grafter and she wondered what life, if any, this woman led outside the charity.

'Just one last question, you do have somewhere to live?' said Toni as she replaced the top on her pen.

'Yep, and I share it with my best mate. Someone I met in Her Majesty's Grand Hotel.' Amber paused for a moment and whispered, 'And, not somewhere I will be making a reservation to stay again.'

Removing her glasses for another polish on the blouse from the box, Toni took a deep breath and said, 'Which prison were you in?'

'Fairfield.'

Toni's eyes lit up. 'That's where I help out once a

month on a Saturday. I befriend the ladies and give out information on charities like ours. I work closely with the probation and welfare staff. What saddens me is how many prisoners go on to reoffend, often because they have nowhere to live. My heart goes out to these women and I'll never stop trying to help them.'

Stunned by Toni's kindness, Amber wondered why she hadn't seen her when she was still back in the prison. 'That's a really good thing to do.'

'Well, it still leaves me the rest of my Saturdays to help in the homeless centres; that's where much of the money from our charity goes.'

Amber rose to leave and dropped into the conversation that she would work hard.

With a cheeky smile growing on her face, Toni mumbled, 'I'll kick your ass if you don't young lady. Just hold on a moment and I'll give you some literature on our code of practice and history behind how I started this charity.'

Toni moved away from her desk, opened a door and walked into a tiny room without a window. A single bed with clothes draped over the duvet and some personal possessions came into sight. In the corner stood a pine table with a large screen TV perched on the top.

Amber felt her eyes well up as her new boss returned with the documents and partially closed the door behind her. 'Sorry about the mess in my bedroom.'

***

On returning home, there was great excitement as Amber hurriedly announced that she had been successful in securing work. Whilst it was limited to seven hours every Saturday, another milestone for improving their income had been reached.

Excitedly, Liz handed over an envelope addressed to her friend, 'Who's this from?'

Amber's eyes lit up as she started to read the letter. 'I can't believe it; the bank is reinstating the stolen money after all.'

'Wow, that's amazing. Do you think we should go out to dinner to celebrate?'

'Definitely not, I'm holding on to my money. It just needs me to reset the username, and password. Things are really looking up, Liz. But, do stop jumping up and down on the sofa.'

Amber mused over the strangest interview she had ever attended and the eccentricity of her new boss living in the storeroom. On the whole it had been a good day especially with her savings being returned. The icing on the cake would be hearing from the council about an interview.

Chapter 26

Barefoot as they walked along the Burriana beach, Kane gripped the hand of his ex-girlfriend, Sue, who had recently returned to live in Spain. Her new job in the UK hadn't worked out. After a lunch of paella, cooked on an open fire in a pan the size of an enormous TV satellite dish, they strolled on the sand. It was the perfect start to a sunny afternoon that Kane hoped would slip into lovemaking back at the villa.

Three months had passed since Kane removed the red scarf that had mostly hidden his disfigured face and life had become more bearable. The feeling of being the centre of attention each time he ventured out to the village or beach was no longer an issue. His first outing had been the worst as some of his friends and shopkeepers failed to recognise him. There followed much embarrassment by all parties once he spoke to them.

The old men sitting on the concrete benches, with hats riding high on tanned foreheads, had whispered to each other before turning back for another glance. On another occasion, Kane approached a couple of young Spanish housewives that he had always greeted and they blanked him. Just as disturbing, were the over-the-top reactions of looking past the injuries and pretending nothing had occurred. A few weeks on, entering shops in the main square had become easier as the conversation moved away from Kane to the trials and tribulations of everyday life in the scorching heat.

Now that Sue was back in town, she was the person closest to him who looked deeper than the scars. Her work abroad had only lasted a few months as the publicity company laid off most of its staff. She was missing Kane and managed to obtain employment in a villa rental shop on the busy shopping streets of Torrox. Kane was elated to have her back. Their relationship was never destined for greater things. No love affair, just a mutual understanding between the two friends that carried no commitment to stay together.

On returning to Kane's home, the two friends were excited with the prospect of making love again and hurriedly undressed in the master bedroom that had the incredible view of the lower mountain terraces dotted with gnarled olive trees. This was a unique property that was not overlooked and afforded a high degree of privacy.

Sue lowered her naked body onto the bed and ran a hand along the crumpled skin of his face. He feared that the much-altered lip line would put her off kissing, but this was not the case. How many times in his mind had he mentally undressed her and sunk down on the gigantic bed to satisfy the eager young woman? Their exchanged moments of togetherness always left him content and in no rush to rise from the comfy mattress. This was a special friendship made in Spain.

Sue was the only person that Kane let touch his face. She bathed the troubled skin with cold water and told him to not frown. Her warm kisses moved delicately across his head to the lips that longed for attention. She handled his emotional outbursts and turned a moderate day into a brighter one.

Taking a shower together in the wet room with the water turned to full, they took turns to wash each other. There was much laughter as the shampoo plastic bottle ended up on the tiled floor. Kane managed to put his full weight on the container making the base sticky and encased in bubbles.

Wrapped in white fluffy bath robes, they sat on the

edge of the pool dangling legs into cold water. When Kane returned indoors to don swimming trunks, Sue disrobed and dived in to swim an entire length under water. Climbing up the aluminium steps she stood naked on the tiles and gazed at the tops of the mountains and birds of prey that were circling a clump of trees.

Kane returned with two red towels and nervously said, 'Cover up – you never know someone might be watching with binoculars. Only last week I saw a drone close to the villa.'

Shrugging her shoulders, Sue reluctantly took the towel and pulled a sun lounger closer to the villa where the shade was inviting and served as a respite from the penetrating sun.

Kane opened his book, removed the bookmark and proceeded to read. He was aware that his friend was more excitable than usual and wanting to chat all the time. The paperback was firmly closed and, when he managed to get a word in edgeways, he asked, 'Something is bothering you, I recognise the signs, what's up?'

'Not sure what you mean.'

'Come on, level with me. You started to tell me something on the beach and then went all quiet on me.'

With his head buzzing with scenarios that Kane feared would involve the statement that she was leaving him again, he waited patiently for an answer.

Sue moved a hand down to her naked belly and rubbed fingers in a circular motion. 'I'm pregnant.'

'Oh, my God, I know you weren't on the pill because of medical reasons but we were always careful.' He was momentarily puzzled and said, 'Hang on, you have only been back three weeks and today is the first time we have slept together. I can't possibly be the father.'

'Of course you aren't. I only found out just over a week ago. It was a guy in the London office and a one-off. He didn't mean anything to me.'

Kane clenched a fist in an attempt to stem the temper that was brewing in his head and shouted, 'I can't believe we've just made love and somehow I feel dirty. Have you no shame?'

The exaggerated shrugging of shoulders was followed with a nonplussed look on her face. 'I can't turn back time, can I? I have to deal with the consequences and I'm keeping the baby. You are not being asked to support my child when it is born, so chill out.'

Kane scooped up his jeans from the patio floor that had been taken off in a hurry and held them at waist height over his towelled body. 'You should tell the father.'

She shook her head forcefully. 'No way.'

He looked at the girl he thought he knew and despaired. Over their time together their relationship had suited both parties – she was never going to be the next Mrs Boulter. Today she had revealed her true colours with the morals of a loose woman. The thought of her becoming pregnant and then jumping into the sack with him was too much to take in. What was she thinking?

'What I can't get my head around is that we've just spent the most incredible time in bed before you tell me you are having another man's child. We should never have made love; it just doesn't seem right. Can't you see that?'

Kane stared at Sue's naked body as she lay on the sun lounger. She applied a generous squirt of sun tan lotion to her breasts and casually said, 'Stop being so dramatic, me being here today was mutual, wasn't it?'

'You are missing the point. I can't believe you could slip seamlessly from his arms into mine and make light of what has occurred. You can't jump into bed with every man that smiles at you.'

'Let's rewind, shall we? We had broken up and I was miles away in London and lonely, so what's your problem?'

'I couldn't spell it out any clearer if I tried – you just don't get it, do you?'

Chancing what he said next was definitely going to fuel their argument. 'Are there any other relationships I should know about? Just get some clothes on and go. I can't get my head around all this.'

It took Sue considerably longer to get dressed than it had to undress and she stormed out without saying goodbye.

***

Kane struggled to come to terms with Sue's bizarre take on shifting from one guy to another without any conscience. Strolling back into his life, only to drop this bombshell, was unacceptable. How could someone who had helped him through all his troubles act so irresponsibly?

With a wobbly hand he momentarily unlocked the drinks cabinet. He was wavering over risking having just the one drink to calm his nerves. Grasping the key, he pulled open the glass door and ran fingers over each of the bottles of wine and selected a Rioja. **His automatic warning system kicked in**, prompting him to back off; any thoughts of slipping were dismissed as he relocked the cabinet. Ten years had passed since his last drink and that was the way it was going to stay.

Still shocked with Sue's revelation, he acknowledged that for the foreseeable future remaining unattached was on the cards. Women had come and gone in his life since the brief ties had been broken with Amber, and she was never coming back.

Chapter 27

The eight o'clock bus to Alperton had pulled into the stop fifteen minutes late and Amber increased her pace to reach the charity shop. Not a good start for her first day's work with Toni Ceedar. On reaching the shop door, she spotted her new boss seated behind the counter spooning breakfast cereal into her mouth. Amber knocked gently on the glass and got no response. A marginally louder tap did the trick with the lady walking over to let in the new employee.

'Sorry, I know you said eight o'clock but the bus was late,' Amber hurriedly said as she was let into the cramped and cluttered shop.

With a confused look on her face that threatened to form into a frown, Toni reversed the plastic sign to 'open'.

'You are too early and I'm having my breakfast.' She raised a hand to her face to run fingers along chapped lips. 'Didn't you read your job offer letter. I do hope your attention to detail will improve when you price up items for sale.'

Amber had to stop herself challenging the starting time. The text in her letter was poorly written and typed with three spelling mistakes. Toni definitely mentioned in the interview the starting time of eight o'clock and there was nothing that referred to hours of work. 'I must have got confused – sorry about that.'

'Don't give it another thought, dear. Now, before we start, did you study the staff manual that I gave you?'

Amber nodded her head suspecting that the well-composed document was not from the pen of Toni but had been copied from another company's handbook.

'Do you want something to eat? I have a toaster

downstairs …' There was a pause before she continued. 'I don't suppose you could do without butter, I haven't any butter.'

'No, I'm fine, just tell me what you want me to do. Shall I make a start on the hoovering?'

Toni looked impressed. 'Yes, please and whilst you are at it, tidy the rails as we got a bit behind yesterday.'

Glancing around the oblong room, Amber took in the jobs that needed attention and smiled. 'No problem, I'll soon have the place looking like a new pin. You will need to show me how the till operates and any keys for doors.'

'All in good time. I'm going to be around for the next two Saturdays while you get up to standard. Did you say you wanted toast?'

Once again Amber declined the offer.

She was relieved with the knowledge that, however strange her mentor was proving to be, she was not being dropped in at the deep end.

'I run a tight ship and like things tidy and organised,' said Toni in a triumphant voice. 'Nothing escapes me. I have eyes in the back of my head and possess a good memory.' Her attention turned to the counter as she frantically searched for her glasses case.

Amber was gradually beginning to realise that Toni had a terrible memory and wondered what else would be revealed as the day progressed. There was a deeper side to the sad divorcee who lived with little comfort in the basement of her shop. She was a kind-hearted person who placed others before her own interests. With a heart that was set to maximum power, Toni's whole philosophy lay in helping the less fortunate.

Frantically searching for the key to the till, Toni repeated twice that someone must have moved it. On locating it on the floor behind the counter, she gleefully informed Amber, 'I'm popping out to the newsagent to get milk and biscuits for the volunteers who will be here just before we open.'

'And some butter,' said Amber.

'No, I think I've got plenty of butter.'

Alone in the shop, Amber noticed an ancient Dyson hoover which resembled a grey spaceship that had survived the long haul to the moon and back. She was startled as Toni popped her head around the door. Had she forgotten something?

'You do eat biscuits and are there any allergies I should know about? I don't want you dropping dead on the carpet from eating nuts, especially after the superb job you are going to do with that hoover.'

Amber roared with laughter. Toni's phraseology and management skills were certainly entertaining. 'No allergies to report.'

Meeting the two volunteers just minutes before opening time, the ladies made their introductions. They smiled encouragingly at Amber who was struggling with unlocking the storeroom door. The older of the two, an Indian woman with a worried look permanently on her face, kept asking her colleague what she should do next. They were both beautifully dressed in blouses and mid-length skirts that showed off their neat figures.

Twenty minutes into being open, a male customer wobbled his way to the till and stopped to lean on his wooden walking stick. Out of breath, he asked if his wife had come into the shop. He was offered a seat and chatted to customers who were patiently waiting to be served. He remained there for at least thirty minutes before leaving without saying goodbye. One of the volunteers said he was a regular to the shop and had lost his wife a few years ago.

Amber went to find Toni to check on a customer's claim that they took in electrical items. Having told the man there were no trained staff to test and certify the goods, the conversation grew from frustrating to unreasonable. The small TV with side speakers had been lugged in from a car and his threat to leave it on the floor had been issued.

Toni was wiping down and pricing stock when Amber entered the stale-smelling stockroom that was piled high with books and children's toys. The boss lady avoided eye contact and said in a dispassionate voice, 'You've worked in a charity shop before, so know the answer, can't you see I'm busy?'

Amber wondered if there was ever a good time to seek advice. It was her first morning and the man the other side of the wall was throwing his toys out of the pram. She'd managed to stop him storming out and leaving the TV in the shop. He was adamant that she fetched someone more senior.

'Sorry, but this guy may have already scarpered but he's insisted on seeing the manager.'

Toni's attitude moved swiftly to concern. 'Not a problem dear, you only have to ask. We get the odd person who can't be bothered to go to the council tip. Don't you worry, I'll deal with this.'

Back in the shop Toni worked her charm to calm the situation. The man with plenty to say bent down to pick up the heavy and cumbersome item and refused any assistance to carry it out of the shop.

'How did she do that?' queried the new Saturday manager.

The volunteer with the long, silver hair tied back in a ponytail shrugged her shoulders and muttered, 'She can sort out anything.' She quickly added, 'She can also be a bit weird at times.'

Amber's reply was accompanied by a chuckle in her voice. 'I haven't noticed anything on those lines.'

Despite the chaos that existed in this charity shop, there was a steady flow of customers and takings were encouraging. At the end of the day Toni shook Amber's hand and thanked her. Feeling tired and grubby from handling the stock, the bus ride home seemed never ending as she recalled the events of the day. Being trusted to work in a business again and handle money felt good. Yes, Toni was a character but what an operator. It was her guess that this woman not only raised huge amounts for her cause but worked untiringly with little thought for her own health.

***

Back in the flat, Liz had been busy heating up a lasagne. A bottle of red wine to celebrate Amber's new job was hastily opened.

'I didn't know you could cook – it smells great.'

'Just one of Tesco's ready meals and the wine was included in the price.'

Liz handed over a letter and watched Amber carefully open the envelope. She was elated to discover the interview details with the council for the Waste Operative role.

'That's great news – well done. All we need now is for me to pull off that job with the packaging company,' said Liz proudly.

'Too right. I'm sure you will get it. Now let's just hope that business isn't owned by our elusive Italian, or not so Italian man, called Luca.'

***

The interview with the council went well with a friendly trio of HR staff and management supervisor outlining the work involved for collecting household rubbish. The requirement to obey all health and safety rules was spelled out in detail. When the conversation switched to her criminal record and subsequent imprisonment, Amber swallowed hard. Her determination to lead a responsible life was accepted with cheery smiles. She was asked if she could cope with the manual work and the early starts. Confirmation was given there and then of her employment with the council subject to a DBS search, a health check, references and three months' probationary period.

Amber shook hands with each of the smartly dressed female interviewers and the man with his tie at half-mast who had introduced himself as the despatch manager. Daniel Godding, smelling of cheap aftershave, advised that she would be reporting directly to him. He was reasonably good looking with a sea of freckles on his cheeks and wore blue designer glasses.

The scheduled induction period would be over three days and involve safety aspects including vehicle knowledge, manual and mechanical handling guidelines. The grey manual had clearly been used before which suggested a high turnover of staff was common place. One of the reasons could relate to injuries due to repetitive heavy lifting and poor physical fitness for the work in question.

Fresh starts are always challenging and on the designated morning, at 5.00 am, Amber pulled on the uncomfortable orange trousers and coat with the words Waste Operative emblazoned on the back and climbed into her assigned vehicle. The members of crew seven, Raymond and Felix, were stunned to discover their new buddy was indeed a beautiful woman.

'Hello, I'm Amber.'

'They didn't tell us who was starting,' said the driver.

'My name is Raymond and this is Felix. We'll show you the ropes but expect you to pull your weight.'

'Don't you worry about that as I will work hard.'

They made a fuss of Amber offering to show her around the monster truck that looked clean but smelt terrible. Odours of rotting food and general household rubbish would take some getting used to.

Inside the cab, Amber sat next to Raymond, the driver, and was offered a seat belt that would be regularly fastened and unhooked due to the nature of the work and the constant climbing in and out. Young Felix, who was in his mid-twenties and with a mop of ginger hair, sidled up to Amber on the uncomfortable brown bench seating. He pulled out an enormous chocolate bar from his high visibility jacket and stripped the foil wrapper down. He broke off a piece for Amber who politely declined the offer. Only minutes before the young man had mentioned that he had been checking the mechanism for lifting wheelie bins. His gloveless hands had been in contact with the leftover grime of bins and black bags. He apologised for his sneezing that he blamed on hay fever which puzzled Amber as the season had moved on. The dreaded sniffing and running of eyes continued for some time.

Driver Raymond's totally bald head shone in the early morning sunshine and his constant whistling amused Amber. He was the keeper of immaculately trimmed fingernails and wore a gold wedding ring. It soon became evident that he was a proud man and enjoyed being in charge of the relatively new Mercedes refuse vehicle with a payload of 7,320 kilos. A brown teddy bear that was tied to the dashboard was patted on the head each time the powerful engine was fired up.

Raymond ran a tight ship and, despite having to return to the site to empty their load, the bodywork on the monster truck shone. Even the tyres were regularly washed. Amber was later to learn that once a week they were expected to use the pressure washer to loosen the grime. Raymond went that bit further and polished the windows and enormous wing mirrors. There was the distinct smell of lemons in the cab and Amber spotted an air freshener tree that swung from the volume control on the radio.

It was a strange experience travelling in the front with much rattling from the plastic door panels and tools under the seats. Riding the speedbumps Raymond responded to Amber's questions with one syllable answers as he changed gear and guided the heavy vehicle into streets packed with parked cars. He commented on seeing the same dogwalkers each week and waved at early morning residents who were setting off for work.

Their first pickup point was Turville Road in an area of North Harrow that Amber knew well and where she desperately hoped she wouldn't be recognised. The tree-lined street was littered with wheelie bins, many with lids propped open with excessive rubbish that prompted their leader to mutter, 'They were warned two weeks ago about mixed rubbish and over-filled bins. Mr Godding insists we crack down on the rules.'

Gripping onto her seat, Amber offered, 'I thought we had to take everything.'

Felix, the younger man, shook his head and replied, 'We have to be fair and educate people but make examples of residents who abuse the rules.'

As they piled out of the heavy doors onto the grass verge, Felix stared at a mass of mixed waste and sighed. 'Some people bung together recycled with waste and we get pulled up by the depot manager for bringing it back. Just watch what I do.'

The young man leant into a black wheelie bin with the

house number six crudely painted in white and extracted a bag of recycled packaging and plastic bottles. 'See what I mean. They have a green one for this stuff.'

The full bin was wheeled back onto the driveaway of the semi-detached house where a smart, new red Ford was parked.

Amber heard the loud bleeping of their vehicle reversing and it made her jump. It was followed by a recording that warned of operatives working in the road.

As Amber's mentors put her through her paces, the young man's questions kept coming, and she was convinced he was going to enquire about her marital status or whether there was a boyfriend in the wings. She was spared any further interrogation as they got on with the back-breaking task of collecting rubbish. Dragging the wheelies off the pavement and experiencing the jerk of the heavy container was no easy task. Her early attempts on lining the container up with the clamp failed and it took three goes before the roar of the motor tipped the waste effortlessly into the jaws of the collector.

'God, is that oil I can smell?'

This time Felix's voice was one of impatience. 'We've got loads to do so let's not waste any time. You'll get used to the hydraulics, it's quite safe – grab those wheelies and you can have another go at emptying them. You'll need to put your back into it.'

Amber dragged a heavy bin away from the pavement and tried to hide her breathless voice. 'I'll soon get the hang of it.'

'Just remember to close the lids after emptying – you keep forgetting.'

Back in the cab, the drive to the next location took less than thirty seconds. The cul-de-sac with a tight entrance looked a challenge for the driver. Raymond's eyes never left the mirrors as he reversed with only a few inches to spare each side taking care not to damage the parked cars.

Before Amber jumped out of the cab, she put a hand in the air and nervously said, 'Hold on, there's something I need to get off my chest.'

Felix, with a cheeky grin forming, joked that all clothing had to remain on during their shift.

'Very funny; now if you don't mind, I'll cut to the chase – I'm not that long out from serving time in prison and …'

Both men gasped in unison. 'Prison. That's where they take the murderers, isn't it?' said Felix who removed his glasses to stare at the smeared lenses. With a quick rub with the edge of his tee shirt, the interrogation continued. 'Does boss man, Godding, know you have a criminal record and why were you in prison?'

Irritated with this line of questioning, Amber's inner voice was howling advice: *Stay calm, you chose to bring it up. Best they know the truth – you are going to tell them the truth, aren't you?*

Gripping the seat to avoid her shaking arms being too noticeable, she raised her voice. 'Yeah, he knows. I had to declare these things during the interview. I wasn't in for killing anyone; it was housebreaking and I'm ashamed of what I did.'

'Oh, I see. You a posh girl riding the trash with us and all along you're a jailbird.' Raymond moved his wallet away from the dashboard and pocketed it in his jacket.

Amber felt like the world was once again swallowing her up. Surely if he knew the entire story that included her sorrow and desire to make amends he may think otherwise.

Raymond touched the arm of her hideous orange jacket. 'Just kiddin …You can't expect to drop a bombshell like that on us without any reaction. My son and I are not judgemental and we respect you for being up front.'

Amber gasped, 'Did you say son ... Felix is your son?'

'Yep, he's the good looking one and I just do the driving. We make a great team.'

'What happened to the last guy who worked with you?'

The older man giggled. 'Swallowed and minced up in the back, it took a week to get the truck clean again. Truth is he couldn't take the pace and swapped his job for a P45. Let's hope you grow some muscles and stick with us. It's actually not a bad job and the pay has improved.'

Amber saw the funny side and chipped in with, 'No funny quips from your son about my muscles please. Be assured, if I put my mind to doing something, I stick at it. Not sure about the smell of lemons in here though and the back of the truck stinks.'

'Never had a woman working the bins before and it's going to be fun,' said Felix who jumped out of the cab and encouraged Amber to do the same. 'Bins won't empty themselves.'

Mouthing to herself, Amber said, *'They never had a girl in the team before.'*

As she slid along the bench seat, Raymond urged her to hang on for a moment. 'Only if you want to tell us about your ordeal, do so later over a cuppa.' He raised a hand to high five and then wound down the window to shout to his son. 'Keep your hair on – she's coming.'

Mid-morning saw the team return to the landfill site to offload the morning's collection in preparation for a further run within the Middlesex catchment area. Amber was exhausted and chose to hide her weariness by staying upbeat. Donning regulation cloth masks, Felix and Amber stood well back whilst Raymond tipped the contents into an area designated for burying in vast pits.

There was an almighty squawking of seagulls as they took wing to swoop on the treasures laid out on the ground below.

To be fair, there wasn't that much to learn about collecting rubbish. The common denominator for all employees was in remaining safe while undertaking the potentially hazardous work. Raymond revealed that majority of the public obeyed the guidelines on what to put out for disposal. There were exceptions as dead animals, paint, chemicals, electrical goods were sometimes stored in the rubbish awaiting collection.

Amber's first day had been an eye-opener and her shoulders and arms ached. The relentless pace of lifting and climbing in and out of the truck was proving to be a strain on the body. The plus side was that she enjoyed being with the father and son team who were good people.

She had worried that there wouldn't be enough toilet breaks but her fears were short-lived as this crew knew where to stop for bathroom facilities. The combination of new medication and a calmer lifestyle had practically ruled out the urgency that commonly relates to a urinary tract condition.

***

Over the period of two months, Amber settled into her work and got on well with her crew members. Unlike their colleagues on the other wagons, no swearing existed and it came as no surprise to Amber to learn that they were church-goers but definitely not Bible-pushers. Sharing a table in the canteen, Amber's heart went out to Raymond as he revealed that his wife had died of breast cancer three years ago. Both father and son continued to live in the family home. Amber moved the subject on to whether Felix had a lady in tow which brought out much laughter from the two men. Felix batted for the other side.

For some unknown reason, the despatch manager, Daniel Godding, chose to swap operatives around for one week only. Unhappy with the change, Amber found herself working with another team on the Wembley route. Gone were the two gentlemen who treated her as an equal as she was thrust into a farmyard of vile behaviour. The two men on this larger vehicle looked past her face to the obligatory heavy suit she wore and made lewd jokes about her being top heavy. The driver, an opinionated older man, looked down on the new girl and commented on her posh accent. He had the annoying habit of snapping his fingers every time he spoke and thought nothing of interrupting others. Although they were testing her, she could see past the silliness. However, it hit home just how caring her normal crew were.

These were a rough group of individuals who included a swear word in every sentence that fell from their foul mouths. The older of the two men, a large man with a heart of granite, offered no apology for breaking wind in the cab. He activated the windows to fully open and blamed Amber. There were roars of laughter as they climbed out to drag the wheelies leaving the frightened woman sitting in the cab.

Unlike Raymond's clean and tidy wagon, this vehicle was the pits and was littered with fast food containers.

In-between driving to the next avenue or cul-de-sac, the conversation centred on the awful bosses in charge of them. Loyalty was a one-sided affair with the management being blamed for everything. Their supervisor, Mr Godding, took the brunt of much of their groundless claims about being overworked. He was branded as the enemy.

Most of the moaning and bad behaviour was reserved

for the cab or canteen and strangely not with their customer skills on the streets. They briefly passed the time of day with residents and, on the whole, carried out the vital role of removing rubbish without any problem. During her time with this team, Amber also met other crews back at the depot who were more welcoming. Just her luck to be landed with the moaners and groaners.

Amber longed for her week to end and a return to normality with the colleagues she felt drawn to. At the end of a particularly hard day her heart rose a beat on reading a text from young Felix that read: *Not too much longer to endure. Dad says do you fancy coming to dinner at our place on Friday night?*

The reply that flew back was instant: *Count me in.*

Chapter 28

Amber always looked forward to her Saturday work in the charity shop and to seeing Toni when she returned late afternoon from her visits to help the homeless. Once a month her boss helped out at HMP Fairfield where she thrived on assisting the welfare team with counselling inmates. The offer of lunch was always refused and she took her own bottled water which she kept in a bag that never left her side.

When the shop closed at five-thirty, the two women would chat and Amber knew that from deep inside her bag, Toni would produce doughnuts or caramel slices. The regular phrase she came up with was, 'Now, how did they get in there?'

Getting to know Toni was fun and, underneath the tough skin, she was a one in a million person who cared deeply for others. Having sold her two-bedroom house this freed up funds to run the charity shop and allowed her to donate so much money along the way. With relatively few personal possessions to call her own, living in the converted storeroom with a tiny washroom and dodgy electric shower, was all she needed. Her outlandish behaviour took some getting used to, as did the remarks she came out with. Amber worked hard to revamp the shop and was thrilled when Toni rewarded her with a fish and chip supper, saying they were now the best charity shop on the high street. Watching the pennies and budgeting was also something Amber knew all about and Toni was impressed.

Late one Saturday afternoon, Toni entered the busy shop with a smile on her face and Amber instinctively knew she had good news to convey. Her boss stopped to talk to customers and when she popped her head around the stock room door, it was evident she could no longer contain her excitement. 'You know that woman I was telling you about in the west wing of Fairfield that I helped when she reoffended, well she's due to be let out next week. It turns out she's written a book about her experiences and some fancy publisher has given her a book deal. She's mentioned me in the dedication page as helping her to see the light and I'm over the moon. I can't wait to get a copy from Amazon.'

'Wow, that's incredible. Just shows you how valuable your counselling is to the inmates.'

Nodding her head, Toni pulled from her bag the expected doughnuts and prodded them with a suspect finger that looked far from clean. The sticky treats oozed raspberry jam. 'After two of these beauties and a cup of tea that will be me done for dinner.'

Amber stared at the tired woman in the faded blue jeans and felt concerned by the obvious weight loss and unhealthy diet. It was sad to think that when the shop closed for the evening, she may not eat anything else and would simply retire to the makeshift bedroom to watch TV.

'A few gooey buns are not a meal. How about tonight I treat us to an Italian in that new restaurant opposite – do you fancy some pasta or a pizza? We can celebrate your news and I have something to ask you.'

Toni warmed to the invitation but still had to comment on Amber not wasting her money.

'Behave, won't you? I'm in full time employment and also have my earnings from the Saturday job here.'

Toni's expression changed to deadpan serious. 'That's really kind of you but no thank you. This isn't easy to say but sadly I have to let you go. I really like you and we get on so well but I need to keep the overheads to a minimum.'

Amber was used to Toni's foolery and smiled. Once

again she had forgotten that just under a week ago, she had used the very same words in an effort to wind her up. It had been hilarious at the time and here she was playing the same prank again.

Play-acting, Amber grabbed her handbag and headed for the basement steps. 'Oh, I was wondering how long it would be before I would lose my job. Please don't feel bad – we can still be friends.'

Toni looked worried and shouted out, 'Only kiddin! You should have seen the look on your face.'

'Oh, no, not another of your jokes, well you nearly had me there.'

The two women burst into laughter and Toni whispered, 'I will come out to dinner and I may try some of that fancy lasagne you keep going on about. Are you sure you can afford a posh meal like that?'

Seated in the virtually empty Italian restaurant in Alperton High Street, the two friends nibbled on breadsticks and studied the menu. The waiter, who certainly didn't speak with a sing-song voice or look Italian, was uninterested in his customers. Their choice of lasagne and two large glasses of house red wine was recorded on a tiny notepad that was duly stuffed into a baggy trouser pocket.

A man in a grey suit, who could only be the owner, came out of the kitchen and welcomed them to his restaurant. Judging by his accent he was indeed the real McCoy, a true Italian with a boyish face. He had all the charms of a Mediterranean *signore*. Amber thought of her mystery man Luca and dismissed any chance of him having come from wonderful Italy.

The waiter returned with their drinks and Toni cradled her glass as she said, 'I'm ready for this. Now, spill the beans old gal, what were you going to tell me?'

Amber took a deep breath and went for it. 'I've spent

the last few weeks planning how we can raise extra money for our charity.'

'Oh yeah, I'm all ears.'

'I've researched things on the internet and am convinced that crowd funding could be the answer. We just need to register and set up a page, but first we need a story, something that touches people's hearts and encourages them to delve into their pockets.'

'Not sure what you mean by crowd funding.'

'Well, basically your business hinges on people's generosity and this would be done online and there are greater chances to raise money and…'

'You mean it goes through the banks?'

'No, Toni, it is all done on the computer and the money is forwarded to the charity.'

'That sounds clever but I don't know anything about computers. Could I do it on my mobile?'

Amber smiled. 'What happens is crowd funding helps to improve lives by raising money and, in our case, it will go to the homeless charities you support locally. The internet is really powerful, especially if the message goes viral.'

'Is it really that easy?'

Amber reached for her drink, took a small sip and leaned back on the wooden chair. 'What I do know is the subject matter has to be something special to kick off the process. I've been in contact with a marketing lady who reckons she could help us reach the right people, maybe even worldwide. She would assist with the script and help me with the video. What we need are real people's stories that make you sit up and think.'

Toni shook her head. 'Marketing lady you said, that's going to cost big time.'

'Not really, she's knows monies are tight and would charge two hundred pounds and I will pay this out of my savings. When it's ready to roll, I'm also going to donate some money.'

'I won't let you do that. You have your own problems.'

Before Amber had a chance to reply, the waiter appeared with the lasagne and awkwardly placed the square dishes at an angle in front of them and turned to leave.

Leaning over the table Amber straightened their meals and whispered. 'I've never been so sure about anything in my life. If marketed properly, the potential to raise funds will undoubtedly snowball. It is crucial that the images and story are portrayed in a sensitive manner. I want you to feature in the appeal that will bring a lump to people's throats.'

'Me...? I couldn't pull that off. I'm just a scatty lady with more frowns than smiles.'

'For the record, you are the kindest person I have ever met – you have to do it.'

Amber stretched out a hand to run a finger along the tired and wrinkled skin of Toni's cheek and said, 'You'll do just fine.'

***

Back home, Amber was excited to share her news with her flatmate but Liz insisted she spoke first. With no work on the horizon, she was moving on.

Shocked and saddened, Amber pleaded, 'You can't just up sticks, and anyway, where would you live?'

'I rang my mum and she's on her own again, so I'm going to stay in Durham. She reckons that I should be able to get a job where she works in the meat packing factory.'

'Think carefully before you make a decision as I'm

not putting any pressure on you to move on. We get on so well and I don't want you to leave. It takes time to get employment and we can survive on your benefits and what I bring in.'

Liz placed her arms around her friend's shoulders and said, 'That's just it, I need to stand on my own two feet. If it wasn't for you, I'd probably have reoffended and ended up back in prison. I now have a different perspective on life and am forever grateful for your help.'

With eyes welling up, Amber sighed, 'If it doesn't work out, you can just slot back in here. Anyway, it rains up there all the time and you can't speak the lingo.'

'Yeah, and I know Mum will drive me mad. I'm going up this Saturday so I'll give you some rent from my benefits and you can keep my things in the fridge. Not sure about the mince that's past the sell by date though.'

Amber waved a dismissive finger in the air. 'You will not pay me anything. Anyway, you can't go on Saturday, it's your birthday and I'm making you a banana cake. Stay a few more days, say you will. You'll need to give notice on walking the dogs, won't you?'

'Both my contacts told me yesterday they were making alternative arrangements, so there's nothing to stop me going. I'll have to pass on staying for my birthday as Mum is expecting me.' Pausing for breath Liz caught the worried expression on Amber's face and tried to console her. 'We won't lose touch and I'll be down to see you soon. It's not like I'm going to live in Australia or worse, Fairfield prison. Now, tell me about your day.'

'Don't even mention that prison.'

Liz nodded her head. 'I asked about your day.'

'Yeah, it went well. Toni thought my idea for crowd funding was worth a punt. I'm convinced it will make a difference to her charity and life. She's running on empty and I'm going to put the spark back in her life.'

'Just like you did for me.'

Chapter 29

The passenger in seat 14A on the mid-morning flight to Gatwick nervously pulled on his seatbelt and looked out of the window as the plane lifted off the tarmac and climbed steeply over Malaga. The view of the beaches and mountainous backdrop was spectacular.

Kane was going home for a visit. It had been well over a year since he last travelled to stay with his mother and catch up with sibling Jason who always managed to spoil things with his bitter reminders of the past. Aware that his fellow passengers were staring at him, he reminded himself that he was past getting upset. The scars no longer looked so fierce but there was no getting away from the fact that the misshapen and changed face was drawing second glances.

The short vacation had been hurriedly put together with a not so cheap reservation on an airline with a poor record of customer satisfaction. They were all about quick turn arounds and minimal passenger comforts whilst charging extortionate rates. The plane was heaving with passengers.

Two girls with dark, painted eyebrows and silver fingernails sat next to Kane and, apart from initially staring, went on to ignore him. Enormous bags that should have been stored in the lockers were extracted from under their seats. They proceeded to unload a mountain of phones, iPads, makeup and bottled water. An elbow was pushed into Kane's side and no apology was forthcoming.

It was to be a short flight of two hours and fifteen minutes and it was proving difficult to shut off from their constant chatter and awful language. The 'f' word featured every ten seconds as the young women discussed their conquests with lads whilst visiting the all-inclusive holiday complex in Torremolinos.

Within a short time of the seatbelt warnings being turned off, the aisles filled with travellers keen to use the toilets or others clinging to the fronts of seats to talk with their families or friends. The cabin crew were working hard to settle people down as the refreshment trolley was loaded for doing battle with the crowded aisle. A few rows back there was the sound of a baby crying with anxious parents taking turns to stand to rock the infant. There was an unpleasant smell of brie and bacon paninis as Kane's fellow passengers tucked into their food. The girl, with the low-cut blouse that required so few buttons, appeared to have an opinion on most matters. She dropped her credit card and leant down to the floor where Kane's immaculate brown lace up shoes fought for space. Her demanding voice rang out, 'You'll have to move your feet.'

Kane was fuming. Just his luck, having paid for a window seat to be next to such annoying youngsters and he vowed never to fly with the airline again.

He sat rigidly still in the hard seat and concentrated on the purpose of his short trip back home. He was to meet up with a number of people from his past and had taken the precaution of warning them about his new appearance. Lessening the initial shock had to be the best way forward.

Kane told himself that whilst he was the ugliest man on the mountain, there had been much passing of time since his brush with death. The necessity to reboot his life was paramount. Seven months on, the English man had ventured fully into the wider Spanish world and things were settling down. The scarf that hid the terrible scars had been binned, as had all the worries of being the guy who everyone stared at. A desire now existed to get on with everyday life without feeling sorry for himself.

He regularly spent time with his immediate neighbours before heading up for a coffee in his favourite bar with a view of the road that led to the village. Sitting at the rustic table with a cappuccino and complimentary tapas, the view never failed to impress.

Kane's recovery and determination to rise up from feeling so low was partly down to his ex-girlfriend, Sue. They had stayed friends with a strict agreement to never cross the line again. The heavily pregnant young lady had once again become his saviour, she was the one who never gave up on him. Deep down, he was definitely a glass half full man who wasn't going to give up either.

Today, he was going home to meet up with the family and visit his lawyer to sign off the sale of the remaining flat that had been rented out for a number of years. The funds would help with his early retirement plans. During the stay, he planned to remain strong and resist the temptation to track down Amber or for that matter quiz Jason for an update on her.

The remainder of the flight passed quickly and, shortly after mid-day, the plane touched down on a rain-soaked runway. The process of clearing airport security and collecting luggage proved easier than on previous visits.

Walking through the automatic doors into the arrivals' terminal, his eyes scanned the faces of hundreds of people, including taxi drivers holding up A4 sheets with names on. Within the crowd, there stood his mother who was waving both arms in the air to attract his attention. Jason smiled briefly as he stood rigidly still holding his car keys.

Tucking themselves away from the crowds, Kane hugged his mother and slipped a hand into Jason's cold and sweaty palm. His brother swiftly pulled away and offered to carry the suitcase. He led the way to the short stay carpark.

Jason's silver BMW looked as if it needed a wash, on closer inspection, a hoovering and clearing of possessions wouldn't have gone amiss. Anxious to clear the airport he hooted the horn at an elderly couple who struggled to reverse their car from a narrow space. 'So Bruv, how's the good life been treating you. Swimming and pulling birds all day long, no doubt.'

Kane laughed at the ridiculous comment. 'It's been great and I've joined in with a number of activities. I enjoy the walking group and social evenings. As for a new lady, that's all on hold.'

'Oh, I see, then again, there have been a few in the past, haven't there?'

Kane ignored the remark and switched the topic to his brother's legal practice.

Reaching for a mint from the glovebox, Jason held the plastic container up to his lips and between crunching and swallowing said, 'Anyone else for one of these?'

'No, I'll pass on that. How's your work going, are you still busy?'

Now on the dual carriageway that linked with the M25, the car sped up to sixty miles an hour and Kane's mother shouted from the back. 'Not so fast, you'll get clocked on one of those speed camera things. You are a legal man and should know the penalties for breaking the law.'

With one hand on the steering wheel Jason looked into the driver's mirror and spoke directly to his mother. 'I wasn't going that fast – I just want to clear the lorries.' He smiled at Kane and in a confident voice boasted. 'I thrive on work and a legal man like me is in much demand. Divorces and conveyancing mainly – or as we say in the business, splits and moves.'

Kane sucked in air and questioned why his brother felt

he had to show off.

It was their mother who brought up Kane's accident. 'I'm amazed how much better your face looks.'

'Really.'

'Yes, it's not so angry and the surgery has vastly improved things. We are so proud of you for the way you've coped.'

Feeling pleased with himself, Kane replied, 'I had loads of help and reached a day when I said to hell with it, take me or leave me.'

'Yeah, and he's got a new set of front teeth,' said Jason who was once again overtaking cars. Judging by the expression on his face, he was moved by his brother's comments. He nodded his head a number of times before flashing a motorist for undercutting him.

***

Both Kane and his mother were to stay at Jason's large flat in Wembley that afforded a view of the football stadium arc that was like a brushstroke across the London sky. The trepidation regarding the three of them living in such close proximity for a few days was building in Kane's head. All he wanted was a happy reunion and not a falling out about the injustices of the past.

Jason's antediluvian flat was a flashback to the seventies that housed the worst of flatpack furniture. It just lacked a budgie in a cage, a bevelled mirror on chains, lava lamp, joss sticks and orange painted walls. Looking out of place in this setting, a top of the range smart TV on the wall above a sealed-up fireplace dwarfed the room. A smoked glass dining table revealed fingerprints and crumbs from previous meals. The occupier of this home was indeed a leftover from the past, someone who rarely smiled and carried a heavy weight on his shoulders and stomach. This man loved all things retro and for a person still in his prime, his bizarre tastes and attitude must have thwarted his chances with the fairer sex.

Exhausted from travelling, Kane slumped down on the springy sofa and acknowledged that his brother lived in a time warp. Distressing as it was coping with their quarrelling, he loved Jason and longed to tell him so.

Accepting a cup of tea from his mother, Kane thanked her and watched as she straightened the faded cushions with the ghastly green paisley designs. She rubbed a finger along the edge of the bookcase and held it up to show her son the dust.

Craning his neck to look at the far corner of the room, an unpleasant sight met Kane's eyes. Hanging crookedly in the alcove on the painted wood chip paper was his picture. The poorly painted London scene with incongruous images of animals dominating the skyline brought back the disturbing events that led to his final showdown with Amber.

Kane's head felt fit to burst as his inner pestering voice screamed out the words for the hundredth time: *Why did she have to see your picture? It was the link that revealed she stole from your apartment.*

Jason appeared from the kitchen with a tea towel over his shoulder and looked puzzled. 'You look like you have seen a ghost. What's up?'

Sitting bolt upright Kane composed himself and nervously said, 'It was seeing my old painting. I wish you would get rid of it; it gives me the creeps.'

'Oh, the one Amber saw when she burgled your flat. It reminds me of the Pink Floyd album cover, only better. I don't usually pay you compliments but it would look good in a gallery. I've got it on my laptop at work. When I fire up the box of tricks, up it comes – I can let you have a copy if you want.'

'I just wish she hadn't seen it. As soon as she described the painting, I knew she had been the thief and that was the end of our friendship.'

'Oh, my God,' sighed Jason. 'I do believe you still have the hots for her.'

'Don't be so vulgar.'

'Keep your hair on. The last time I saw her was on Facetime and she looked stunning. If she really meant that much to you, can't you forgive her?'

'NO NEVER,' came back the terrified voice.

Jason shrugged his shoulders and left the room. A fight had commenced in Kane's head as his heart desperately wished to make contact with Amber again.

Playing his music loud, Jason prepared their evening meal and the appetising smells wafted through the flat. He was a superb cook and tonight the roast beef was going to go down a treat with slabs of Yorkshire pudding that hung over the side of the plate, roast potatoes and Brussels sprouts bathed in thick gravy. They were treated to a blast from the past with seventies and eighties pop hits that now sounded dated. Somewhere in the three-bedroom apartment there would undoubtedly be vinyl records on the Music for Pleasure label that had been purchased many decades ago from the local Woolworth store.

Over the meal, Kane's mother revealed that a friendship with a man in the theatre club she belonged to was becoming more serious. The passing of time since her husband died had at long last softened the pain allowing her life to begin again in earnest. Both brothers were shocked, as well as happy for her, and pressed for more details on the silver-haired man who lived on the same street in Luton.

When their mother retired to bed, Kane topped up his

brother's wine glass and stared at his own non-alcoholic drink. He took a deep breath. It was time to address their chequered past.

'Thanks for letting me stay and for running Mum over here, it means so much to me.' Pausing for thought, he nervously coughed before continuing, 'There's something that needs clearing up.'

Jason partly closed his eyes. 'Here we go again. Why is it when we meet you go over the same old problems? Brothers often fight and that's what we do.'

'I'll cut to the chase. You never forgave me for accepting all that money from Dad to buy into the travel agency business and I just want to say …'

Bringing his fist hard down on the table, the bottle of wine wobbled and Kane reached out to steady it. Jason's explosive voice filled the living room. 'You had him twisted around your little finger and when I needed funds to buy into the legal practice, there was nothing left for me.'

Kane sighed. He still felt bad after all these years especially as he had failed to restore the friendship they had once enjoyed. 'Hold on there, when our father died you know he left debts and it fell on me to sort out the finances to buy Mum that flat. You were at Southampton reading law and unable to help out.'

'What's your point, Bruv?'

'You got your money in the end, didn't you? So, what's the 'I hate Kane for life' all been about?'

Now on his feet, Jason parked his chair at an angle under the table and turned to face Kane. His hard reply was fast in coming. 'When I graduated Mum found an old ISA of hers and that's what she gave me to finance buying into the partnership. All of this tension stems back to you being the older son and always getting what you wanted.'

Kane could hardly control his temper and wrung his hands together, squeezing fingers so firmly that he momentarily cried out in pain. His eyes moved up to his brother's face and then over to his painting on the wall that he wished would find its way into the bin.

He composed what he was about to say and calmly said, 'There was no ISA, no forgotten pot of money, it was me who gave it to you. I made Mum promise not to tell you, it was me. I felt bad with Dad not looking out for you so I stepped in. I know it was wrong not telling you the money came from myself but, at the time, it seemed like the right thing to do. Can't we draw a line under the misunderstanding?'

The revelation was too much for Jason who had tears welling up in his eyes. He steadied himself on the doorframe and it was a while before he responded. 'Oh, my God, I had no idea. You should have told me. I've been horrible to you and it's all down to my unfounded jealousy. I even did my utmost to break up your relationship with Amber.'

'Don't worry about her.'

In a whisper of a voice Jason offered, 'I know where she lives and I'm going to put things right for you.'

'NO, definitely not. I've come to terms with living without her.' He stifled a sob. 'I just want you and Mum.'

***

Spending time with the family was important to Kane during the three days spent at the flat. Jason kept apologising which resulted in the occasional man hug. All that needed to be discussed had been said leaving hope for the future. An agreement was made for Jason to stay at the villa, only this time he would be introduced to some of the locals and friends who had stood by Kane during his ordeal.

Kane's preparation for visiting friends and acquaintances in the UK had been made through telephone calls. He had forewarned them of the way he now looked. The last thing he wanted to do was turn up on the doorstep and frighten people. No doubt there would still be a few uncomfortable moments before being invited in to catch up on all the news.

The first visit was to the two men who ran the florist in a parade of shops in Greenford. They had put out a banner with Kane's name emblazoned in flowers and the welcome inside the back of the shop included coffee and pastries. In-between serving customers, Brian and John, proudly showed him their wedding photos and discussed plans for a honeymoon in northern Italy later in the year.

Most of the reunions took place in wine bars and when his friends got over the initial shock of seeing him, it was like he'd never been away. Yes, there were stares from shoppers and the woman who drove the bus up to Sudbury Hill, but nothing was going to spoil the few days left of the mini vacation.

Entering the offices of Kane's old company was an eye opener as, unbeknown to him, a further two floors in the building had been secured. Including the staff in all three branches, the head count had swelled to one hundred and ninety. The call centre was enormous and was kitted out with the latest technology for handling customer service activities. It had been a fair size company when the founder, Kane Boulter, sold his controlling share and just a few years later the business was literally flying. Fellow directors and staff made a fuss of him and told him if he wanted a holiday, he knew where to come.

On the last day he visited his solicitor and signed off the sale of the remaining flat to a property developer who was buying up much of the leafy Middlesex rental market.

When Kane left for the airport, his mother hugged him and whispered she hoped he would find someone to settle down with.

'Plenty of time for all of that, anyway I haven't met the right girl yet.'

***

On returning to Spain Kane slotted back into his routine of seeing friends. Swapping the busy pace of life back home for Andalucía was the best thing he had ever done. The true Spaniards had nailed a happier path through life with their laid-back *mañana* approach and he was keen to resume a calmer existence.

Kane took a call on his mobile from Sue's friend, Mars, an older woman she shared a house with. She hurriedly told him they were in the maternity wing at Malaga hospital and that mother and baby were doing well. Mario weighed in at nine pounds and two ounces and was by all accounts a chubby baby with large cheeks and a mop of dark hair.

The news thrilled Kane as he thought of Sue who had become so excited at the prospect of giving birth. He was pleased for her yet concerned about how she would cope financially. There were her well-off parents helping with the rent but a day would come when she would probably return to the UK. Kane would miss her company but told himself that she was a walk-on character who came into his life in an instant and would leave just as quickly.

Chapter 30

The day that despatch manager, Daniel Godding, called Amber into his office, a feeling of edginess crept through her body. Recent redundancies had left her unsettled, especially as she had only been in employment for the relatively short period of time. The office, with a view of the fleet of waste disposal vehicles and servicing bays, was where people started or ended their employment with the council.

Sitting with her legs crossed in the uncomfortable plastic trousers, Amber remained silent and bent and twisted her nervous fingers as she waited for the meeting to begin. Her boss, the man with the freckly face and poor taste in colourful ties, apologised for keeping her waiting. He positioned his hands in a pinnacle shape on the immaculate desk with stapler and pens standing to attention like soldiers.

'You said you wanted to see me. What's it all about?'

Grinning like a Cheshire cat, the man's face changed to thoughtful. 'That's right young lady, there is an opening on garden waste collections and you may be the person to fill the post. It's a less physical job and not so smelly – are you interested?'

Unsure if a refusal would offend, Amber took a chance. 'That's really kind of you to think of my welfare but I'm really a tough bird and smells don't bother me so much now. I'd like to remain on Raymond's team as I'm really enjoying it.'

'I think you may regret your decision but if that's what you want.' Checking his watch, he huffily added, 'I really thought you would jump at the chance of this vacancy but I was obviously wrong. Opportunities like this don't come up that often.'

In an attempt to appease her disgruntled boss, Amber said, 'Possibly, in the future, a move may suit me – you will bear me in mind again, won't you?'

The manager's voice lacked conviction as he mumbled a feeble reply. He frowned and tapped stubby, sweaty fingers that left moisture and fingerprints on the highly polished surface of his desk. Manoeuvring the car-shaped mouse, he stared intensely at the giant computer screen. Amber's name was deleted in a second from the short list of candidates.

Mr Godding never said goodbye, leaving Amber anxious that she may have blotted her copybook. The easy route would have been to accept the transfer but she wasn't going to risk losing the companionship of the father and son team. They were great to work with and she would never forget the day young Felix dealt with the racist remark that spilt from the lips of one of the other drivers. He stood up for her and warned the animal to back off. Friends like these didn't come along that often.

***

As Amber climbed into the cleanest waste disposal vehicle on the site, she smiled at Raymond who was grinning. She shunted up next to Felix on the cramped bench. 'Sorry I'm late, I got called in to see Godding.'

'No problema; what did he want?' quizzed Raymond.

'Nothing important – just to transfer me to garden collections and had a right strop when I declined the offer. Judging by the way he conducted the end of the meeting, I suspect my card has been marked.'

'Picking up the garden stuff, you say – that's girlie work.' He paused and turned his attention to starting the engine and quickly added, 'No offence intended.'

A smile grew on Amber's face. 'Plenty taken, now

let's get this show on the road.'

Raymond turned to his son and punched him gently on the arm. 'Are you going to tell Amber that on her day off we found a dead cat in that bin in Sudbury Hill and used her gloves to shift it?'

'Stop lying, our run doesn't cover that area,' replied Amber with laughter in her voice.

Guiding the heavy vehicle out of the yard and onto the dual carriageway in the direction of route five, the happy team of waste operatives chatted about their respective weekends.

Young Felix extracted a leaflet from a carrier bag that held his lunch. Amber cringed as she read the word 'church'. She had been tactful in the past to avoid getting involved with their worship and here was another handout. 'Have a look at our crowd funding for a woman with cancer who has been helping others by fund-raising. It's going really well. Come on Amber, dust off that pretty purse of yours and support her.'

Amber felt like her eyes were going to bulge out of their sockets as she focused on the print and photo of a mother and child. She was thrilled to learn that their church was running a crowd funding appeal online. She pondered on whether there was someone who could share a few tips on how to register and take her own appeal to market?

'Yes, of course I'll pledge some money but tell me more about how it works as I've got this idea to do a similar thing for Toni's charity.'

'Not really sure, all I know is we've had almost four hundred pounds promised from loads of people who have seen it online. If it goes viral that will open the world up to seeing it. With a fair wind, the donations could snowball. James Forester is ace at raising money. I could get you two guys together for a chat.'

Amber felt her heart pounding as the adrenalin raced around her body. This was an exciting opportunity to gather some more ideas. She decided there and then to call their appeal after her boss Toni.

As they arrived at the first pickup point, she jumped down from the vehicle to start herding the wheelie bins ready for tipping into the back. It never got any easier shifting heavy rubbish around and today the smell was particularly bad. Raymond remarked that it must be another dead cat.

Halfway through completing a street, one of the bins became jammed in the lifting device and there followed a loud grinding sound from the gearing. It took both Amber and Felix to free the container. On moving it back to the driveway, the owner, a young man clutching his car keys, looked at the broken lid and challenged them on the damage. On this occasion, her colleague handled the situation badly with the two men at loggerheads and it was Amber who arbitrated offering to report back to the depot. She pulled out her mobile phone and recorded the, now much calmer, resident's name and address. A photo of the damage was taken.

It takes a good person to apologise for their bad handling of a situation and Felix took off his gloves to shake the householder's hand. Felix held his head down low.

***

On Sunday morning, Amber anxiously waited in the hall for the church service to end. The smell of furniture polish reminded her of the old days when, as a child, she used to visit an aunt who lived in a house full of antique furniture. She also recalled the smell of gravy and roast potatoes that always made her hungry.

It had certainly been a lively hour listening to the hymns and through the partly open door she gazed at the charismatic congregation, many of whom were throwing their arms in the air. She listened intensely to the sermon from a woman in ceremonial robes and long blonde hair that swept around her shoulders. With a voice that would have filled a cathedral, the message hammered out referred to loving your neighbour. At one stage the preacher left the pulpit and handed out flowers to the ladies in the front seats before airing the inevitable repost, 'Praise the Lord.'

Raymond and his son respected Amber's wish not to participate in the service, hence the hour and thirty-minute wait in the hall where she listened to all things godly. She had no set views on religion but verged towards being an atheist.

The meeting room was where coffee was to be served and judging by the three enormous electric kettles, she speculated on the number of worshippers that would be present. With all the noise that accompanies a gathering, she wondered if chatting about crowd funding would be feasible. Amber grasped her note book with the prepared questions in readiness to meet Mr Forester.

'James meet Amber, Amber meet James,' said Felix with a grin on his face.

The outstretched hand was gently squeezed by Amber who experienced a tingling sensation that ran along her arm and felt incredible. The young man was certainly good looking with hair tied back in a ponytail and his brown eyes that focused on hers. A navy-blue denim jacket hugged his trim body and the white tee shirt revealed a bony chest. Her first thoughts were how thin he looked and whether he ate enough.

'Felix said you want some help in setting up a funding site for the charity you support. With the right angle placed on your homeless story, I'm sure I can be of assistance. I have done two so far and one even went global and brought in a lot of money. Fill me in with your progress to date.'

Aware of others listening in on their conversation, Amber had an audience and momentarily smiled and waved at the sea of faces. Many whispered a hello as they clutched their service sheets and Bibles before edging forward to the refreshments table.

Turning back to James, she nervously fluffed her words. 'W… w… well, not that much. Actually, nothing yet.' Her confidence started to build as he encouraged her to continue. 'I thought about uploading something that touches the heart and features those already helped rather than just depressing scenes of life on the street. The plight of the homeless is dear to my heart and I might know just the right person to tell his story.'

'Good start.'

'I've contacted a lady who can do the filming and she's going to find out more about crowd funding. I think she's going to Google it. She won't charge too much and I thought if I put…'

Interrupting the stranger to their church, James looked shocked. 'Hang on, this is all about helping the needy. Let's get one thing straight, there will be no paying anyone money to set it up. I can see you really need a hand. We'll shoot the video and register the launch. If we work hard, we'll be up and running in no time. What are you going to call the project?'

'Oh, I've named it after my boss Toni. It was working in her charity shop on Saturdays that gave me the idea to promote it. I'm so excited you want to help us.'

'Is this about someone called Toni who has died and the cause lies in helping future sufferers who find themselves homeless?'

James' quizzical stare and bizarre remark stunned Amber. 'No, she's quite alive. What I meant to say is it's all about her drive to help the homeless. She's a shining example and if only we can expand the message, I'm sure we'll get support from a wider audience.'

'Oh, I see. Toni, you say, is the instigator and her name would feature. Not the best title for crowd funding as it sounds like we are raising money for her. Let's try and find another one that resonates with our audience.'

'Oh, okay, I'll give that some thought.'

James then said a strange thing. 'During the service, I was aware you were waiting in here to see me and I said a prayer for you. I just knew you needed help. I know nothing about you except that you have had a rough time yourself.'

Spellbound by the handsome man, Amber's eyes drifted to his long fingers where there was no sign of a ring. She muttered, 'How did you know that?'

They were interrupted by a man carrying a tray of coffee cups and mostly broken digestive biscuits. Sipping the not-so-hot drink, James made his excuse to mix with fellow church-goers and waved a hand at head height to a woman clutching some leaflets. James mentioned the need to visit Toni's charity shop to draw up a blueprint. A hurried exchange of contact numbers took place on their mobiles before he turned to leave. Amber high-fived her friend Felix and mouthed a heartfelt thank you.

Chapter 31

After leaving the church Amber headed for the charity shop and, turning the key in the lock of the door, viewed the shelves and rails that looked untidy. She bent down to pick up a blouse that had fallen on the floor and searched for its hanger. One of the rails that held men's trousers was leaning at an angle and needed repairing. She knew instinctively that Toni had started on one of her jobs and had become distracted. When Amber had finished her Saturday stint, she had tidied up and hoovered the entire shop and now, the next morning, it looked a mess.

Toni appeared in a red dressing gown that had definitely been on offer in the window on the previous day and was surprised to see her. She stared at Amber's cheery face and short curly hair. 'You do know it's Sunday and not your work day?'

'Very funny. I've just been to church and there is some exciting news.'

Feigning a laugh, Toni sarcastically said, 'Church you say; don't tell me that you've met the Messiah and are turning all happy-clappy?'

Amber ignored the remark. 'Stop mucking around and make us a drink. I just need to pop downstairs to the loo – I'm bursting.'

Making her way down the narrow iron staircase, a stale smell hit her nostrils. Definitely damp she thought that needed checking out. She used the bathroom and frustratingly there was no toilet roll available and no sign of a replacement. Later she would check under the sink in the kitchen in case a visit to the corner store was required.

Still aware of the damp smell, she ventured into Toni's bedroom. The depressing room with no window looked less welcoming every time she set foot in there. A hideous floral lampshade hung from the unpainted plasterboard ceiling that had never been properly skimmed and still revealed the heads of the nails. She spied the cheap carpet that Toni had laid herself which held various stains and sighed. It upset her to think of her boss living in such squalor. The long and short of the matter was she paid herself very little to keep overheads down to maximize her donations to the needy.

Her eyes were drawn to the damp patches on the walls where Toni's single bed had been pulled further into the room. The plaster revealed spores of black mould that could only get worse.

Back upstairs Toni had hurriedly dressed in jeans and jumper and was running a brush through her long hair. The dressing gown now hung on a peg in the hallway alongside her blue anorak.

Sipping the hot tea from the chipped Charles and Diana mug, Amber broached the subject of the damp in the bedroom.

'Yeah, I know it's getting worse, so I've got a decorator coming in on Wednesday to paint some of that damp blocking stuff. It will be fine.'

'No. it's not fine. I've had the same problem at my place and it's not a paint job. A builder needs to hack off the plaster to a height of one metre and return at a later date to make good.' She paused and then added, 'I can lend you my dehumidifier.'

Toni looked bored with the conversation and changed the subject. 'You know that guy yesterday who brought in the Star Wars figures, well, he rang after you had gone home and to be honest …'

'Oh, give me strength,' interjected Amber. 'We were talking about your bedroom and I'm wondering just how unhealthy it must be to sleep in there.'

'Oh, wind your neck in young lady and tell me what

right you had to poke around in my room. For your information, I sleep with the door open for ventilation. I'll get it fixed. God, you do worry about things.'

A plan was forming in Amber's head that just needed fine tuning to persuade Toni to see sense. She took a deep breath and went for it. 'I'm looking out for you because you are not just my boss but also a good friend. I won't see you getting ill with breathing difficulties from all that damp. Who would run the business if you pegged out? My flatmate Liz has moved on and you can have her bedroom for a while.'

Toni looked genuinely moved by the kind offer and surprisingly, without any hesitation, agreed to the arrangement. Taken aback by the ease of turning around a tricky situation, Amber smiled. The routinely stubborn lady, who normally fought her corner, had caved in without so much as a moan or protest.

'I insist on paying my way and will do the housework. I could also cook the meals. I'll cancel the decorator man and ring a builder as it's a bigger job than I first thought. The deal has to be that if you get fed up with me or I outstay my welcome, then I'll be on the first bus back to Alperton.'

Amber nodded. 'Only one thing, no disrespect intended, your take on housework and mine differs greatly, so leave all that to me. Also, I'm not eating any ready meals warmed up in the microwave.'

'Nothing wrong with the meal deals I buy; I just wish they did liver and bacon. I'd better pack a few things. I won't be more than ten minutes.'

Thirty-five minutes later, Toni's relatively new suitcase crammed with clothes and personal items was hauled up the basement staircase. They left the charity shop in the direction of the bus stop. Even on a Sunday, the traffic was gridlocked on the North Circular Road which would undoubtedly delay the arrival of their bus. Fumes from the polluting vehicles left a warm, stale taste on the tongue and Amber covered her mouth with a hand and coughed. It was a deadly mix of chemicals that was mostly accepted as being part and parcel of residing in the London area.

'We'll take a taxi to Harrow.' Amber never took taxis; she couldn't afford the fare and taking one today would lower her weekly budget.

'We could walk,' shouted Toni over the noise of the traffic.

'Too far. There's a rank near Halfords – give me your case please. Really sorry about all this.'

***

On arrival at the flat Toni wandered from room to room and commented on how tidy everything looked. From her bedroom she shouted, 'Have you changed the sheets on my bed? I don't like the idea of sleeping under other people's grubby duvets.'

Amber appeared in the doorway and gave as good as she received, 'Well no. Liz only slept in them for about a month and she regularly showered. Of course I changed them.'

The rest of the evening panned out well with a fish finger and chip supper. They watched a DVD that featured a Sicilian Mafia boss who woke up one morning with no recollection of his evil past or, for that matter, his long-suffering wife. His attempts to delve into his background revealed not only gangland activity but a colleague who desperately needed his help. Half way through the film Toni mentioned that her ex-husband had enjoyed watching movies like this one and he could, at times, be a violent man. Amber was surprised by the disclosure as Toni often spoke fondly of him and said they started the charity shop together.

***

That night, the sound of Toni's volcanic snoring had kept Amber awake. With only two hours to go before her boss needed to leave for work, she placed her alarm clock next to Toni's bed. It was loud enough to wake the dead and the repeater button had been activated for two sessions of Big Ben thumping out seven o'clock. Notes on locking up the flat and which bus to take were propped up on the kitchen table that was laid for breakfast. The toaster had been stored away in the hall cupboard. Toni's charcoaled slices brought back memories of her smoke-filled kitchen and craziness on inserting a fork into the appliance to free the charred offering.

As Amber walked to the bus stop, her thoughts were on her charismatic but frustrating friend and, taking into account that the workmen hadn't been booked in yet, the duration of Toni's stay could escalate to at least a month, possibly two.

Learning more about Toni had revealed a sad and complex life that involved a husband who broke her heart. Her revelation about his violent mood swings had been another piece in the jigsaw as she drip-fed her life story. Since their divorce her interest centred on raising funds and ignoring her own life. Muddling along with little comfort or personal horizon to aim for, she was fast becoming an eccentric old woman.

The day that Toni came to stay her tuneless whistling had grated in Amber's head. The normally peaceful surroundings, since Liz had left, were to be a thing of the past. Toni had commented on the orderly accommodation; if only she knew the whole story. Not so many years ago, the place had been a tip. The extraordinary transformation from slovenly and chaotic to clean and tidy had all been down to the shame that still hung like a heavy rope around her neck.

Amber had brought up with Toni the subject of crowd funding and James' kind offer to kickstart the appeal. He would contact her by e-mail with suggestions and arrange a date to meet up. Her duty lay in finding someone to be featured in the short video of less than a minute. The message had to harness a lifeline for the mostly silent homeless. The ultimate goal was for their appeal to go viral to create awareness and a commitment to pledge.

Toni's response had been fast in coming. 'Do you think James will message you tomorrow?'

'Give him time, won't you?'

It was the roar of the bus pulling in that brought Amber back to her senses and she realised her lunchbox was still back in the flat. As she swiped her contactless travel card, the driver's expressionless face reminded her of a number of the women back in prison. Sometimes it was easier not to enter into conversation and ignore the unresponsive hollow look that hid decades of unhappiness.

The bus lurched forward and she staggered towards a vacant window seat. The fifteen-minute ride would soon be over leaving the short walk to the depot. She checked her watch for the third time since leaving home and drew out her mobile phone. Breathing on the screen, the fingerprints were polished away with a tissue. On loading mail, her heart beat rose. James Forester's message was in the waiting to be opened box.

His greeting was warm and he sent his best wishes saying he looked forward to seeing her again soon. There followed a detailed account of how he helped another church member attract support and monies through crowd funding. He continued by saying he would ring on Tuesday evening to firm up their meeting and that Caroline would accompany him as she would help with the video and editing. There was an attachment photo labelled with the woman's name. Amber clicked on the file and up came a plain looking girl in her twenties with enormous round glasses and a cheery smile. On rereading the text, this time her eyes homed in on the PS that read: *Caroline is my partner and I know she will be thrilled to meet you. Bless you Amber.*

Amber tutted loudly and swiped the screen away to the home page. She then saw the funny side and laughed out loud. A noisier than usual voice inside her head held her attention: *Here you go again. Don't assume every man with a pulse will be interested in you. And now, pay attention as your stop is coming up and you don't want to be late for work, do you?*

***

The shift started well with much banter between the crew. As Raymond reversed into a cul-de-sac, the heavens opened with a torrential downpour crashing on the metal cab roof. There was no let up and, despite the waterproof clothing, on leaving the vehicle the soaking made working difficult. Over all the months Amber had been on the bins this was one of the worst really bad weather days she had encountered and it brought home the hardship of the job. Dragging bins through puddles was hard and grimy work. Her hair was drenched as was the tee shirt she wore under the orange jacket. She kept telling herself the rain had to stop soon but it showed no sign of abating.

Inside the cab, Amber sat uncomfortably and observed

Raymond continually applying the blower on the windscreen to clear the steamed-up glass. Felix drew the short straw and braved the weather to buy the bacon rolls. Returning to the depot to drop off the rubbish, their not-so-favourite supervisor, Mr Godding, handed over three manila envelopes. The annual pay rise had been agreed by the union and management. Raymond and his son sighed when they read out the minimum increase of one per cent that had been awarded. Mental arithmetic had never been a problem for Amber who quickly calculated the extra monthly salary minus the tax. The net figure of fifteen pounds a month was not to be sniffed at. She was back in work and, yes, it wasn't the best pay rise but she was covering bills with a little left for the odd night out. Life was panning out well.

Chapter 32

Two days into Toni's stay in the flat she received the estimate for the damp problem. It was the best part of eight hundred pounds to strip the plaster back to bricks and restore. The builder commented that everything on that side of the room had to be pulled away and covered up. Paying for the repair involved lowering Toni's savings to a bare minimum. The initial work would take three days with a further six weeks for the wall to dry out before the plastering commenced.

'Oh, no, I'm stuck with you for the best part of two months,' joked Amber.

Toni tapped the table top and said, 'You said that James and his girlfriend are visiting tonight. He asked that we give some thought to the message for the video post. My mind has gone blank. Have you any ideas?'

Amber suddenly had a brainwave for the name of the project. 'Let's not call it after you as it may detract from it going viral on the web. How about 'Concrete Pillows'? It weighs up perfectly the difficulties of sleeping on a hard and dirty pavement.'

'That's brilliant, I never wanted any of this to be about me. It should focus on the plight of the homeless and your title is just the ticket.'

That evening, arriving on time, James was let into the flat and Amber craned her neck round the front door. 'Where's Caroline?'

Dropping his damp coat on the laminate flooring James sighed. 'Still bucketing down out there.'

'You've come on your own?' asked Amber anxiously.

'Oh, yes, we fell out, we're always falling out. It's my fault, I've got a relatively short fuse and we quarrelled. She won't be helping us. Not a problem as I'll borrow a camcorder from someone in our church.'

In an unconvincing voice Amber muttered, 'Sorry to hear about you guys.' Her thoughts lingered on his words that spoke of impatience and heartache. As fit as he looked, this would be the wrong person to date. Why couldn't he have had Kane's temperament as well as the good looks?

Seated in the lounge sipping coffee, it was Toni who had a headful of questions for James. 'So, how much can we expect to draw in with this promotion thingy of yours?'

James laboured his reply which lacked any conviction about raising massive funds. 'Oh, not sure. It all depends on whether it goes viral and even then, just because the world views the message, there is no guarantee of pledges. I've helped on a few of these and the last one was really encouraging – we got over a thousand pounds.'

Unable to supress her laughter, Toni raised both hands in the air and said, 'That's nothing. I thought people pulled in huge amounts like a million or more.'

James' short fuse triggered a grinding of teeth along with a face that no longer exuded any warmth. Amber glared at Toni for making such a statement and whispered, 'Thanks a bunch.'

Their guest's wonderful deep voice hardened like a displeased school teacher. 'Well, that's me done, I'm off. Why don't you do it yourself? It's not a walk in the park as you will soon discover.'

He gathered up his files and rose from the sofa leaving Amber with little choice but to apologise for her friend's acid tongue. 'Ignore Toni, this is all new territory and she didn't mean to sound off at you. I also need to tell you that I've come up with a more plausible title for our pitch – what do you think of Concrete Pillows?'

Lowering himself back onto the sofa their visitor switched back to Mr Charming and congratulated Amber on the excellent play on words.

The friendly smile returned and the discussions resumed as if nothing had occurred. James made copious notes and went on to draw an incredible sketch of a close up of a man's face with large and frightened eyes staring back.

James revealed his occupation as being a book cover designer for a London publisher. His suggestion was to open the video with a line drawing of a homeless man. The image would transform from graphic to real life. A few meaningful words would be narrated before the filming switched to the appeal details. The strap line of Concrete Pillows would be repeated twice in the post.

'She's a bloody genius dreaming up those words,' said Toni who was silently clapping Amber.

James' cheeks took on a bright red shade as he turned to face Toni. 'Let's just stick with genius and leave out your colourful adjective.'

'Yes, don't swear Toni,' said Amber who was dreading another confrontation.'

'Sorry, it just slipped out.'

James took back control of the meeting. 'More to the point, there's a guy at work who writes the back-cover teasers for novels so I'll get him on board. He'll stitch together incredible words for our video which needs to be dynamic and seamless.'

Amber could hardly conceal her excitement as she knew of just the right person who might agree to be filmed. It was a man she had befriended whilst helping out at a soup kitchen. It all depended on whether, after all these years, he was still around. She wondered if he had the same mobile or whether it had been stolen like the previous one. Hopefully, she would be able to track him down. It would be great to meet up with Gerrard again. A moment of doubt rattled around her head as a cruel scenario made her question whether to go looking for him. Their last meeting must have been over four years ago and this was a long time for anyone living on the street. If he had been fortunate, he would have found accommodation; if unlucky, he may possibly have passed away.

Amber was brought back to the meeting with a shudder as James asked if she was all right. Her anxious face and eyes that stared blankly at the wall spoke of a fear that was not to be shared. 'Yep, I'm fine. Is it hot in here or is it just me?'

Toni muttered, 'Not pregnant, are you?'

Laughing off the remark, Amber replied, 'Not much chance of that with my track record with men. It's a while since I…'

James coughed loudly. 'Too much detail ladies.'

A timetable was drawn up and James' statement back in the church hall that the project would only take a few days was amended to however long it took. The structure of the message had to be right and no timescale should be imposed. Harnessing the power of social media to spread the word about Toni's charity required detailed planning.

***

The man with the enormous cheeks and a smile that never failed to please had to be tracked down, only it was proving more difficult than Amber first thought. He was not answering his mobile. She was able to establish that Gerrard, a Jamaican man in his forties, was back on the pavements and possibly living in Chalk Farm in North London. The prospect of locating him was tantamount to losing a fifty pence coin down a drain and trying to fish it out with a stick. The concrete jungle of London, with its myriad of streets and hideaways, remained a difficult place to navigate.

Amber's Oyster travel card proved to be good value as over a two-week period she took the train into North London to commence her search. Having gone straight from work, there was no time to freshen up from her grimy day on the bins, or have dinner with Toni. The haunts of Camden Town and Chalk Farm were somewhere Amber had never ventured before and she drew a blank with the search. She took the advice of a shopkeeper who suggested trying the Finchley Road where many of the homeless congregated. Amber walked the busy road that led from Swiss Cottage to Golders Green where so many leftover souls ended up in alleyways, shop doorways or on street corners.

It took a considerable amount of legwork to cover the ground. There was much sadness as she spoke to different people who each had a story to tell. They were mostly good human beings seeking a second chance who had experienced heartache along the way. Many shared the need to befriend the silver needle. Drugs were often the bane of the homeless.

There were others who lived on the wrong side of the law and ripped off the public. The common factors for ending up on the streets were losing employment, their home, loved ones and friends. Mental health issues played a massive role in the theatre of the streets. Personal hygiene obviously became an issue as was damp bedding and illnesses that related to being out in all weathers. Sheltering in cardboard, makeshift homes and keeping thieves at bay was not for the faint-hearted. There were never enough hostel places and many were too proud to accept help. Climbing back up the ladder became a fading dream with many people only lasting three to five years in the open.

There were a few mistaken sightings of the man she used to visit in the hostel and Amber wondered if returning to Chalk Farm would be fruitful. The light at the end of the tunnel came when she met two young women who had spoken to a man that fitted his description. He was usually to be found in an alley behind the Europa Club in Finchley Road.

It was early evening and Amber slowed her pace to enter the gap between two buildings, dodging the dog mess and litter. Syringes and foil accompanied used condoms that glistened in the moonlight and littered a filthy concrete yard. The smell was nauseating and it became obvious that the bushes and walls had been used as a toilet. A police helicopter hovered above and Amber found the clackety sound of the blades cutting hard into the air hurt her ears. She pressed on and the sight of legs clad in filthy blue jeans poking out from a cardboard box came into sight. Worry swept through her head with the warning that the person may actually have passed away or be a danger to her.

Her gentle greeting rang out, 'Hello, can I speak to you. I'm looking for someone called Gerrard. Are you Gerrard?'

There was a snort and much movement in the makeshift home that was cluttered with bedding and clothes cascading from an Asda carrier bag. Amber stepped back as the giant of a man with a shaved head and cuts to the face wriggled out into the alley.

There was no mistaking the kind voice as his eyes homed in on Amber. The six-foot-six Jamaican man, who spoke with a South London accent, greeted her with one of his smiles that exposed an almost perfect set of white teeth. He looked puzzled and muttered, 'I know the voice but can't place the face. Who are you?'

'It's Amber. A few years back I used to chat to you in the soup kitchen and hostel where you lived. I even gave you a mobile phone. You look like you've been through the wars and that haircut really doesn't suit you.'

'Oh, it's you. I didn't recognise you. Have you been on a diet?'

Amber nodded and continued to stare at the unwashed face that was covered with scars. She wondered if he had been in a fight.

After a few minutes of catch up, she switched the conversation to the filming for the video. A brief explanation followed on the meaning of crowd funding that she was sure he struggled to grasp. There was no hesitation on his part in agreeing to participate in the appeal. Amber passed him one of her old pay-as-you-go phones that she had already topped up. The plan was made to return on Sunday with James who would bring the camcorder.

Amber lied when she said the organisers had granted a payment for Gerrard's role in the video. She pulled out her purse and kindly said, 'And, of course, this is for you for your twenty-five seconds of fame. It's not much but it's all yours.'

Gerrard's eyes lit up at the sight of the crisp twenty-pound note that Amber had earlier withdrawn from her account at a cashpoint in Finsbury Park.

As she said goodbye, Gerrard looked blankly at her for a moment and it came as a shock when he asked her name again. Before she had a chance to reply, he muttered, 'Of course I know who you are, Amber, it's just myself that I don't know any more.'

Reaching to shake his weathered and torn hand that held traces of dried blood, Amber stifled a sob. There were thousands of lost Gerrards out there who were fighting a losing battle.

Chapter 33

'What do you mean, he won't speak to you?' said Toni who was mopping up the remnants of her evening meal with a finger.

Amber ignored the question and sighed. 'You really do have terrible table manners, it's all over your chin.'

'But you gave him a phone and all that money.'

'The guy was in a bad way and he's just the sort of person we are trying to help. I got through to the mobile but he told me he really didn't want to be filmed and to stop bothering him. I wonder if he's got mental health issues.'

'Oh, that's awful.'

'Yes, and doesn't it just pinpoint how many unfortunate people there are on the streets. On a positive note, I've spoken to James who reckons he knows of someone who will be ideal for the opening sequence of the video. That's great news, isn't it?'

Toni nodded and then said, 'When I was at work this morning the builder had a chat with me and the good news is, I'll soon be out of your hair. The plaster doesn't need to be stripped back so the bill will be much lower. He's going to install some air vents and is confident that the blocking paint will solve the damp. Your de-humidifier is continually on and should do the trick. I'm going to treat myself to a new carpet and duvet to spruce the place up. I reckon in two weeks I'll be packing my bags.'

An unsettling feeling of being alone again swept through Amber's mind. With Liz having moved out and now Toni planning her departure, it was going to be terribly lonely in the flat. The last few weeks with Toni had been fun. Yes, she could be annoying but what a good friend she had become at a time when she herself was still picking up the threads of her life.

'That's a relief as I thought your room was going to cost loads to repair.' Amber took a deep breath and continued, 'We get on so well, why don't you move in here on a permanent basis? I really don't want you to go and I'm sure we can come to an agreement on a minimum rent.'

'But you said I was your worst tenant and I annoyed you.'

'Did I say that? I have a suggestion that may change your thinking. Space is a premium in the shop and you are hogging a valuable storage area that could be used for that stock you just invested in. All those greeting cards, scarfs and bags of sweets need to be looked after. You should live here.'

The sound of Toni snapping her fingers always set Amber's teeth on edge. 'I can see that makes sense but what would I do with my furniture and everything in my room? Also, if we fall out, I'll have to go back to the shop, won't I?'

'Easy peasy, my mates at work can bring your furniture over here. The flat is big enough for two grown up girls to argue and hide, so shut up and make me a cup of tea.'

'You are not bunging my stuff on one of your dustcarts.'

***

With the script all signed off by James, the next phase of the appeal was to commence the filming and editing. The paperwork had all been registered and as many avenues for posting on social media as possible were being explored. James' Facebook and Twitter accounts held over three thousand friends and followers to reach out to which would make a brilliant start. Thirty people in the church were active with their daily posts and offered to lend a hand by spreading the word.

It was hoped that a high degree of retweeting and sharing of the video would take place. Achieving the status of 'viral' on the internet necessitated a powerful message becoming extremely popular in just a matter of hours or days. It could appear on social media thousands of times, even millions of views. The ultimate goal was to be picked up online by the press and TV stations.

They also had to be transparent about the distribution of any monies received. Recently the press had revealed the despicable behaviour of a so-called crowd funding individual who was only interested in lining his own pockets. Their pitch had to be truthful and ultimately achieve the goal of bringing relief to the needy.

On the day the video was recorded, fortunately, the Met Office slipped up big time with their weather prediction for London. It had been forecast that a warm sunny morning would prevail. Instead, the conditions for filming were just what was required: thumping black clouds that swept across the sky with a noticeable drop in temperature. Out in the open, the odd roll of thunder in the distance became louder as the storm gathered pace. The driving rain-soaked James' and Amber's coats as they set up the filming in the hostel yard in Wembley where permission had been given to film.

Amber thanked the tall man with at least a week's stubble on his face. He walked with a pronounced limp as he shuffled to the pitted brick wall of an alleyway. Homeless man Paul's delivery of heartfelt words for the opening scene were recorded in one take. Adjusting the focus on the lens, James closed in on the wrinkled face. He kept blinking his eyes to free them from the wetness that, to all intents and purposes, could have been tears. The rain was falling so heavily and drenched the long lank hair that clung to the man's haunted face.

They all looked over to where a lightning fork illuminated the arc of Wembley Stadium. Amber drew breath and counted the seconds before the next explosive crack of thunder was amplified from the heavens.

Paul's role in the video was over in a few moments.

There were no retakes as the man's natural performance resonated with James and Amber. They treated him to coffee and a bun purchased from a cafe in a parade of shops that lined the main drag to the tube station.

Enquiries were made about his health and why he had turned down offers of a roof over his head in the hostel just yards away from where they were standing. The reply clarified the disadvantages and dangers of staying in these institutions and being in contact with so many menacing people. Continually watching one's back was testing, especially for a rough sleeper like him. Amber placed twenty pounds of her own money into the man's hand and he pocketed the notes in the grey anorak with the broken zip which had seen better days. He turned to leave but first crossed over to Amber to thank her again.

James frowned at Amber for breaking one of the most important rules - handing over money was never to be encouraged. They watched as Paul moved slowly, tilting slightly to the right with every step he took. Avoiding an enormous puddle, he hobbled into an alley and out of sight.

'That went well, didn't it?' said Amber in a triumphant voice.

'Yes, I think God was looking down on us today and we captured something powerful here. Just one thing though that you slipped up on.'

Amber was puzzled. 'Sorry, what did I do wrong?'

'You broke the golden rule on not handing out money. Far better to give clothes or food than feed the need for drugs and booze. I just thought I would mention it. Apart from that, you did an incredible job and I'm proud of you.'

Of course, James was right. There was a lesson to be learned and she thanked him for his guidance on the matter.

When Amber got home, she hung her coat to dry on a hanger over the bath. Emptying the pockets, she extracted her Oyster travel card, tissues and glasses case. Her fingers delved deeper and, puzzled by what felt like paper, extracted the money that had been passed to Paul. Tears streamed down her face and she let out a desperate cry. He must have returned the notes with the speed of a pickpocket, only Paul was no thief.

***

Within two days the voiceover, wording and images of homeless Paul were signed off by all parties concerned and uploaded onto Facebook and Twitter. The sites were checked every few hours and after three days exposure, disappointingly, there were relatively few responses in terms of likes and shares. The website that directed people to pledge attracted only three hits and two of those were from James and Amber.

In a call to James, Amber expressed her concern. 'What about all your church friends, didn't you say they would get involved and also share the post to reach others? It's not the video, is it?'

'We have to be patient. Often what happens is people don't see the appeal or fail to respond quickly. It's a bit like a dripping tap – softly, softly, catchee monkey. My plan is to send it out again in a few days' time. Just remember, there are still the other internet sites to load it onto. Stop worrying.'

A week passed and Amber was elated with the news of the response figures. The number of likes and comments had swelled to over six hundred and pledges totalled two thousand pounds. James was right, they just had to market the message in the right way and gradually draw in funds for the charity.

The big breakthrough came when a footballer, who played in the reserve team for Tottenham, tweeted the appeal details to his friends and followers – the uptake was overwhelming with over two thousand hits. This was the catalyst for drawing in monies from all over the UK. A couple in Edinburgh donated one hundred pounds and forwarded the post to their friends. There was a message from a girl in Lisbon who typed in broken English that she was joining in and hoped they were having a good day. County Longford and Mayo in Ireland showed interest and pledges as the links snowballed internationally, even as far as America.

The funds were swelling and a teaser post was rapidly sent out and that's when one of the local newspapers in Middlesex contacted Amber for an interview to discuss the phenomenal response the charity was achieving. The gifting had now reached seventy thousand pounds.

In an excited voice, Amber relayed the news to Toni who was emptying the washing machine and had dropped many of the underclothes on the floor. 'They want to interview me but I think it should be you as this charity is your baby, isn't it?'

Toni shook her head and bent down to scoop up the fallen black bras and looked up to her friend, smiling. 'No, I'm useless with words and would make a mess of it. It was your idea to do the people funding thingy.

What's it called again?'

'Crowd funding.'

'And that as well,' replied Toni with a cheeky grin on her face.

***

Two days later, after Amber's shift, she met up with a junior reporter for the local rag. The young man in his grey suit with tie at half-mast promised to help the appeal with his story. Amber liked to think of those who were kind enough to donate to the cause were virtual carers. She vowed to post regular updates on their website and social media about how funds were benefitting individuals.

Amber was nervous of the recording machine that looked like a mobile phone and hoped the article would help reach even more people.

'It will be edited so don't worry. This is really a great story, now tell me about your occupation as this will be of interest to our readers.'

'Turn that thing off as I want to say something off record.'

Confident that the device had been paused, Amber's tone of voice changed to serious. 'This cannot be about me. My friend and founder of the charity should be the one to be praised as she has worked for years to raise money to support the homeless, not me.'

The reporter pulled from his bag a file that had Toni's name included in the title of charity. 'Let me stop you there Amber. I have spoken to Toni and she is determined that you should be the spokesperson. It was your idea to organise crowd funding and I can assure you a story like this can only help with your efforts. Now, tell me about your work as the only female waste collection operative in this area of Middlesex.'

'How did you know that? Was it my mates on our route?'

Grinning, the reporter swiped record on the device. 'Tell us about your work and how you have organised your time to concentrate on this wonderful appeal.'

Amber spoke with conviction about enjoying her job whilst she planned ways to improve other people's lives.

As the interview drew to a close, an alarming thought raced around her head: *This guy has done his homework and what if he reveals my criminal past? It was the sort of thing reporters did to enhance their story.*

***

One week later, Toni showed Amber the newspaper article. The reference to Amber was indeed an insight into an extraordinary person's determination to kickstart proceedings. Luckily for her, there had been no digging into her past which could have tainted the project.

Following the coverage by the newspaper group, the exposure was pumped up with a local BBC radio station interview featuring Amber as the afternoon guest. Viral status had been reached with worldwide interest secured.

Chapter 34

After an overnight stay in Manchester city centre, Amber arrived by taxi at Media City for her guest spot on the BBC breakfast show. She gazed at the enormous studio buildings and to the lake and bridges. On arriving at reception, she handed over the paperwork and underwent various security checks. Seated on a comfy chair, she crossed and uncrossed her legs as the nerves set in and the necessity to use the bathroom arose. The clock on the wall read seven o'clock and she still checked her watch for reassurance. Her interview was scheduled for eight-twenty and the thought of appearing on live TV scared her. The presenters would want to know about the appeal and, with cameras filming her every move, what if she fluffed her answers or her stomach rumbled?

On the far wall of the reception, a massive screen the size of her bedroom wall was broadcasting the news headlines She recognised the two presenters and the red couch that she herself would soon be sitting on.

She asked if she could use the toilet and, on returning, the floor manager for the show was waiting to escort her to the guest lounge. As they rode in the lift to the third floor, the chatty man with a shaved head and silver earring, asked for her mobile to be turned off. It was placed along with her handbag in a cellophane bag and he handed her a receipt. Her small overnight case had already been stored in the administration offices. He assured her it would be returned before she left the studios.

Amber thanked him and muttered, 'I'm a bit nervous about going on the programme.'

'You'll be fine. The presenters are really friendly and it will be over before you know it.'

Sitting alone in the glass visitors' lounge she sipped a coffee and watched the show which was featuring a report on the Government's handling of the recent flooding in East Anglia. It wasn't long before she was asked to make the short journey along a corridor with wide bi-folding doors to allow access to the sets and equipment.

Her heart was racing as she stood quietly with the floor manager waiting for a green light to be illuminated to complete the journey to the red couch. The microphone lead that ran under her shirt felt scratchy and she wondered if the adhesive tape had become loose. How she wished she still had her handbag to check her face and apply extra perfume.

Watching the screen that hung from a bracket on the wall, she homed in on the presenters who were reading from the autocue that would shortly include a reference to herself. The minister for health was being interviewed live from the London studios and was dodging questions on the NHS. This was followed by an update on the latest forecasts from the Bank of England and finally an announcement about their next guest. On hearing her name, the adrenalin started to pump around her veins.

Panic set in as a young woman holding a walkie-talkie appeared in the doorway. The moment had arrived to move to the studio. Amber was settled on the couch and shook the hands of the presenters whilst a short recap on the news headlines was screened.

The cameras zoomed in on the female presenter whose serious expression softened as the cameras filmed the interview. 'The lovely Louise will be here with the weather shortly and there will be more from the health minister after eight-thirty. Before that, we have Amber McCarthy who has been instrumental in raising awareness of a charity supporting the homeless by crowd funding which had now gone global.'

With the robotic camera running on its silent rail, Amber was in full view. The lights were really bright and she was aware of the floor staff going about their duties. 'Hello Amber – tell us more about the work you have been doing for the homeless and the incredible title of the project: Concrete Pillows.'

Amber smiled and the words flowed easily from her mouth. 'It came to me as I thought of the homeless people living on our streets and their hardships that many of us are not fully aware of. Concrete Pillows sums up the harshness of bedding down on a cold pavement or in an alleyway. I have a Saturday job in an independently owned charity shop that reaches out across projects in North London and Middlesex. The founder, Toni, and I have made it our duty to make a difference to people's lives. We concentrate on the shelters and soup kitchens. The response so far has been incredible and I wish to thank the public for their continued support.'

'Well, you certainly have done that. Your exposure on social media has really taken off and produced unprecedented funds for the nominated project. The figure stands at just over one million pounds with pledges still flooding in from Europe and as far away as New York and Australia. The ball just keeps rolling.'

Feeling confident, Amber nodded. 'Yes, that's right. People's generosity is overwhelming and our promise to all those kind people who made pledges is to give them feedback regularly on where and how their money is being spent. We are facilitators giving the guarantee of extra income for homeless projects. The monies raised will enable us to improve on the shelter accommodation and soup kitchens we already support.'

The male presenter then pointed to the TV screen behind the sofa. 'Now, let's have a look at that video and the heartfelt message that has gone viral.'

The opening image of the man's weathered face and carefully chosen words never failed to bring a lump to Amber's throat and she nervously blinked a number of times.

Both presenters genuinely looked moved and faced Amber to say, 'The filming has been beautifully crafted and the invitation to get involved is so powerful.'

Amber put a thumb up in the air and smiled. 'I want to pay tribute to everyone who has worked on the project and, of course, the charity shop owner, Toni Ceedar, who inspired me.'

'Now, you have a rather unusual job, Amber. Tell us about your work as a waste disposal operative.'

Panic set in as Amber's inner voice whispered: *Please don't ask me about my time in prison.*

Above their heads the screen showed a picture of her in the hideous fluorescent orange uniform emptying a bin into the back of the vehicle. Her colleagues were grinning as they stood back and watched.

Amber inwardly sighed – she wished they hadn't used that wretched press photo, the one with her working the bins. The tabloids had a field day with their coverage of the story. Amber took a deep breath and said, 'I enjoy getting my hands dirty and the job description 'waste operative' is pretty impressive, don't you think?'

The questions reverted back to crowd funding, details of the website and methods for pledging. Amber urged the public to share the post as many times as they could to reach even more people.

The interview came to an end with camera two focusing first on the image of the man on the video and then to a rain-soaked pavement. The male presenter smiled all the way through the interview and closed the chat with, 'Thank you, Amber, come back and see us again soon. Good luck with Concrete Pillows. Now, on to the weather and Louise who is looking very summery by the Media City lake. Over to you, Louise.'

***

One viewer who was unable to take his eyes off the screen was Kane's brother, Jason, who happened to be watching the programme as he ate his breakfast. He had no knowledge of the amazing work Amber had undertaken and was suitably impressed.

He immediately rang Kane in Spain and waited some time for the call to be answered. 'Not still in bed, Bruv, are you?'

'Oh, it's you. I was just getting out of the shower when the phone rang. I'm all wet.' Exaggerating his yawn, he said, 'What do want at this ridiculous hour?'

Jason rushed his words. 'I'm gobsmacked as I've just been watching morning TV and who do you think was on it?'

'I don't know – Neil Sedaka.'

'Who?'

'Oh, forget it – who was it?'

'It was Amber,' replied Jason excitely.

'Did you say Amber?'

'Yep, I've just learnt she's all over the press and now on breakfast TV. She's organised crowd funding for the homeless and the response has gone mental. She's raised well over a million. What an interview, she did really well. You should see how pretty she looks.'

'Goodness, do you think I can use catch up to watch it?'

Jason spoke softly, 'Yes it will be on there. It's got me thinking that we let her slip out of your life too easily and I played a big part in that. Can you ever forgive me for our misunderstanding on Dad and also Amber?'

'That's all water under the bridge and you know I love you. Look, I'll cut this short. What time was she on and which channel?'

'It was just after eight and on the BBC.' Jason hastily added, 'I'm so proud of her and am going to watch it again. It's over to you Kane if you want to win her back.'

***

Kane selected the news channel and swiped the bar to rewind the show. Just after the NHS discussion, there was Amber sitting on the sofa and Jason had been spot on when he said she looked beautiful, but then she had always looked beautiful to him. He hung onto her every word and realised what a fool he had been in losing touch. She had certainly turned her life around after prison. His heart was beating like a broken pump stuck on full power; the decision to call her became paramount. Did she still have the same mobile number, if not he'd search for an e-mail address or jump on a plane to see her. However much she had hurt him in the past, this was the catalyst to renew their friendship.

Chapter 35

It had been a long day travelling back on the train and Amber collapsed into her favourite chair in the lounge and mulled over her trip to the studio. Unusually for her, her mobile phone had been switched off all day. She physically shook as her eyes homed in on the notification of three missed calls and a message from Kane who sounded anxious to speak with her. What did he want after all this time? Memories flooded back of the handsome man who still managed to quicken her heartbeat.

She clicked on the recall number and when Kane picked up the call, she nervously said, 'It's me.'

'Oh great. It's so good hearing your voice. I just saw your TV interview and I'm so proud of you. The work you are doing for the charity is mind blowing with that massive amount raised. Well done.'

'Thanks, but there's a few of us involved and not just me. In essence, the real hero is my charity shop friend.'

'Modest as ever. Look, what I'm going to say may shock you but here goes. I'd like to catch up with you as you are still dear to my heart. We should never have lost touch. We had a good thing going and I think we should meet up soon. What do you think?'

'My sentiments too, but Kane let's not forget you made it clear I wasn't included in your life plan and who could blame you after my despicable behaviour. I really have turned over a new leaf. I fear it may be too late for us though.'

There was a pause before Kane spoke again. 'Look, we both made mistakes. I understand all that but can we at least meet? I could come over to you.'

There was no hesitation in her voice as the hasty reply

bounced back over the air waves. 'No, I'd prefer to make the journey as I've always wanted to go to Spain. I'm owed some holiday but need to check out some dates with my boss. I'll stay in that town Nerja – how does that sound to you?'

Amber could hear the excitement in his voice. 'Are you sure? I'll pay for the trip and I can't wait to show you where I live.'

'There is no way you are going to fund my little holiday. I'll leave booking the flight until a few days before flying to get the best price. My guess is if I get the dates approved, I should be over in just over a week, would that suit you?'

'Yes, definitely yes. What's your e-mail and I'll send you my home address? Let me know when you are coming so I can meet you at the airport.'

'No, I am happy to get myself to your villa and we can meet up there.'

***

Amber sat perfectly still and gazed at her mobile waiting for Kane's message to ping into the inbox. She heard the sound of Toni's voice as she let herself into the flat. 'I'm glad you are home; you must be shattered. You were an absolute star today and I can't wait to watch the recording again.'

As Toni poked her head around the door frame of the lounge, she caught sight of Amber who was grinning from ear to ear.

'You really did enjoy your interview, didn't you?'

Holding her phone at chin height Amber excitedly said, 'He rang me and…'

'What, the producer of the show phoned you?'

Amber's eyes lit up as she clarified her exciting news.

'No, Kane called and I'm going to fly over and meet him in Spain.'

**

The next morning it was back to work for Amber as she climbed into the bin lorry with buddies Raymond and Felix. They had watched her moment of glory on television and both men kissed her on the cheek. Felix explained, 'As I said last night, we are so proud of you and there has been an amazing increase in new pledges.'

'I'm still on a high and can't thank you enough for all your help.'

'No sweat. The other thing is Joyce in our church, who handles the accounts, is about to issue an update to post on social media. It's well over the million now.'

Amber relayed her own news about visiting Kane in Spain and Felix said, 'I just hope old man Godding gets us a decent replacement while you are away. And, don't forget you wanted to take James out to dinner as a thank you for all his hard work and support.'

'Thanks for reminding me, but I've already arranged it for tomorrow night.'

On returning to the depot with the first load to be dropped, Amber became anxious about tackling her despatch manager who, at times, could be quite prickly. On this particular day, her boss was in a good mood and welcomed her into his office patting the hard chair for her to sit on. Today she felt pleased for him as he was excited about becoming a grandfather. He readily agreed to the leave dates and confirmed that holiday cover would be found for her period of absence. Only at the end of their meeting did he mention that he had tuned in to watch her TV debut and was really impressed with her.

On arriving home, Amber powered up the laptop and

spotted what she thought was a good deal on a budget airline's site. She immediately messaged Kane with the dates. As she was about to confirm the booking, to her delight, there was a keener deal that involved travelling a day earlier. This was secured along with a budget-priced hotel in Nerja.

She made the decision not to contact Kane again with the revised dates. Her plan was to surprise him with an earlier visit.

Chapter 36

Touching down at Malaga airport fifteen minutes earlier than scheduled, Amber cleared baggage control and customs in record time and left the busy terminal. Out in the hot sun she wheeled her small case and vowed to buy a sunhat at the first opportunity. The wait for the bus was under half an hour and it wasn't long before she was on her way looking out at the sea on the right and mountains to the left. The fifty-minute drive past the seaside towns of Torre del Mar and Torrox soon gave way to the beautiful coastline that borders Nerja and the surrounding Andalusian villages.

The drop-off point at the bus station was a longish walk to the town centre where her hotel was located. The mid-day heat was hellish and, even with the white hat she had bought in a gift shop, there was little relief from the high temperatures. The sight of tourists in beach attire making their way down to the sea reminded Amber of just how long it had been since she had taken a holiday. Passing countless bars and restaurants, the narrow streets with whitewashed buildings widened into the main shopping area. Cloth sails suspended from buildings partly shielded holidaymakers from the fierce heat that was bearing down on the town.

On reaching the Balcón de Europa, Amber queued for an ice cream and dragged her case to sit on a bench. The incredible view of the sparkling sea and mountains littered with holiday homes and steep terraces reminded her of a travel programme she had watched on the Costa del Sol. She spied the highly-coloured parrots in the palm trees that were particularly noisy. There was much chatter from tourists who were congregating in the square to stare at a wedding that had just ended in the church.

Street artists and performers were drawing the crowds with souvenirs and CDs being purchased. Walking to the end of the **Balcón**, Amber recognised the bronze statue of King Alfonso XII from her internet search. The lonely figure stood close to the iron cannons that once protected the town from invaders intent on securing the Spanish mainland. She posed for a selfie on her mobile phone and duly posted it on Facebook.

Her hotel in Calle de la Cruz was central to the town and beach and, after a shower, she ventured into the busy streets to have lunch in a small restaurant. Seated at a table overlooking the picturesque white church she relaxed and watched the world go by. Families en route to the Burriana Beach carried inflatable dolphins and all the paraphernalia attached to holidaying in the sun.

Savouring traditional tortilla, crusty bread with a large glass of red wine, this was the most relaxed Amber had felt for many years. She was so excited at the prospect of seeing Kane again and wondered where all this might lead. Her mind cast back to their enjoyable weekend in Lisbon when they both declared feelings for each other. She then thought of Toni and promised herself that whatever the outcome with her and Kane, she would always be there for her dear friend. She also remembered young Liz and promised herself she must let her know the outcome of her meeting with Kane.

After lunch she would take a ride in a taxi to Frigiliana to surprise Kane with her unscheduled visit. If he was out for the day, she would return the following morning as previously arranged.

It would have been less expensive to have taken the bus, only today she chose to travel in comfort. The taxi weaved through countryside with derelict farmhouses and donkeys tethered to trees with no protection from the sun. The last few minutes of the journey were on steep roads with splendid views down to the golden beaches that lined the coast road to Nerja. The taxi driver, who spoke perfect English, brought the shiny red Chevrolet to a jerky halt in a small village close to the main tourist haunt of Frigiliana. Amber climbed out of the back of the vehicle and paid the driver who pointed to a magnificent villa set back off the road.

Today's cicada performance was set to frenetic clicking and, on entering the grounds, there was a small puddle on the concrete path where a hosepipe with a sprinkler swung from side to side. Judging by what she could see, the property was set on a large plot with an incredible panoramic view of the mountains and countryside.

Trembling with the anticipation of seeing Kane again, Amber counted to ten and went for it. There was a delay before the front door glided open and there stood a tall, thin man with a horrendously scarred and disfigured face.

Amber drew her arms into her sides and turned her head away in an effort not to stare. It was a shocking sight and she felt sorry for the man who stumbled back into the safety of the hallway.

'I, I am so sorry; I must have got the wrong house. I was looking for Kane Boulter,' said Amber in a trembling voice.

She was about to turn away when she heard Kane's gentle voice. He had now moved back into view. 'Oh, Amber, what are you doing here?' I thought you were coming tomorrow. You don't recognise me, do you?'

Traumatised and unable to take in that this was indeed Kane, Amber had to steady herself against a wall and gasped. He now looked so shockingly different to the handsome man who had turned her heart all that time ago. It took a moment to find her voice. 'Oh, my God, I can't believe it is you – whatever has happened to your face?'

Edging forward into the bright sunlight, Kane stood directly in front of Amber and once again his appearance alarmed her.

'It looks awful, doesn't it?' said Kane who was trying to control the shaking of his hands.

Amber moved forward and touched his arm. 'Oh, my God, how terrible. Now, I can see you properly and I've got over the initial shock, I'm sure with more healing it will soon look better. I'm just thrilled to be here and see you. But why didn't you tell me?'

Kane interrupted her. 'It was with all the excitement of talking to you on the phone, it went completely out of my mind to tell you about my accident. I'm so used to looking like this I plain forgot.'

'Accident! What happened to you?'

'Why didn't you ring to say you were arriving a day earlier? You said you were coming tomorrow. I'm really sorry I should have warned you.'

'I got an earlier flight to surprise you. It's a terrible thing seeing you like this and you gave me a real fright.'

'Come in and I'll tell you everything.'

She followed him through into the air-conditioned lounge with modern furnishings and came to a halt by the doors that led to the garden and pool. Gazing briefly at the view of mountain scenery she waited for his explanation.

'It was over a year ago when I went to the carnival in town that I fell under a horse.' He hesitated and then muttered, 'I was trampled and nearly died.'

Amber closed her eyes and silently mouthed the word 'trampled'. It was hard taking in his news and the thought of anyone being trampled by a horse, let alone Kane, was horrific.

When she did speak, her voice sounded angry. 'Why

didn't anyone ring me? I had a right to know.'

'That was my decision not to worry you and, to be fair, we weren't talking, were we?'

He momentarily touched the side of his face. 'If it's any consolation, it looks so much better than it did after the accident – there's been loads of surgery. Over time, I've got used to looking like this. I've joked that I'm the ugliest man on the mountain, only nobody ever laughs. I'm just upset my appearance has scared you.'

Attempting to lighten the conversation, Amber replied, 'Ugliest man on the mountain, I don't think! You haven't lost your sense of humour, have you?'

She moved closer to him and kissed her fingers before placing them on the scars. 'I can't believe what you must have been through and the pain suffered. You are still beautiful to me and I'm so happy to have you in my life again.'

Kane looked less worried and said, 'It means so much to me you making this trip to see me. I just want to clear the air between us so we can remain friends. Why don't you go outside and I'll get us a cold orange drink?'

Hearing the words: remain friends, confused Amber. She was still in love with him and was convinced he shared the same feelings for her. What wasn't he telling her?

Stepping onto the brightly coloured tiles that felt warm through her sandals, she approached the pool area, Amber turned her head to the side where a palm tree was giving some shade. To her amazement, seated on a garden chair was a young woman who was breastfeeding a baby. The woman quickly lowered the child to her lap and pulled down the flimsy white tee-shirt as she tonelessly said, 'Who are you?'

Amber's eyes were fixed on the baby. The worst of scenarios was gathering speed as her hasty conclusion was that this could only be Kane's wife or partner.

Amber returned to the lounge where Kane was hovering with the drinks. She was gritting her teeth and trying to remain calm. 'I'm leaving, so get out of my way. I thought we had something special between us – I was obviously wrong.'

Puzzled by the outburst, Kane sounded desperately upset. 'I don't want you to go. What's wrong?'

'Do you really need to ask?'

The penny dropped and Kane sighed. 'I'm really sorry I forgot that Sue and the baby were out there. A lot has happened since we last met. I should have made the introductions but my head was in a whirl with you turning up like that and I forgot she was there.'

'You seem to do a lot of forgetting these days. I'm done here.'

'Now just hold on and let me explain …'

'I can't believe you would invite me into your life again and do this.'

'It's not like that,' said Kane as he watched Amber grab her bag and rush out of the villa. He shouted after her, 'I can explain – I'm not …'

***

Kane's body momentarily froze as he tried to process just what to do next. When Sue sauntered into the lounge smelling of baby sick, she queried who the visitor was. He hurriedly explained that Amber had obviously thought they were a married couple with a child. Sue's face creased with worry as she urged him to leave the villa immediately to find Amber and make amends.

There was no sign of Amber in the lane that led to the village. Kane increased his pace. He anxiously glanced into a bar hoping to spot her sheltering from the heat.

He frantically swiped the screen of his mobile and selected her name from the large list of contacts. The call rang out but was not being picked up. Desperate to leave a message he became cross that the facility was not available and sent a text instead.

Kane checked Amber's e-mail that revealed where she was staying. Hotel Cordo was a dump and he should have ensured she had somewhere better to stay. Still no response on the phone and no sign of her, she must have found a taxi. The bus was leaving in a few minutes and there wasn't a moment to lose before the bumpy journey down to the coast.

***

The bus was crowded with tourists, many of them looked exhausted from walking around the village in the extreme heat. Kane gave up his seat to an elderly woman and kept checking his phone. He had to remain calm and told himself that even if Amber was in the process of rearranging her flight, the earliest would be for the next morning. The breakdown in communication was all his own doing and needed sorting.

Arriving at the bus terminal in record time, Kane pulled on his sun hat and made his way into town. He knew the exact location of Calle de la Cruz and dodged the holidaymakers on the narrow pavements. On reaching the shabby exterior of Hotel Cordo, that never reversed their vacancies sign, he sighed. Locals spoke badly of the establishment that was housed above a bar with loud music. His heart went out to Amber who must have struggled to afford the trip. He had really messed things up.

The girl on the reception desk with an almost expressionless face was checking her mobile phone and ignored Kane's request for help. He just needed her to ring Amber's room. This time he raised his voice and there was a reaction from the Spanish youngster who reluctantly called room seven. The call kept ringing out.

Kane's eyes lit up as he spotted Amber entering the hotel and went to open the door for her. She stepped back into the street.

'Leave me alone – I'm going home as soon as I can get a flight.'

Grasping his phone, Kane's emotionally charged voice rang out. 'Just read the text I sent you and I'll go.'

Amber pulled out her phone and her eyes welled up as she read the message: *I have no partner, wife or child.*

Sue is a friend who was visiting. I love you, Amber.

Chapter 37

Lying on towels on the grass, the sun was pleasingly warm as Kane cradled Amber's hand and told her that he loved her. The view of the woodland was spectacular with the cloudless blue sky that was creased with the jet streams of aeroplanes coming in to land.

Today, the beach was busy with families enjoying the July heatwave. Children were swimming in the cold water of the Ruislip Lido in the borough of Hillingdon. The massive lake with the glorious sandy beach was technically a large reservoir, known as the only London beach that had been around since the early Victorian period.

Amber's first visit to the Lido had been on a school trip and memories of running free in the country park with friends came flooding back. Today was Kane's first visit and, whilst he missed the beauty and quietness of his pool in Spain, he had never regretted the decision to move back to the UK. Home was now a semi-detached house in one of the leafy roads that lined North Harrow Park.

The happy couple had been married on a sunny afternoon in the **Church of El Salvador** that overlooks the **Balcón** de Europa. They now visited the villa only as guests. Gifting **Casa** Emilia to Jason brought much happiness to Kane who now had both his brother and Amber back in his life.

Gazing around the glorious Lido, Kane observed the faces of people who were enjoying the wonderful weather and location. Happiness was everywhere to be seen.

He looked down to his wife and smiled. Amber was the stunning butterfly that had flitted in and out of his life but thankfully had returned stronger than ever before.

Other titles by this author include:
**Phoenix and the Blue Jay
Shadow with Nowhere to Fall**

Website: **marklaming.co.uk**

www.blossomspringpublishing.com

Printed in Great Britain
by Amazon